DEAD CHRISTMAS
A ZOMBIE ANTHOLOGY

EDITED BY
ANTHONY GIANGREGORIO

DEAD CHRISTMAS
Copyright © 2011 Open Casket Press
ISBN Softcover ISBN 13: 978-1-61199-033-1
           ISBN 10: 1-611990-33-5

Table of Contents

FOREWORD BY ANTHONY GIANGREGORIO....................4

HOW SLAPPY ENDED CHRISTMAS BY MARK CHRISTOPHER 6

A FAMILY TRADITION BY DANIEL LOUBIER...........................22

MERRY CHRISTMAS, CLAIRE BY KEVIN LEWIS 36

A WHITE CHRISTMAS: LIVE FROM 1941!.............................55

MIDNIGHT SERVICE BY CHRISTOPHER NADEAU....................76

KEEPING WARM BY JAMES JEFFREY PAUL.........................87

A CHRISTMAS CARD FOR KATHY BY KEN L. JONES 100

AXE TO GRIND BY REBECCA SNOW 108

A ZOMBIE FOR XMAS BY ASH HARTWELL 122

A CHRISTMAS DINNER BY VINCENZO BILOF..........................135

RED CHRISTMAS BY SUZANNE ROBB 151

EVEN ZOMBIES LOVE CHRISTMAS BY A. GIANGREGORIO 173

HOLLY JOLLY CHRISTMAS BY KELLY M. HUDSON 189

SECRET SANTA BY JONATHAN TEMPLAR 205

THE CHRISTMAS HELP BY 218

ABOUT THE WRITERS.............................234

Instead of some boring foreword where I talk about the joys of Christmas and zombies, how about a poem instead?

Dead Christmas

ANTHONY GIANGREGORIO

Twas the night before Dead Christmas, and all through the land,
Not a living creature was stirring, except a few severed hands.

The last family left alive, was barricaded inside,
While visions of death and carnage, danced in their minds.
The undead were hungry, as they searched for food,
And the humans knew their time was short, all of them in dire moods.

But then in the backyard, of this particular house,
There came a loud noise, and it wasn't a mouse.
Away to the back door, the family ran with haste,
For the dead were breaking in, there was no time to waste.

Moonlight bathed the new fallen snow,
As the family searched both high and then low.
But then did their searching eyes finally find,
It was a dead man in a Santa suit, and behind him more of his kind.

Though hard to believe, he was not false but the real deal,
And as he stumbled from his sleigh, eight undead reindeer snorted with zeal.
His eyes were glazed, his flesh pale and white,

And as he let out a low moan, anyone within earshot was chilled with fright.

Zombie Santa waved the undead horde onward,
And hundreds of animated corpses began to stumble forward.
As the ghouls began to break into the home,
The family cried out, their screams swallowed by undead moans.

The living dead began to feed, and the carnage was great,
As Zombie Santa looked on, the last human family suffering a terrible fate.
When all were killed and only bloody shards were left,
Santa climbed back into his sleigh, carrying a single severed head with some heft.

He held it aloft for all the zombies to see,
And reached inside to pull out the brains, and handed them to two ghouls, not three.

"The last humans are dead and we rule the land!
We are the true creatures God wants on hand.
Humans were weak, and we are strong,
And this night, our reach is long!"

"The dead walk the Earth, and so the world will burn,
Humans are gone, never to return.
So the next time you hug your loved ones, don't take them for granted,
Remember, how fast they can be supplanted."

HOW SLAPPY ENDED CHRISTMAS

MARK CHRISTOPHER

There was nothing particularly special about Slappy the elf. There was also nothing bad; or nothing especially good. Slappy fell somewhere in the middle; just sort of average. Mostly ignored by the other elf supervisors, Slappy was content at his job as a third level toy truck assembler. Here he could sit on his special little elf bench and tirelessly plot along at a seemingly never-ending task.

The long assembly belt would carry the base models of toy cars and trucks where a line of elves would work to assemble the parts into one entire unit. Slappy's job was to tack on the wooden wheels before they were ushered on to the paint department and lastly, to waxing. The other elves would chat amongst themselves, mostly discussing how many days there were until Christmas.

For elves, Christmas wasn't a one-day holiday; it was a carefully scheduled project that lasted 364 days a year. There were a few elves that didn't quite share in the Christmas cheer. These elves were usually ushered away and were never heard from again. Their fatal flaw was speaking out against the holiday. Slappy knew better. He'd grown tired of Christmas a long time ago, but since he never heard from the ones that had been removed, he deduced it was best to just keep quiet and go with the flow.

Besides, it really wasn't that bad. The other elves were pleasant enough and the toy factory had a warm, enticing atmosphere that contrasted perfectly to the frigid climate of the North Pole. The pleasant aroma of nutmeg and peppermint floated in the air, and the occasional odor of holly and cranberry could make the gloomiest elf smile.

Slappy inhaled deeply and took in the smells around him, sighing as he exhaled. The sharp pain that splashed suddenly across his back snapped him out of the dreamy moment.

"Get back to work, *Sloppy*!" Knuckle, the car assembly supervisor, yelled as he cracked Slappy's back with a leather strap. "Those wheels aren't going to put themselves on!"

If Slappy had to choose one thing he did hate, it was Knuckle, who was different from the other elves. He stood nearly a foot taller, with ears that ended in sharper points. His bushy eyebrows resembled fat, gray caterpillars that had come to a rest above his beady, red eyes. He wore the traditional elf garb: green hat lined with white fur, black leather shoes, and white gloves. What made him stand out was he wore a blue shirt and pants that signified him as a supervisor; the other worker elves wore green. If one thing made Slappy's little heart start to pound in anger, it was being called *Sloppy*.

"Sorry, sir. I didn't realize I was stalling," Slappy replied quickly, not turning to confront his tormentor.

"Damn it, *Sloppy*! We don't have time for your day dreaming! You know how many days we have till Christmas?" It was a rhetorical question. Everyone knew the countdown and if they had forgotten, the large digital display hanging from the wall, constantly counting down the days, was quick to remind them.

"Thirty-seven days, sir," Slappy replied.

"Well, no shit," Knuckle replied sarcastically. "Glad you wheel boys know how to read a calendar. Now get back to work, *Sloppy*." He began walking away.

"It's Slappy, sir. Slappy. You know that."

There was a collective gasp from the other wheel assemblers as Knuckle froze in place. Turning sharply, he quickly walked to where Slappy was sitting. Grabbing Slappy's shoulder firmly, he spun the much smaller elf around. Face to face, Slappy could feel Knuckle's hot, sour breath. The smells of Christmas had been eliminated.

"Listen to me, you worthless little shit. One more word out of you and I'll make sure you're removed. Do you understand me?" He spoke in a slow, menacing tone.

"I...I do sir," Slappy stammered, unsure what the larger elf was going to do next.

"Now get back to work. All of you get back to work! I want double the number of cars finished before your shift ends! Get moving!" Knuckle screamed as the entire assembly line threw themselves back into their tasks. He cracked the leather strap against a workbench as he walked away, causing some of the elves to jump.

"Nice going, Slappy," Jewel, a particularly pretty, blond-haired elf whispered.

"Whatever," was all Slappy cared to mutter as he tacked a wheel onto a truck base.

Four hours later, the horn blew loudly throughout the workshop, announcing shift change. Twelve hour days were grueling, but as Knuckle had so elegantly put it, the toys weren't going to make themselves. Slappy joined the rest of his crew in the locker room. There the elves showered and changed into clean clothes before returning to their housing units. Slappy was heckled slightly by the rest of the crew for his outburst at the line. Only his good friend, Pips, welcomed him with a compliment.

"That was pretty brave of you today," the second level toy car painter told his glum-looking friend. Pips was identical looking to

Slappy in almost every way. In fact, there wasn't much difference between any of the elves. Usually hair or eye color was the only way to tell many of them apart. Pips, however, had a rounded gut protruding over his pants. His love of cinnamon cake had finally caught up to him.

"I'm glad someone thinks so," Slappy replied with a half-smile. He was looking forward to going to his room at the housing unit. There he would enjoy a nice hot cider and lose himself in a good book. Slappy was almost salivating at the thought of the cider.

"Are you assholes still dicking around in here?" Knuckle screamed as he burst into the locker room. "Move it so the next shift can come on!" He slammed the locker room door hard as he left. He was gone as soon as he'd arrived, almost like he'd never been there. His loud voice left its ghostly presence as a high-pitched ring in Slappy's ears.

"Man, I wish Santa could see how he acted," Pips said, shaking his head in disgust.

"Santa? Ha!" Slappy laughed. "When's the last time he ever showed his face at the shop? Pips, he doesn't care about us. We just make the toys and he gets the credit. If he was here, he'd probably just tell Knuckle to drive us harder."

"I don't want to think that," Pips said, now taking his turn looking glum.

"Well, you think whatever you want," Slappy said as he closed his locker door and slung his shower bag over his shoulder. "I'm out of here."

"You want me to walk with you? I'll only be a few more minutes."

"No, that's okay. Take your time. I kind of want to be by myself for a while." Slappy pulled his thick jacket on and walked out of the locker room, giving Pips a gentle squeeze on the shoulder before departing.

Poor guy, Pips thought as he ran a comb through his thin, brown hair.

The sharp, cold air of the North Pole struck Slappy in the face like a jilted lover. His eyes immediately began to water as the swirling winds and bitter cold began drying out his steel blue eyes. The walk to the housing unit was a relatively short one, about ten minutes, but in the bitter, driving cold it felt like miles.

Slappy stood outside the building and looked up. Standing twenty stories high, the elf housing unit was a boring, windowless monolith set against a white backdrop. Its brown brick stood in sharp contrast to the emerald green trees and fluffy, snow-covered hills. He brought his hand to the door to let himself in, when another idea came to him. The urge to go for a walk filled him, and even though the cider beckoned, he was unable to shake the thought that a stroll in the cold would do him some good. The verbal thrashing by Knuckle had left more of an impact on him than he could have imagined. Turning away, he headed away from the housing unit, and into the untouched splendor of the magical North Pole.

He plodded along best he could as the wet snow gripped his legs with each step. His calf muscles started to burn and tighten as he cut a path into the thick snow. Finally, he came to a clearing and the ground was more like crunchy ice. His calves thanked him. He walked through the pine trees, their branches ripe with red berries, birds chirping and jumping about. The forest was thick, but he knew of a crystal blue lake that resided on the other side.

Maybe some time watching the tranquil water will ease my mind, he thought as he reached the end of the forest.

He stepped out into a clearing and could see the blue lake ahead. A few quick strides later found him standing at the bank of

Gingerbread Lake. He'd heard stories about the lake from the other elves in the housing unit. Mostly it was the older elves telling eerie tales to the women and younger elves about the lake's magical powers and the creatures that resided at the bottom; creatures that would rise up and snatch an elf, bringing them to an instant watery grave, especially elves that spoke out about Christmas.

Slappy thought the stories were ridiculous. It was just a lake. In fact, he could almost see the bottom, and at the moment, no creatures were ready to make a meal out of him. Just white rocks—most likely ancient sediment deposits—littered the lake floor.

He sat down at the bank and gazed out into the atmosphere, concentrating on the space where the water and the air met. His mind was adrift, hectically sorting the events of the day, when a sudden rush of air bubbles came boiling to the surface of the lake, snapping him back to reality and causing him to jump to his feet. In the serene environment, the break of bubbles was like mini thunderclaps.

Suddenly, a mess of white hair appeared on the surface followed by a face that bobbed up and down like a cork. Slappy couldn't believe his eyes. He wanted to turn and flee, but his curious nature gripped him.

Was this one of the elves that had been removed? he wondered and knelt down. He used his arm to move the water to pull the floating corpse closer. He couldn't believe how swiftly the body came to him; he wasn't moving the water very quickly. Soon, the corpse was within arm's reach and Slappy was able to examine it. The skin was a lifeless gray and appeared almost melted by the water exposure. The eye sockets were empty and clumps of white hair were visible in patches. Slappy couldn't tell if it had once been a man or a woman. Then the corpse he would have sworn was lifeless made a noise.

He fell backwards and immediately felt the seat of his pants grow damp from the snow. It wasn't a loud noise, more like a gurgle-groan, but that was more than most corpses made.

"You're alive!" Slappy yelled and rushed back to the water's edge. This was what must have happened to the elves that spoke out, he realized. They were thrown into the lake and somehow were kept alive! To live at the bottom of a lake in silence and devoid of sight was monstrous. Slappy could feel his blood turn icy, and it wasn't because of the near-freezing temperature.

"I have to get you out of here," Slappy said to the bobbing corpse, reaching his hand out.

Taking hold of the water-soaked and faded green coat, he pulled the corpse closer to him. Then suddenly the corpse sprang to life. With a quickness that shocked Slappy, catching him off guard, the corpse grabbed his arm. Slappy could feel the tight pressure of cold, dead flesh press into him. He screamed loudly and tried to pull back, but found the corpse's grasp was too tight. The corpse opened its mouth, sinking its jagged teeth into his hand.

"Aughhh!" Slappy screamed and jerked away, causing the corpse's teeth to shred the soft flesh of his palm. Immediately the crystal blue waters turned a faint purple as the red blood mixed. Bringing his other hand forward, Slappy smashed his intact palm into the forehead of the corpse. The head snapped back as the water-softened flesh broke apart along the neck. Water immediately rushed in, filling the body and like a stone, it sank back into the depths.

Tears of pain welled in Slappy's eyes as he held his palm. The feel of hot blood flowing down his hand was making him sick. He gazed down at the water and saw a sight that almost caused him to faint. Dozens of white-haired heads peppered the floor of the lake. He'd thought they were rocks when he first glanced down, but now the mystery of the cast-out elves was definitely solved.

A wave of nausea swept over him like a tidal wave, causing him to release his stomach contents onto the white snow, making a horrible abstract of greens and browns. Composing himself, he packed snow into his wound; it ached horribly.

Away from Gingerbread Lake and through the pine forest Slappy ran. He ran for the safety of his housing unit and fellow elves, the same elves that only an hour ago he wanted nothing to do with. He was able to stop most of the bleeding as the cold snow worked its magic on the wound. As he reached the front door of his housing unit, he took a deep breath and shoved his injured hand deep into his coat pocket. There was no need to cause alarm.

Opening the door quietly, he slipped in like a shadow. He made sure to do his best to avoid detection as the shouts and laughs of the elves enjoying the community area filled his ears.

"Slappy!" Pips yelled when he spotted his friend. "Where've you been, buddy?" Pips was holding a mug of hot cider. Several other elves looked up from their game of cards and gave Slappy smiles and waves. "Come and join us. We're almost done with this hand!" Pips yelled.

"Okay, just let me go clean up a little first," Slappy said, trying not to garner any more attention.

"You should be clean enough!" Pips said with a laugh. "We did all have showers!"

"Yeah I know, but clumsy me fell down while walking and my clothes are wet. I'll be back shortly," Slappy replied and entered the elevator. His voice was amazingly calm, but as the doors closed, he had to steady his shaking hand to push the button for the tenth floor.

Exiting the elevator, he turned down a narrow hallway and entered his room. The room was small but it was his personal space in a world that gave little privacy. Tossing his coat on a small cot, he walked quickly to the bathroom. He ran his hand under the warm water and applied a liberal amount of soap, scrubbing the wound. He was relieved to see it wasn't as bad as he thought. Wincing, he pulled away the loose ribbons of skin; they came away with a slight elastic pull. Slappy wrapped his hand in clean gauze from a first aid kit. Looking himself once over in the mirror, he took a deep breath.

"You won't breathe a word about this. Not to anyone," he told his reflection. The thought of being thrown into the lake to live amongst the eyeless monsters terrified him. He would hold on to the secret all the way to his dying days, and for an elf, that was a very long time—normally.

"So...where'd you go?" Pips asked, sliding a hot cider to Slappy.

"Just walked around a bit in the forest," Slappy said as he brought his gauze wrapped hand up to grab the cider, forgetting about his wound.

"Santa help me! What happened to you?" Pips asked, eyeing the gauze.

"It's nothing," Slappy replied nonchalantly. "Just hit a tree root when I fell. Cut my hand a little. Nothing serious."

"I hope it doesn't slow you down from tacking tires," Pips said, concerned.

Slappy hadn't thought of that. The thought of Knuckle tearing into him was causing his heart to race. With it so close to Christmas, what if they removed him! What good was an injured elf when the Christmas countdown was so near?

"I'll be all right, Pips. You worry too much," Slappy said, sipping his cider. The spicy taste of cloves helped sooth his nerves a bit.

The elves socialized, drank and played cards for several hours before the buzzer went off, signaling it was time for lights out. Tired elves were not productive elves.

Slappy said his goodbyes and headed for his room. He hand ached slightly as he crawled into bed. Pulling the covers over his head, he took a deep breath and closed his eyes.

He was visited by the most horrible dreams that night; dreams of fire, death, and destruction. Dreams that should never enter the mind of an elf.

Something in him was changing.

When Slappy opened his eyes the next morning, he knew something was horribly wrong with him. He was extremely ill and his body ached from head to toe. Gazing down at his bandaged hand, he was startled to see the gauze was soaked through with a bloody pus mixture.

He leapt out of bed—which only made him feel worse—and entered the bathroom. Removing the gauze slowly, his heart dropped as he revealed a festering, infected wound. Globs of goo oozed forth from where the corpse's teeth had broken his skin.

This is really bad, he thought, staring slack-jawed at the wound. Running it under the water, he made sure to thoroughly wash it with soap before wrapping clean gauze over it.

He looked at himself in the mirror and was shocked at the face that greeted him. His skin was almost a faint purple and his lips were dry and cracked.

Dark circles were forming under his eyes and his hair looked stringy and lighter in color.

His stomach rumbled and he immediately dropped to his knees in front of the toilet, once again spewing forth its contents. The cider that had resided in his stomach burned with apple acidity as it passed out of him.

Slappy was sick, really sick. He considered going to the infirmary, but knew that wasn't an option. They would ask him too many questions and eventually someone would discover where he'd been.

Who could he trust? What would become of him if someone found out? It wasn't a risk worth taking.

I'll just pay extra attention to it, he thought, slipping his bandaged hand into a glove. All he had to do was tack tires onto wooden cars like he did every day. If he could do that, then there was no reason anyone would need to know.

He washed up the best he could and then dressed.

He'd just exited his room when Pips' voice filled his ears. "Holy Santa! You look terrible!" Pips exclaimed at the sight of his friend.

"I don't feel too hot either," Slappy said, coughing out the end of the sentence.

"You can't go to work like this?" Pips said, concerned. "It's not smart. You need rest."

"I don't really have a choice," Slappy said sadly. "I'm an elf. I work. That's all I'm good for, and if I don't, they'll get rid of me."

"I know you don't feel well, but do you have to be so dark?"

He didn't reply, something in him felt missing, a certain peculiar emptiness he couldn't place. As he exited the building and into the frigid atmosphere of the North Pole, he was surprised to discover the cold didn't bother him.

He really couldn't feel the cold air that should be nipping at him. Jack Frost was clearly still in bed. Walking in silence with the other elves, Slappy saw the once bright world through eyes of gray. Everything was gray. The sky, the snow, the trees—all colorless. What was happening to him?

"Where's my mind?" he wondered aloud, unaware.

"You say something?" Pips asked.

Slappy chose not to reply.

Entering the toy shop, he couldn't smell the enticing aromas he knew had to be wafting through the air. Why couldn't he smell them? Everything was the same, yet it was all different. Slappy sat down at his designated bench and waited for the assembly line to begin.

"All right, assholes! Today we're going to work harder than ever. The night shift did a real shit job and it's up to you to pick up their slack!" Knuckle screamed and cracked the leather strap. His boisterous screams were grating on Slappy's nerves. The urge to get up and kill Knuckle flashed through his mind; thoughts no elf should ever have, yet they were there.

At that moment Slappy wanted nothing more than to stand up and tear Knuckle's throat out. The thought of the warm blood was causing him to drool.

"Will you pull it together?" Jewel pleaded. She lightly pushed Slappy. He shook his head and the morbid thoughts left him.

"*Sloppy!* You worthless elf shit! You better be ready to tack some wheels today!" Knuckle screamed as he threw on the switch to start the process. The assembly belt gave a metallic groan and slowly began inching forward, picking up speed as the seconds passed. Soon the line was full of wooden car bodies. The elves began collecting them and tacking on wheels. Slappy kept up as best he could, his gloved hand making it difficult to grip a hammer or a car frame.

A rush of cold swept over Slappy's body like an icy flame. A dull burning started deep in his stomach and rushed its way to his heart. He could feel his heart's rhythm pound faster and faster as droplets of sweat poured from beneath his hat. He gasped as his throat became tighter, and each breath resulted in less oxygen. A sharp pain, like a spear piercing his body, came upon him as his heart separated from its ventricles. Darkness immediately filled his vision and he pitched forward. He was dead before his head hit the assembly line belt.

"Slappy!" Jewel cried when she saw him pitch forward. She knew he'd looked odd this morning. *Poor guy has to be really sick*, she thought as she stopped work and ran to his side.

"*Sloppy*, you lazy elf turd! I'll teach you to fall asleep on my line!" Knuckle screamed, bringing the leather strap down hard on Slappy's back. There was no reaction. Puzzled, Knuckle struck again, the result the same.

"Slappy?" Knuckle said, concern starting to fill his voice.

"He's dead!" Jewel wailed as she shook him. "Slappy! Wake up!" she screamed, shaking him violently.

Slappy slowly raised his head.

"You dumb bastard! I knew you were faking!" Knuckle yelled. "I don't know how you didn't react to my last two hits, but this time you're going to feel them!"

Slappy couldn't make out what Knuckle was screaming about. All he was fixated on was the pulsing neck in front of him. His lifeless eyes caught Jewel's and she gasped. It was all she had time to do before he lunged forward, his snapping mouth latching onto Jewel's throat. With a swift jerk, he removed her trachea. The sensation of hot blood filled his mouth, driving him wild.

"Santa help us!" Knuckle stammered when Slappy turned to face him.

With a primal howl, he leapt onto Knuckle as swiftly as a jaguar pouncing on a small deer. He tore into Knuckle's body, ripping his shirt off, and digging his hands deep into the elf's stomach. He felt the skin give as his hands found plump organs. Knuckle's screams were silenced quickly as Slappy began chomping on his liver. Slappy fed for only a few short minutes before his attention was drawn to the other elves that were running and screaming around him. He attacked any he could get near.

As these events transpired, the entire toy shop went into a panic. Jewel had bled out quickly and had only been lying on the floor for a few minutes before the change took hold of her. Lurching to her feet, she immediately took a large bite out of the shoulder of a plump female elf with red hair. The red-haired elf screamed and knocked another elf off a tall ladder, causing him to tumble to the floor and snap his neck.

Knuckle was quickly on his feet again, his organs falling freely from the hole in his gut as he pursued elves that were too terrified to move. As elves were slain, it took only moments for them to rise up and continue the attack.

The toy factory supervisor, having been stationed above the entire shop floor in an enclosed control room, saw what was transpiring. His mind couldn't grasp the situation, but he knew madness had over taken the elves. All he could think about was that this might be revenge from the elves they had tossed into the lake, the outspoken elves that were now weighed down by heavy stones and sent to the bottom of the lake, to suffer in waking death for all eternity. With tears streaming down his face, he flipped open a plastic cover and pressed a yellow button he hoped to never have to press. The doors to the shop sealed closed, trapping both the living elves with their zombie brethren. Using a walkway, he exited from the roof. He could hear the screams in his ears as he closed and locked the roof hatch.

"What the hell happened?" Santa roared at the factory supervisor.

"I don't know, sir. Everything was fine and then they just started attacking one another." He was too terrified to mention the idea that they were paying for their sins.

"We have to get back in there! Christmas is approaching soon and we need those toys made!"

"But sir, I don't think *you* understand. They were ripping each other apart!"

"I don't think you understand," Santa said in disgust. "Move aside. I'll put an end to this uprising right now. Good thing the lake is deep, because it's about to get a lot of new occupants!"

Santa waddled forward and approached the main shop doors, his fat little legs moving quickly under his large frame. He punched in his code at the door security pad to override the shutdown feature. The doors unlocked with a loud click. Pushing the doors open, he strolled into the shop.

"You little monsters have just royally fucked up!" he screamed as hundreds of dead faces turned to face the sudden noise source. Just as he was about to summon his jolly magic to put an end to this uprising, his foot slipped on a bit of entrails. Hitting the floor hard, his breath left him as he struggled to move—a fat turtle trapped on its back.

Before he could do or say anything, the elves were on top of him. All he could do was scream as dozens of mouths latched on and began ripping off his suit to get at the flesh beneath. His belly, like a tub full of jelly, was scooped clean from its cavity. His rosy cheeks were devoured and his cherry of a nose was bitten clean off. The elf factory supervisor screamed and fled, not bothering to close the doors. The zombie elves soon wandered out of the shop floor and into the magical North Pole. In no time, the clear blue sky was consumed with ash and fire, the beautiful white snow turning a deep crimson red.

Christmas was officially cancelled.

Slappy stumbled through the massacres, holding onto the severed arm of Santa. Then his eyes caught something familiar. There, nestled in a large shed, was the infamous red sleigh. The old way of pulling the sleigh with eight tiny reindeer was outdated and this new, sleek sleigh had a simple touch screen that could instantly teleport to any part of the world. All he needed to do was ride it and the sleigh would bring him to the Earth realm. All the humans he could eat!

Slappy sprang to the sleigh, and to the other zombies gave a whistle.
And away they all flew, like a psychotic missile.
Slappy exclaimed, as he took another bite,
"No more Christmas, you're all going to die tonight!

A FAMILY TRADITION

DANIEL LOUBIER

Christmas is my favorite time of year. My brother Patrick's as well. It's the only time of year when the delightful scents that fill our home can change from one day to the next. Today it smells like pine; tomorrow, maybe fresh-baked gingerbread cookies; the day after, hot apple cider. You never know. And that's what makes this season so special. You never know what kind of surprise will greet you each day you wake up.

It's also special because, on Christmas Eve, Dad, Mom, my brother and I all gather in our living room, next to the tree, and shoot the zombies that congregate on the lawn and on our front porch.

There was a time when people were afraid of zombies. At first, no one knew what the hell was going on. All we knew was that some people seemed to lose their minds and began to bite other people. Then, those that were bitten turned into zombies themselves. So naturally, we all panicked. We ran, we hid, we tried to fight them; it was utter chaos.

We heard stories about people in the major cities being forced from their homes by squatters looking for refuge. Some were even dragged from their cars by others who were desperate to get away from the undead. Some people were even killed on sight for suspicion of being a zombie. We used to stay in our house, mostly out of fear of being bitten, but also out of fear of the 'normal' people.

But then, one day, people began to realize that the chaos was in large part brought on by us. After all, the zombies were stupid and slow, so unless you were crippled or blind—or dead already—you really weren't in much danger.

People started to come out of their homes again. They went back to work, those whose offices hadn't been closed or damaged, that is. In time though, most businesses reopened and simply put up barricades around their buildings. This kept out the zombies and allowed in only the humans. In the meantime, we just decided to ignore the zombies. They weren't very reactive and they certainly weren't going to catch us in the unlikely event we had to run away from them.

And that's why Christmastime means so much to my family. It's the only time of year that Mom lets Dad, Patrick and I shoot the zombies.

"You guys ready?" Dad asked. He half-skipped, half-galloped down the stairs, full of excitement and pride. He held three rifles in his hands. "Think either of you can break last year's record?"

"Thirty-one zombies!" Patrick exclaimed. "That's impossible!" He eagerly held out both hands as Dad handed him one of the rifles.

"Not impossible," I said. "Just improbable."

"That's right," Dad agreed, handing me a rifle. "You never how many we might see this year." He turned toward the kitchen. "Honey! You coming?"

"I'll be-*urp*-I'll be there in a minute," Mom called from the kitchen, her words slurred from her drinking. She was already drunk. Mom liked to hit the sauce early on Christmas Eve. It was her way of dealing with what she called 'the madness' in which the three of us partook. She was also putting the finishing touches on her world-famous homemade brownies. She made brownies with M&Ms mixed into the batter, so when the brownies cooked, the chocolate candies would melt and spread through the mixture. They were amazing.

"All right, honey," Dad called. "But there's already about a dozen in the street. If they get too close, we'll have to get started without you!"

Patrick and I knelt down in front of the still-closed window and held the rifles close to our sides. We stared at the small horde forming outside our house. See, what Mom didn't know is that every year on this night, Dad would stop by the supermarket for some steaks on his way home from work. He'd open the packages and leave the raw beef in the bushes in front of our porch. The smell of raw meat always attracted more zombies than usual. It was genius.

Mom burst into the family room with a tray of brownies, four glasses of milk and a glass of brandy. She put the tray down on the floor and assumed her position in her favorite recliner. "Anyone hungry?" she stammered.

"Mmmm!" Patrick burst out as he reached over me and grabbed two brownies.

"I think I want to wait until we're done shooting zombies," I said.

"That's my boy," Dad grinned and elbowed me in the ribs. "You don't want that sugar getting you all jumpy, do you?"

Patrick looked down at the two brownies in his hand, frowned, and set them on the end table next to him.

"Holy shit!" Mom yelled. She pointed at the window.

Simultaneously, we all looked at once. There was a zombie on the porch already. Dad loaded a round in his rifle and reached for the sill. "I guess it's go-time," he said.

Patrick and I both loaded our guns. Then we waited until Dad gave us the nod.

"One…two…*three!*" Dad said. He threw open the window and Patrick and I took aim. Patrick fired the first round, which hit the zombie in the shoulder. I fired next and blasted a chunk off its head. It went down in a sloppy heap.

"One-Zero, Ethan!" Dad yelled.

"That's not fair! Ethan's closer!" Patrick whined.

"Shut your mouth and reload!" Dad instructed.

"Bill!" Mom scolded. "Don talk to your son like that!"

"Charlene, this is a sport, and Patrick knows that." Dad turned to Patrick. "Right, son?"

Patrick nodded weakly.

"Okay then." He turned back to Mom. "See? He gets it. It's all goo…"

"*Dad*!" I yelled. "In the driveway!"

He spun and raised his rifle. The window was open wide enough that he didn't need to get closer. He squeezed the trigger. The bullet made a crater in the zombie's forehead. "*Pow!*" he yelled, pumping his fist. "One-One-Zero! Get your damn head in the game, Patrick!"

"*Bill!*" Mom implored.

"Not now, dear! We've got zombies!"

All at once, the three of us started blasting into the street and on the front lawn. The sound of the rifles all going off at once was deafening. We didn't care. Tonight was our night. One by one, we picked them off. I punched Patrick in the shoulder each time I scored a kill. Patrick was a few years younger than me, not quite a teenager yet, so I have a little more experience with handling a gun. But for his age, he's actually a pretty good shot. Dad, though…he's a *machine*. He could waste these zombies with his eyes closed. He's that good. The 'thirty-one' was his record. I don't know how he did it. It's not like there are *that* many zombies around; he just knows how to shoot.

After about an hour of shooting, we didn't see many more zombies. We'd killed a lot of them already and thinned out the herd quite a bit. Every couple of minutes or so, we'd see one stumbling around the side of a neighbor's house or one would rise up from behind a car parked in the street. But that seemed to be it.

The unexpected sound of footsteps on the roof scared the hell out of us. Confused us too.

"What was that?" Mom asked, half-awake.

"Can zombies climb up on the roof?" Patrick asked.

"Shut up, Patrick!" Dad whispered.

"Bill!"

"Sorry, dear. I mean, *please* be quiet, Patrick."

All at once, our eyes tracked the sound of movement above our heads. It was too muffled to be coming from the attic. There was definitely something—or someone— on the roof.

"Maybe it's one of the neighbors," I suggested. "They might have gotten scared by the gunfire."

Dad didn't take his eyes off the roof. "Nah, Bert knows we're doing this tonight. I'm sure he told everyone else. That man couldn't keep his mouth shut if his lips were stapled together."

"*Bill!*"

"Ethan," Dad said, ignoring Mom. "Hand me the poker by the fireplace."

I rested my rifle on the floor and reached for the poker. I gave it to Dad, and without turning his gaze away from the ceiling, he placed his gun against the chair behind him. He had a quizzical look in his eyes.

"I think it's moving over to the chimney," he said, his voice low.

We waited and listened. Indeed, the sound did seem to be approaching the chimney. Then we heard what sounded like a scrape.

Then a shuffle.

And another shuffle.

Patrick started to get up but Dad held out his hand. "*Wait,*" he mouthed.

Suddenly, a loud *whoosh* came from the chimney and a huge cloud of debris blew out from the fireplace. We were all temporarily blinded, rubbing soot and ash from our eyes and faces.

"Is everyone okay?" Dad yelled. He dropped the poker and held up his hands to shield his face from the smoke and dust.

"Fine."

"I'm fine."

"I'm okay."

Then a loud groan emitted from the ash cloud. Panic crawled over my body like a colony of ants. I looked around but couldn't find my rifle, the air too thick with ash and dust. I couldn't see Patrick, but I assumed he was too stunned to know where his rifle was. A loud 'click' to my right finally assured me that Dad had found his rifle. That's when we heard a strange voice.

"Don't shoot!" the voice bellowed out. "Don't shoot, goddamn it!"

I saw arms clothed in red sleeves, waving like helicopter blades through the dust cloud. I could just barely make out a face in the ashy mess. The giant, white beard all but gave him away.

"*Santa?*" I asked, bemused.

He hacked and coughed and dusted off his red jacket. "Jesus Christ! Is this how you people greet St. Nick?"

"Who the hell are you?" Dad demanded.

Santa stopped dusting himself off and stared back at Dad. "Really?" He made a gesture with his arms as if to say, *look at me!* "You're really going to ask me that? What's the matter with you?"

"*Urp!* Ohhh," Mom drunkenly moaned, sounding a lot like a zombie.

With amazing speed, Santa grabbed the barrel of Dad's gun, ripped it from his hands, and aimed it at Mom.

"No!" we all screamed.

With no hesitation, Santa squeezed the trigger, putting a bullet through Mom's head. Skull fragments and brain matter slapped against the wall behind her.

"*Oh my God!*" Dad screamed.

"You can thank me later," Santa insisted. He was amazingly calm.

Dad looked at him, his eyes wide. "That was my wife!"

Santa looked down at Mom, sprawled on her chair, then turned back to Dad. "She sounded like one of *them*."

"She was drunk!"

Santa wrinkled his forehead. He took another look at Mom, dead in the chair, the remains of her head splashed against the wall. "Huh," he said. "I couldn't tell the difference." He handed the rifle back to Dad, who was too confounded to take it, and let it fall to the floor. Patrick and I were in complete shock. Mom had just been blown away by the swift gunmanship of Santa Claus. We quietly stared at her body, lifeless and crumpled in the chair. Somehow, it seemed fitting. She'd spent a lot of her life sitting in that chair. It only made sense she would eventually die in it, too.

"Well, don't just stand there with stone faces! There's still work to be done!" Santa yelled.

The break in silence shook my attention. "What do you mean?"

"Looks to me like you have a zombie problem," Santa said. He pointed outside.

I looked to my left, out the windows. Sure enough, there were about twenty zombies in our yard.

"How the hell…"

"The reindeer all wear bells," Santa said, cutting me off. "The noise seems to attract the dead folks when I fly around on Christmas Eve." He paused for a minute, reflecting. "Guess I won't be using the bells next year."

"Reindeer?" I said. Nothing was making sense.

"Sure, you know: Dasher, Donner, Dicker, Ducker, Tucker... the whole crew. Hell, I forget their names. You probably know 'em better'n I do, kid."

"Is...is Mom dead?" Patrick had finally come out of his trance.

Santa looked at me. "*Oops*," he mouthed. He turned to Patrick, knelt down so he was at eye level with my brother. "Yeah, you see...I saw you boys and your father shooting zombies down here, and well, when I got here, I thought your mother was a zombie, too. So I shot her."

Patrick hadn't blinked. "Is she gonna be okay?" His face was emotionless. He was in shock.

"Oh boy," Santa sighed. "Uh, let's see..." He spoke in a condescending tone. "YOUR MOM IS DEAD. SEE?" He turned and waved a hand at Mom's body. "SHE WON'T BE BACK TO TUCK YOU IN TONIGHT!"

Patrick just stared straight ahead. He was back in his trance.

Dad held a hand to his forehead. He paced around in a small circle, tried to find an answer, a solution, anything.

Santa glared at him. "When you're done doing...whatever it is you're doing, you might want to consider this zombie problem you've got out there."

Dad and I looked outside again. There were now more than before. A couple of zombies had broken into our car. They'd smashed in the windows, ripped through the seats, and torn out the steering wheel and part of the dashboard. I'd never seen them be so destructive before; it was kind of bizarre. We heard a window break in the kitchen, then another one in my bedroom down the hall. The zombies had gotten into the house. We had to get out.

Again, Santa tried to hurry things up. "Oooooh! Look at the pretty guns! What do you say we shoot our way out? Huh, fellas?" His eyes were wide and he wore a goofy smile. Under normal circumstances, I might have laughed. Truth be told, Santa was a straight-up jerk. But he was right.

"Dad, we can do this," I said. "We'll load the rifles and make our way to our neighbor's house and take their car."

"I've got a better idea," Santa said. "Follow me." He picked my rifle up off the floor and handed it to me. I removed a handful of bullets from my pocket and started loading. He then picked up Dad's rifle from the floor and handed it to him. Dad was still a bit stunned, but he took it and slowly started reloading.

Patrick was the last one. His rifle was resting against a table.

"Grab your gun, kid," Santa said. Patrick just stood there. "Hey, Stone-face! Let's move!" Patrick flinched, jarred by Santa's booming voice. He spun around and reached for his rifle. I handed him some rounds and he began loading it. When we were done we turned to Santa, eagerly awaiting his next command.

Santa removed a Colt .45 from his waistband and held it up close to his shoulder. "You all ready?" he asked.

We nodded.

"Okay, let's give 'em hell, boys!" Santa shouted.

He charged through the front door and onto the porch. As soon as he was outside, he fired a couple of times and took care of the two zombies that were standing by the front windows. I emerged from behind him and aimed my rifle at a group of zombies in the front yard. One by one, they dropped like bowling pins. Patrick was next out the door. He ran in front of Santa and dropped two more zombies that were walking up the steps to the porch.

Dad was the last one outside. He screamed like John Rambo and fired until his rifle was empty. Five more zombies were dead—permanently.

I looked around and noticed our house was suddenly surrounded by the undead. They were flocking to our home now, likely drawn to the gunshots. I wasn't sure about Santa, but I knew that between Dad, Patrick and I, we didn't have enough bullets to get through all of them.

"If we can get to the roof, we can take my sleigh!" Santa yelled above the gunfire.

"There's a lattice on the other side of the garage that runs all the way to the roof!" Dad said. He'd already finished reloading.

"All right, let's go for it!" Santa shouted. He moved past Patrick and opened fire once more. One by one, the big man in red dropped the undead all over the yard. Patrick and I moved together, side by side, and shot any zombies that were within ten feet of us. Dad picked them off when the zombies reached the sidewalk and the driveway.

"Keep moving!" Santa shouted. He'd made it down the porch steps and onto the driveway. Patrick and I scurried after him and Dad moved swiftly and cautiously behind us.

As we crossed the driveway, a familiar figure stepped out from around the side of the garage. Santa raised his pistol and took aim.

"*Wait!*" Dad yelled. "It's Bert!"

"Who?" Santa asked.

"That's our neighbor," Patrick said.

Unfortunately, Bert wasn't looking too good. The five-inch gash in his neck and the awkward gait with which he shuffled toward us were two proof-positive signs that he'd been bitten. The bloody severed hand he was gnawing on was also a dead giveaway.

"Son-of-a-bitch, Bert!" Dad said. He raised his rifle and blasted a hole through Bert's head. The body fell backward and into the fence that lined our yard.

"Any more neighbors we should be worried about?" Santa asked.

"I don't know," Dad said.

"Well then, let's keep moving."

We raced around the garage and into the backyard. The lattice that crept up the side of the house was just a little farther ahead. Santa stopped for a moment and let the three of us go first.

"Come on!" Santa yelled, waving us by. "I'll cover you!"

Patrick reached the lattice first. He held his rifle with one hand and began to climb with the other. I let him get a few steps ahead and then followed right behind him. Dad followed me. When all three of us were on the roof, Santa began to climb up.

"Hurry!" Dad yelled. "You've got company!"

Five more zombies had surrounded the bottom of the lattice. They all bumped each other as they reached up and clawed at the fat man in red. Santa turned and fired his gun. He only managed two rounds when his gun clicked empty.

"Damn it!"

"Don't worry about them!" Dad called. "Just get up here!"

Santa shoved the gun into his waistband and continued climbing. He moved pretty fast for a fat guy in a velvet suit. For a moment, I was kind of impressed by his speed and agility.

Then we heard the sound of the lattice cracking and buckling under Santa's weight. Instinctively, the three of us all reached for the top of the lattice, but before we could grab the top, it broke away from the house with a loud *snap*.

Santa fell backwards. We watched in horror as he slammed onto the hard ground, impaling himself on a broken dowel that had snapped off the lattice. The zombies gathered on the ground immediately crowded around Santa, pulling and biting at his red suit. We stared in horror as blood shot upward in spurts and mini fountains. Surprisingly, Santa didn't scream. Or perhaps the sound of his cries were drowned out by the noise of the feeding that was happening fifteen feet below us.

"Hey, what's that?" Patrick asked.

Unaware that Patrick had moved away from us, Dad and I turned and saw what had caught his attention.

It was Santa's sleigh.

"Holy shit," Dad said.

The three of us walked toward the sleigh. It was like nothing we would have thought. It was red of course, and massive. The rear of the sleigh looked similar to the back end of an old Hudson Hornet, but with a much larger trunk. I assumed that was where Santa kept all the gifts he carried around the world. I ran my hand along the shiny exterior as we walked alongside the great machine. It was the smoothest metal I'd ever felt in my life.

"Let's get in, Dad," Patrick said.

"Okay," Dad agreed.

The three of us rested our rifles on the floor of the sleigh. Not surprisingly, there was a single bench-style seat, with leather appointments and chrome accents. The seat was *huge*, big and long enough for ten people to sit comfortably across it. Dad took a seat in the middle, Patrick and I sat on either side of him.

In front of us was a bank of computer equipment; satellite navigation, radar, accelerator/decelerator, wind measurement, fog lamp controls. In fact, it wasn't that different from the cockpit of an airplane.

"I wonder what this does," Dad mused. He reached forward and pressed a button with the words **Lift/Land** on it. We felt a rumble under our seat and the enormous machine came to life. The reindeer, which had been relaxing and standing lazily in front of us, quickly stood at attention. A bar rose up from the floor and rested firmly against our thighs, securing us.

"I think we're leaving," I said.

"Where are we going?" Patrick asked.

Dad looked left and right, his eyes showing the same confusion in mine. "I don't know."

"Is Mom really dead?" Patrick asked.

The question was like a punch in the stomach. I felt the air leave my body and saw the same reaction in Dad, who turned to my brother. Dad's face was somber and a tear formed in his eye. "Yes, Patrick. Your mother's gone now."

Patrick looked away from him, toward the front of the sleigh. I could see in his face that he finally understood what had happened. A lump formed in my throat as the realization of her death finally materialized for me as well. I was sad. It had happened so fast and there was nothing I could have done to prevent it.

The sleigh rumbled some more and we lifted off the roof. In front of us, the reindeer seemed to float upward with the sleigh. I strained my neck to look out and below us. I could see our street. A crowd of zombies had now formed below, and as we floated a bit higher, our front yard came into view. A little higher still and I could see our house. The zombies had amassed an army. They'd ransacked our home and were now inside it.

"Do you think we're going to the North Pole?" Patrick asked; a faint yet forced smile traced across his lips.

I looked at my Dad and raised an eyebrow.

"I don't know," Dad said. "But anywhere is better than here."

The compass on the sleigh's controls indicated we were headed due north. I looked down at the floor and saw what appeared to be some kind of trap door. I reached for the handle and pulled it open. It was a storage space. There were maps, flashlights, some rope; all kinds of stuff you would typically see in a glove compartment. I dug deeper, moved a few things around and found some blankets. I removed a couple and passed them to my dad and brother. Dad helped Patrick wrap himself with the first blanket, then he huddled closer to him and used the second one to wrap them both. I pulled out another blanket for myself and wrapped it around my shoulders.

We rose higher and higher, the reindeer kicking their legs and steering the giant machine up into the clouds.

It was freezing outside. I wondered: if we *were* going to the North Pole, how much colder would it become? And would there be any zombies there?

For the first time in a long time, I was afraid of them. The dead had shown us what could happen if we let our guard down.

We'd become complacent. We'd become lazy. We'd become what they are. I wondered if we were the only humans who had become that careless. And if not, how long would it take for the zombies to find and destroy us?

I hope we're smart enough not to let that happen.

MERRY CHRISTMAS, CLAIRE

KEVIN LEWIS

Even in the bathroom I could hear the pounding on the front door. I was washing my hands in the sink. It seemed like I was doing it for the past half-hour.

The first time you kill someone, especially someone you love, the blood never comes off as easily as you'd like it too. That's life.

My name is Tom Barnes and I wouldn't call myself a violent person. It was just this one time that I let my anger get the best of me. I still can't believe what happened. One moment my wife, Claire, and I were having a lovely dinner. Ham and potatoes, a favorite of mine. The next minute she's dead on the floor.

It was all over my gambling. I admit I have a problem. Claire just couldn't take it anymore. She said she wanted to have some space so I could get help. *Some help!* We got into a heated argument. I called her a "Damn bitch," which I really didn't mean but when you're in an intense argument, sometimes you say things that are not true. Then she slapped me in the face.

It was as if I was someone else. I lost it. I quickly grabbed her and shoved her into the living room where she fell, crashing down on the glass coffee table.

It took a moment for me to realize what I had done. I stared at my beautiful wife of ten years, lying face down in the middle of the living room.

I rushed over and rolled Claire onto her back. The small, porcelain Christmas tree protruded from her bloody chest. Her face was covered in blood.

A large gash stretched across her forehead. Blood oozed from the vertical orifice. Pieces of glass clung to her brown hair.

"Oh, God, Claire!" I knelt down and grabbed her hand. I was so shocked at what I had done, I wasn't thinking clearly. Then I sprang into action.

I grabbed the tree with one hand and placed my other hand on Claire's chest. I slowly pulled the tree out of her chest and when I did, blood sprayed all over me. Claire shrieked in pain.

"Oh, Claire! Claire, hang on!"

I grabbed several towels from the kitchen, which was adjacent to the living room, and applied them to her bleeding forehead and chest.

She kept trying to tell me something but I couldn't understand it until now. It sounded like, "C…all…on…on…" her garbled voice strained. *Call 9-1-1, dumbass!* The one thing I didn't do because I was so confused, shocked, and horrified at what I'd done.

"It's going to be okay, honey. You just hold on."

But she didn't. She lay still while her green eyes, still open even though I knew she was dead, stared at me.

Like most spousal murderers, as well as most murderers in general, I didn't report the incident to the police. Are you insane? I didn't want to go to jail. Hell no! So I did the only sane thing a man in my position could do.

I called the local witch to resurrect my wife.

I'm not kidding.

The pounding continued. I turned off the water and walked out of the bathroom. The light was still on in the living room. That's the one thing I really didn't do was panic and shut off the lights to let anyone passing by know that I wasn't home.

Not that anyone would come by anytime soon because we…I…live on a countryside road, cut off from civilization—the nearest house is about two miles down the road. That's the advantage you get when you live in a countryside state such as Vermont.

When I reached the foot of the staircase, I heard a soft *purring* sound. Oh, Christ! My wife's damn cat, Tabbers, was lapping up her blood! I quickly shooed her away. "Get out of here," I quietly told her.

I opened the door a crack to take a peek at who was out there, fearful that it was a normal passerby, or the police, at which point I would have run the hell out the back door.

But it was not a normal passerby and it was not the police. It was the local witch/wizard/sorcerer, whatever the hell he was.

He stood in the cold, winter night, dressed in a black cloak, one hand clutching a black bag.

What the bag contained, I'm sure I'd find out soon.

Most people would have been petrified at the sight of the man but I just stared transfixed at him.

His wrinkled face was so gaunt with age it was as if he had been born before the invention of the automobile.

Still, it amazed me how much white hair still rested on his head.

"Good evening," the man said.

"Hello, my name is Tom Barnes."

"A pleasure to meet you, Mr. Barnes. My name is Fenton Carnaby. It is mighty chilly out here. I predict we shall have a white Christmas."

The man spoke very elegantly, as if he came from the nineteenth century. I'd be surprised if he swore. Even his name sounded old.

"Won't you come in?" I asked him.

"Thank you."

Mr. Carnaby stepped out of the darkness and into the light of my house.

* * *

"My, my," Mr. Carnaby said as he examined my dead wife. He still wore his black cloak. He probably wore that thing to bed. "This is a pity. And such a pretty woman."

Mr. Carnaby was right. Even in death, Claire looked beautiful, minus the pool of blood around her. She was just as slender as she was in high school where we met. Even at forty, she still looked like she could have been a model.

I stood over by the staircase. I couldn't bring myself to join the mysterious man who knelt over my wife's lifeless body.

Then he looked up at me and said, "Any sane human being would have reported this incident to the police. However, you called me. Why?"

"Because I know what you do. You know things that most…normal people don't know. Witchcraft. It's been widely rumored that you know how to bring back the dead."

Mr. Carnaby stood up and walked over to me. A chill ran up my spine at the very presence of him standing directly in front of me. "Rumors are most often not true. Perhaps I am not what you think I am?"

But I knew the truth. I knew what he was and what he was capable of doing.

And so I told him the story of what I had witnessed.

It was a couple of years ago in the dead of night. I was walking off my anger after a fight with Claire. Same subject: my intense gambling.

Walking along Fairwood Lane always gave me peace of mind, especially at night; the wind blowing against the trees; the crickets chirping in the night.

But not that night.

As I walked, I heard a voice in the woods adjacent to the long road. I knew it was a *really* stupid idea to investigate, but for some reason the idea of something strange going on in there intrigued me.

I saw someone hovering over what appeared to be a dead deer in the woods. The deer was all messed up. It probably got run over in the road and then staggered into the woods where it died.

I couldn't tell if the person standing up was a man or a woman because the person was completely covered in a black cloak.

The person standing threw both hands into the air and started shouting. It sounded like a ritual. Something about resurrecting the dead. I couldn't make out everything despite the fact that the voice echoed across the woods.

Then there was silence. I stood there, not knowing what to say or do. I wanted to run the hell out of the woods, but my feet were glued together because I was horrified at what I had just witnessed.

I heard a rustling sound on the ground. One of the deer's legs had twitched. It stood up and looked at the mysterious cloaked stranger for a moment.

Then it pranced off further into the woods. The thing in the black cloak turned around and I knew who the stranger was in an instant.

It was Mr. Carnaby.

He was the person everyone in my town of Barnestable, Vermont all talked about: the mysterious old man who lived in an old and dilapidated cottage in the woods. There he was in the flesh. The rumors were all true.

He was in fact a witch because it was clear that, at first, the deer was dead.

And then Mr. Carnaby did his magic, which brought the poor animal back to life.

That's why I needed him now.

"Interesting," the old witch said, staring at me. He turned around and walked back over to my wife. "But are you willing to fully go through with the ritual?"

"How hard can it be?" I said.

Mr. Carnaby looked at me. He seemed almost irritated at what I just asked him. Then the grin faded and it turned into an eerie smile. "You'll see."

Mr. Carnaby knelt down and unzipped his black bag. He extracted a large black book, which he handed to me. The title of the book was *The Resurrection*. A pentagram, a common witch's symbol, was emblazoned on the front cover.

I glanced at some of the strangest pages ever imagined. Rituals containing the weirdest incantations: the body of a dead and hated relative to bring back your precious pet, the heart of a rival to further your career…bizarre spells that if I wasn't in a dilemma, I would have cast them off as inane.

"Fascinating, isn't it?" Mr. Carnaby commented, taking the book from my hands.

"Very." I didn't mention the fact that I also found the book to be absolutely terrifying.

Mr. Carnaby flipped through the book. This took a moment. When he found what he was looking for he said, "Here we go," and handed it back to me.

I read the spell aloud, "To resurrect your spouse, you must first bury her in a patch of ground on your property as if she were to be buried for all eternity. Then you must cut yourself and drain a small amount of blood over the gravesite, for the blood of the guilty will seep through the dirt and douse the dead body underneath the earth…"

I stopped reading and looked at Mr. Carnaby. He was smiling at me, clearly enjoying the moment. "I have to cut myself? That's disgusting!"

"You do wish to resurrect your wife, do you not?"

"Yes, but…why do I have to cut myself?"

"Because that is what the spell requires you to do. You and you alone must perform these duties as well as chant the incantation. *And then your wife will rise from the grave!*" He said the last line while raising his hands in the air as if he was some kind of satanic priest presiding over a dead body. I felt as if I was in some B-horror film with a low budget and over-acting actors.

"Unless," he continued, "you don't want to speak to your wife alive again. Perhaps you wish to bury your wife somewhere where no one would find her. And then later on, when her family and friends want to wish her a merry Christmas, what will you say?"

I didn't say anything. I had no answer and that made me realize the strange witch standing in front of me was correct. I had no other choice.

Mr. Carnaby headed to the front door. He opened it and stepped out into the cool winter night.

"I'll return the book as soon as my wife returns."

Mr. Carnaby turned around and shook his head. "That won't be necessary. This book is yours to keep. But use it wisely and may you be happy with your resurrected wife! Merry Christmas!"

Mr. Carnaby walked down my driveway and into the dark night.

I did not procrastinate. I picked up my dead wife from the floor and carried her out into the backyard. I propped her up on a lawn chair while I dug her grave. Fortunately for me there was no snow on the ground. Unfortunately, the ground was so cold that it made digging even the smallest of graves very difficult. It took me about half an hour. Although my wife is a thin woman, I wanted the grave to be big enough so she could maneuver around in it when she awoke.

If she woke up.

I suddenly realized that this could all be some elaborate prank. Maybe Mr. Carnaby was not the weird guy I thought him to be. Maybe he found the deer in the woods and, hearing footsteps approaching, put on the weird act to spook me. But that deer sure looked dead and it ran away very quickly once Mr. Carnaby did his witchcraft stuff.

I don't know. What the hell? I'll try the damn spell and if it works then no worries, I'll have my lovely wife back. If it doesn't work? Well, then, I guess I have two options: Leave her buried in the backyard grave or confess to the police.

Gently, I placed Claire's body into the hole. It took me about two minutes to dump the dirt back into Claire's makeshift grave. I prayed to God himself that nobody witnessed me reciting what I was about to say. That would be embarrassing. Plus, I'd certainly look guilty of murder, and that was definitely not good.

Picking up the book from the ground, I flipped the old and worn pages. The wind started to pick up and the pages flapped from side to side. I found the incantation and spoke its haunting and chilling words.

"I implore you, God of the dead, to resurrect this creature of God. Restore her soul and allow her to rise from her grave."

I set the book down on the stump of a tree that was cut down the year before. Then I grabbed a knife from my pant pocket and sliced the palm of my left hand. Pain surged throughout my entire body. I guided my bleeding hand over my dead wife's grave.

"My blood will be a sacrifice to the evil I have caused."

Droplets of blood oozed from my hand and onto her grave. "Now, let her be free!" I lowered my hand, never once taking my eyes off of Claire's grave.

I prayed this was not going to take long because I felt like I was going to pass out from nausea at any moment.

Nothing happened. There was only silence, save for crickets chirping in the distance. For a moment I thought this was all for nothing and was ready to pack it all in when I heard a rustling. It didn't sound like a rustling of trees. It sounded like dirt being moved.

And it was emanating from underground.

I stepped back for a larger view. I heard moaning from underneath the ground. It was faint at first but I knew its voice instantly. It was Claire. Living with someone for a long time, one knows their spouse's voice through crying, shrieking, conversational talk and, of course, moaning.

The moaning grew louder, which meant she was reaching the surface. I could hear her fingers plow through the dirt.

There was a soft *pough*! Specks of dirt exploded into the air as my wife pushed out the dirt. I wanted desperately to assist her but the demonic book said not to. *They must dig themselves out.*

The book did not give an explanation as to why but I suspect that, since they were somewhat being reborn, they must learn how to take care of themselves.

It didn't matter because Claire seemed to be doing just fine. Her arms rose from the dirt grave and soon her dirt-covered head emerged from the ground.

Her eyes were bulging wide-eyed. She had no idea what was going on. I didn't care at the moment. There she was, standing right in front of me.

I stared at my resurrected wife for the longest time. I couldn't believe it. She was alive and I noticed no physical change to her.

Her blouse was torn but that was about it. I'd love to throw it away, but she'd probably kill me if I did. She also smelled like death. And earth. Her eyes were also the color blue. This was strange because her eyes had been green.

I figured that, since she was being reborn, she, like a baby, would have blue eyes at first. Hopefully her green eyes would return because I had no believable explanation for our family and friends.

Claire glanced from side to side, confused, like she didn't know where she was.

"Claire?"

She stared at me, her eyes wide and very nervous. It was as if this was the first time she had seen me. Then she started to speak. It was guttural at first. Her mouth was probably still filled with dirt.

"Wha…wh…at happ…ened t…to me?"

I hadn't thought of how I was going to answer that question. Part of me wished she hadn't brought it up.

"Nothing," I told her. "You fell in the hole and it caved in on you. Don't you remember?"

That made absolutely no sense but I was definitely stretching here. I had no other sane explanation.

Claire looked in back of her. She stared down at the hole she dug herself out of only a moment ago. "I did?"

Saved!

"Yes. But you're all right now." I gently reached out to take her hand. She stared down at my gesture and was confused for a brief moment. *Is she forgetting how to act?*

But something must have registered in her mind because she finally took my hand. I was relieved. Her hand felt cold but I didn't mind. I was just so glad my wife was alive again.

Slowly, we trekked across the backyard toward our home. Although she had only been dead for a couple of hours, I didn't want to overwhelm her with a fast walk. I steadied her with both my hands; one hand holding hers and another gently gripping her shoulder to balance her.

"I'm…cold." Thank God. Her speech was fully returning.

"I know. I'll make you some hot tea when we get back inside."

Her hunger was coming back as well.

"And food," she added, but she didn't really say it to me. She said it to herself.

Claire suddenly stopped and stooped to the ground.

"Honey, what's wrong?"

She didn't answer me. She brought her hand down and scooped up something so small I could not make out what it was.

"Claire, what are you…?"

Claire held it out in front of her. The moon's reflection shed light on the object she was holding. It was a tiny ant that, from the looks of it, was trying to escape.

"Honey, why don't you put it…"

At that moment she shoved it in her mouth and gulped it down. She didn't wince once for she clearly understood her actions. I was shocked and mortified at what I had just witnessed. My lovely wife just inhaled an ant!

Nasty!

"Claire, sweetheart, what are you doing?"

Her hungry eyes stared at me. "I need to eat," she answered in a painful tone.

"I'll fix you something when we get back inside. But for Christ's sake, don't eat insects."

She looked away from me. I followed her gaze. Her hungry eyes never ceased. I've never seen her act this way in my life. I was concerned. But I was also happy to have her back safe and sound.

* * *

It was five days until Christmas and Claire was not improving. Not that I expected it to be instant, but she was still confused and her constant hunger continued to linger. I decided to take some personal time to be with her while she adjusted to her new lifestyle. I just told my boss that Claire was sick with some virus and needed my immediate care. To save myself, I added that if she continued to be ill, I would take her to the hospital.

Of course I knew in my heart that I could never complete that task. I knew, even then, that Claire was different from the moment she crawled her way out of her grave and ate the ant. I couldn't expose her to the horror from the medical community.

One night we were sitting together at the dinner table. I had made Claire's favorite meal: pasta and meatballs. She wouldn't touch it. She just stared blankly at her food. It didn't interest her at all.

"Claire," I said, sitting across from her. "This is your favorite meal. Eat up."

Her eyes never left the plate. "It doesn't appeal to me."

"Do you want me to make you something else?"

At that moment, Tabbers leapt up onto Claire's lap. Her gaze shifted toward her precious cat. She pet Tabbers softly. "Such a good little cat." Claire was eyeing her cat passively, as if nothing else in the world mattered. Then she quickly brought Tabbers' head up to her mouth and chewed a big gash out of the cat's neck.

I bolted from my chair and ran toward my wife, who still held the cat. She was chewing Tabbers' flesh. Fur dangled from my wife's bloodstained mouth. I glanced at Tabbers who was convulsing in my wife's arms. Blood oozed out of Tabbers' neck.

"Claire, what...what's wrong with you?"

Tabbers suddenly stopped convulsing and just lay dead in my grotesque wife's arms. I reached out to grab the dead cat but

Claire pulled back as if she was a child and I was taking her favorite toy away from her.

"I'm not finished!" she snarled at me. This time she bit off Tabbers' front paw and ate it. Claire smiled triumphantly.

"Not finished, Claire? Jesus Christ!"

"I'M HUNGRY, GODDAMN IT!"

Now I said before that Claire and I had our arguments. However, she never screeched at me at the top of her lungs, nor swore with such ferocity.

I stood there, staring at my wife and thought: This is not my wife. *This is not the woman I vowed to love and cherish until the day I died. What the hell did I bring back from the dead? Who is this woman? This is certainly not my Claire.*

To be on the safe side, I locked Claire down in the basement - for her own wellbeing as well as my own. Claire didn't object, which I was grateful for.

She seemed tired after her dinner.

We never did bury poor old Tabbers. She ate the whole cat.

I eventually returned to work. It was not easy for me to leave Claire alone in the house while I had to pay the bills. I was worried she would escape and eat someone else.

But I had no choice.

I gave her enough food to tide her over until I returned at night. Hell, I even got her scraps from the butcher shop over in Fallsbury.

"What do you need raw meat for?" Stan, the butcher, asked me.

"It's for Claire's cat," I lied. "We're trying a new diet."

"Some diet."

As I was about to leave, Stan shouted out, "Tell Claire I'll be in at 7 tomorrow if she wants to pick up the food early."

I stopped, turned, and faced Stan. "What?"

"The food for your Christmas Eve party? You know? The open house you and Claire hold every year?"

I completely forgot about the party. Everyone is going to be there! Family, friends, and coworkers. What the hell am I going to do? I can't cancel. That would only draw suspicion in my direction. Maybe Claire will be fine by tomorrow night.

I can only hope.

It was a chilly Christmas Eve. The sky was dark the entire day, which meant snow was forthcoming.

I chained Claire downstairs while I prepared for the big night. In the morning, I picked up the food at the supermarket.

Stan asked me why Claire hadn't picked it up. I told him she had a million things to do and that I'd do it for her. He called me a terrific husband. How wrong he was.

Everyone basically arrived around 7:30 p.m. I situated them in the living room—any trace of the accident completely cleaned up. Our five-disc CD player played Christmas music in the background.

It has always been wonderful seeing friends and family at the holidays. I know it sounds cheesy but all of their love and support truly takes your mind off your troubles for the time being.

Or until your snooty brother-in-law ruins the moment for you.

Claire's big brother, Charles, hit the big time in the stock market and had been rubbing it in my face ever since.

He's a tall and be-speckled man with practically no meat on him who managed to marry a trophy wife right after he hit the big time. *She loves him for his intellect. Yeah, right!*

"Are you both enjoying yourselves?" I asked Charles. Claire stood right beside me. In fact, she never left my side when the guests arrived.

Her hungry eyes wandered, though, and that worried me. I could already tell that people were talking in hushed tones.

"Cherry and I are having a wonderful time," Charles answered.

"Yes," Cherry agreed. "I love what you and Claire have done with the place. It's so…festive."

Even in her snooty tone, Cherry was trying to sound flattering. I didn't buy it. I also didn't let it get the best of me. "Well, you know Claire. Christmas was always her favorite holiday."

"About Claire?" Charles chimed in. "I'm worried about her. She doesn't appear to be herself."

Oh, shit!

"Claire's actually recovering from a nasty stomach bug. It really threw her for a loop. Isn't that right, dear?"

I turned around to acknowledge Claire and discovered she was not at my side. Then I heard a horrible scream. It came from upstairs.

I rushed up the staircase to where the scream emanated from and discovered Claire in the bathroom. She stood over Mary Clemens, a secretary at my office, who was cowering on the floor. Mary's arm was bleeding.

"Oh, my God! Mary! Claire?"

Claire turned around. Her mouth was covered in Mary's blood. "I'm not finished," she said in her bizarre tone of voice.

"What the hell is wrong with her?" a frantic and horrified Mary asked.

"It's the medication she's on for her stomach bug. She must be having a bad reaction to it." That was all I could think to say at the moment.

I entered into the chaos and bandaged Mary up as best as I could. As soon as Mary and her boyfriend left for the hospital, I declared the party to be over.

* * *

When I awoke Christmas morning, snow covered the ground. It was a beautiful white Christmas. "Merry Christmas, Claire," I told my wife as I unchained her down in the basement.

I made breakfast and coffee for us. We exchanged gifts, which, in this case meant I opened not only my presents, but Claire's as well.

It appeared that the concept of opening up presents was lost in the resurrection process. Every Christmas I longed for Claire's reaction to the gifts I bought for her.

I enjoyed the moment when her eyes would go wide and her mouth would gape in excitement as she discovered her new treasures. This year, however, I looked at my expressionless wife as she stared at her new perfume and body lotion set, which cost me seventy dollars, with disinterest.

"Claire, don't you like your present? The woman at the store said it's very popular." Of course, I also bought the gift before I killed Claire.

"I'm hungry," was her reply.

She looked up at me but I knew she wasn't staring at me. She was looking right past me at…nothing.

This was not how I expected this Christmas to turn out. Even though Claire had returned from the dead, I figured the holidays would still be a happier occasion—albeit a tad bizarre. Just like the good old days.

But the way Claire turned out, whatever she was now; it was dampening all the Christmas cheer. I was tempted to cancel the annual Christmas dinner with Claire's family but decided to trudge along. I could still make this a Merry Christmas. I could still make Claire happy. I just didn't know how.

Around 10:00 a.m., I chained Claire back down in the basement because I needed to pick up the Christmas ham at the supermarket.

"I'll be back soon, sweetheart."

One Christmas tradition I always enjoy the most is heading out on Christmas morning and seeing the insane traffic. I always imagine that they are last minute holiday shoppers. Morons. They never learn.

This morning, I pulled into a practically full supermarket. I entered the store and witnessed frantic shoppers scurrying to buy food for Christmas dinner. Many people gathered near the deli and were annoyed at the lack of deli meats and cheeses to choose from. *That's for waiting until the last minute!* But not Claire. She ordered the ham a month before.

I walked up to Stan, who was sweating bullets from the insanity, and handed him Claire's slip. He took the slip with a curious grin on his face.

"Claire's still not feeling well?" Stan asked me.

"Yeah. She woke up this morning and was still out of sorts." If only he knew.

Stan shook his head in sympathy for me and disappeared in the back. He returned with a large ham and handed it to me. I placed it in the grocery cart.

My cell phone rang. I answered it. It was Claire. In her undead condition, I was amazed she figured out how to use the phone.

"Claire, honey, what's wrong?"

"I'm still hungry!"

"What do you mean? We just ate breakfast."

"They weren't enough."

"What do you mean 'they' "?

"The people."

The phone went dead. A shiver climbed up my spine. I quickly paid for the ham and rushed out of the store.

When I saw the mini-van parked in my snow-covered driveway, I knew something was up. I rushed inside (not bothering to take the ham out of the trunk) and yelled at the top of my lungs. "Claire!"

Her moans emanated from the basement, so I took comfort in knowing she was still down there. When I reached the foot of the basement steps, the fear crept back inside me again. My basement resembled the kill floor of a slaughterhouse. Straight ahead of me, I witnessed my monstrous wife standing over the dead and eaten bodies of her parents. Claire had practically devoured their entire flesh. Those poor old bastards. It figures. They arrived early, found Claire, and somehow unchained her. Oh, how they must have been shocked! *Merry Christmas!*

I hurried over to Claire. Her face was covered in blood and a strip of flesh dangled from her mouth. "Claire! Claire! What did you do? How could you do this! Answer me!" I grabbed her shoulders and shook her.

Claire just stared at me with those hungry eyes. She shrugged my arms off of her. "I was hungry! I'm still hungry! I can't stop!"

I backed away from her, terrified at what she was. A monster.

Then she looked at me. Stared deep into my eyes. "I need to eat, sweetheart!" She walked toward me, her arms stretched out like claws about to grab its prey. Me.

"Claire, oh Claire, please don't," I said as I backed toward the wall.

"But I'm hungry!" Closer and closer she advanced on me, those ravenous hands never dropping to her side. I backed up against the wall and stood frozen in my tracks. Silently, I prayed that Claire would come to her senses, that she would see that it was I, her loving husband, who wanted nothing more than to have her back in my life. But all she saw in me was food.

Claire stood right in front of me now. Face to face. I could smell her putrid breath and it made me sick to my stomach. For the last time, Claire kissed me. It was a soft and beautiful kiss and for one moment, I thought that she was going to recant her wish to devour me. Claire pulled back and stared at me, her dead eyes locking onto mine. *"Merry Christmas, Tom!"* she said and an eerie expression filled her face. She grabbed me with her cold, dead arms, and shoved me to the floor.

The last moment I had was seeing my wife eat my flesh.

The first thing I wanted when I awoke was food. I was hungry but not for regular food. I touched my neck and noticed that a huge chunk of it was missing. Part of my left arm and leg had been chewed as well. I stared at my undead wife and hunger, as was the case of late, filled her eyes.

"When are we going to have Christmas dinner?" she asked me.

"Soon," I answered. "The rest of the guests haven't arrived."

Our guests arrived an hour later. I answered the door and Charles and Cherry stood in the early snowy afternoon.

"Merry Christmas!" Charles said. Then he noticed my bandaged neck. And arm. "Tom, what happened?"

"I'm fine. Do you want some eggnog?"

Charles and Cherry stepped into the house.

Forget the Christmas ham. Claire and I had the best Christmas dinner ever. The best part was seeing her smile after the longest time. There's nothing like seeing your loved one happy at the holidays.

As I chewed on Charles' left hand, I said, "Merry Christmas, Claire."

A WHITE CHRISTMAS: LIVE FROM 1941!

THOMAS RICHARDSON

September 2010: An incredible find was made today, in the private archives of legendary performer Bing Crosby. Thought lost for sixty years, a recording of the final World Series game between the Pittsburgh Pirates and the Yankees was unearthed by archivists, tasked with cataloguing the extensive collection left to his estate. Oft quoted as one of the most desired games to be recovered by baseball fans worldwide…

There's no question as why the Pirate's game made such big headlines. Go Google it now; '*September 2010 Bing Crosby Baseball*' and you'll get a feel for the magnitude of the find. In a nutshell, Bing, a huge fan and then part-owner of the team, thought he would jinx the team just by being in the country, and thus decamped to Paris while designing to have the game recorded in his absence. Home video recorders were still a decade or so off for all but the most affluent at this point, so any recovery like this, especially of such a sought-after match, is quite rightly heralded by fans of archive TV and radio.

Just to clarify: I'm one of the team that found it. About nine months ago, the custodians of the Crosby Estate got kind of annoyed with the rancid, vinegary smell coming from the vaults, and called a few of us 'experts' in to transfer his records to a digital format for all posterity. However, among the vast collection of Bing's radio performances, TV slots and home videos, there were a few things equally, if not more so, interesting than the Pirate's game which was so heavily reported. I'm talking about Christmas Day, 1941.

Most fans of Vintage Radio know that Bing Crosby was the host of regular NBC show *The Kraft Music Hall,* and 1941 was slap-bang in the middle of his ten-odd year tenure. Again thought lost to the annals of history, this particular show had featured the first ever performance by Bing Crosby performing the classic tune *White Christmas,* and would again have been an incredible find. So you can imagine how excited I was when, in a locked drawer in an old mahogany desk of his, I found a container marked with that exact date, and a simple 'NBC' beside it.

Many 'experts' have dismissed this as a hoax. And to be honest I'm not surprised. Contemporary reports also say that the un-precedented bad weather that particular year interfered with the signal so badly that few outside the immediate area actually heard the original broadcast, leaving us almost no written account of the show's contents to compare this find to. At best, I've heard it suggested that this was a sort of prank, an ill-advised attempt at emulating Orson Well's famous War of the Worlds broadcast from five years previously.

So here it is: publicly, for the first time, as complete a transcript of the broadcast as possible, accounting for damage. I'll let you make up your own mind exactly what happened.

Watch out for the bit where Bing goes crazy on a zombie elf.

Thomas Richardson

Archivist

Now from NBC Short Wave Radio on this Christmas day: The Kraft Music Hall! Starring Mr. Bing Crosby, Master of Ceremonies; Mr. John Scott Trotter, master of his heavily reduced orchestra and few Charioteers. So, without further ado...Mr....Bing...Crosby!

(Rapturous applause. Approx. 43 seconds of heavily distorted, slow-tempo hymn featuring piano, string quartet and male choir, before segue into Mr. Crosby intro)

CROSBY: Many a welcome folks, and a Merriest of Christmases to each and every one of you. Hopefully, you are tuning in from a warm home, a loving family and a neckful of Scotch. (*Audience laugh*) Now to me, Christmas has always been about family. And when it's not about family then thankfully it's about making money. (*Smaller laugh*) That being said, what with this being today of all days, and record snow levels across this fair city, we find ourselves in front of only the most hard-boiled and dedicated Music Hall aficionados. (*The audience applaud themselves*)

SILVERS: (*Interjecting*) Sure; they came for the heat, and they stayed for the seats!

CROSBY: And by that note here is our special guest for the day: He's been called many names, most of them unrepeatable, but here he is, the man who puts the 'speak' in 'speakeasy,' the queen of chutzpah himself, straight from the Hit Parade, Mr. Bill Silvers! (*Large applause, whooping*)

SILVERS: And I'm his brother, Phil. (*Laughter, applause*)

CROSBY: Good to see you.

SILVERS: Good to see *you*.

CROSBY: Unfortunately, not only are we short on crowd this day but we are short on crew, so I would like to apologize both for Ms. Fitzgerald's absence and Mr. Silvers' presence. (*Chuckles*)

SILVERS: Charmed to be here, Bing. I must confess it took a lot of effort to get here tonight.

CROSBY: I'll be beat. Was the snow that bad?

SILVERS No, I just knew I'd have to see your face! (Laughter)

(Tape too damaged to transcribe accurately, approx. 30 seconds missing audio. Mr. Crosby warns listeners again of the unprecedented bad

weather, citing reports of extremely high figures of hospitalization over the last few hours)

CROSBY: Now Phil recently starred as Charlie Moore in small time flop flick *The Hit Parade of 1941.* Say, when did it come out, Bill?

SILVERS: October 15th, about two months ago, Bing

CROSBY: Oh well, I'm sure someone will remember it. (Laughter)

SILVERS: Did you see it?

CROSBY: Did I? Boy, what a hoot!

SILVERS: But it was meant to be a tragedy, Bing!

CROSBY: Like I said, a hoot. (*More laughter, clapping.*)

SILVERS: (*A pause*) Good to see you.

CROSBY: Good to see you. (*Laughter, before subsiding*) Well folks, we've had a few special requests tonight, but we're gonna do them anyway…

SILVERS: (*Interrupting*) Say, Bing, why don't I tootle along on this clarinet, maybe join in a line or two?

CROSBY: What a gay idea, Bill. You show me how it's done. (*The piano starts twinkling, the orchestra slowly building in the background*)

SILVERS: (whispering) More like save the show, say I!

CROSBY: This is a new favorite of mine. The Way it Goes, by Donnie and the Drugstore Cowboys

(*The audience applaud as Mr. Crosby, Mr. Silvers and company break fully into song. The tune is in a quick tempo, and evokes an audible 'buzz' from the audience. Mr. Silvers provides comedy on the clarinet, pretending not to be able to make a sound before breaking into ludicrously complex fills. Mr. Crosby plays the role of the Straight Man, gamely soldiering on throughout the distractions. All lines annotated '( )' represent Mr. Silvers' improvisation, usually derisory lines about Mr.*

Crosby, over the top of Mr. Crosby's performance of the established lyrics)

That's just the way it goes,
That's just the way it seems,
(*Every time that old Bing's horses come in,)*
(*In smoke goes up his dreams!*)
Well you didn't make it big,
No you didn't make it small,
(Folks, if there were two Bob Hopes in town,)
(*He wouldn't make it here at all!*)
Oh…I don't wanna have to be the one now,
Who breaks it to ya, baby:
(*That fat-head here's got a satchel ass,)*
(*And frankly his back is just too hairy!*)

(*Tape too damaged to transcribe accurately, approx. 110 seconds missing audio. As we resume, the tune has finished, and the applause is just beginning to subside*)

SILVERS: Keep clapping, folks, he might leave quicker! (*Laughter*)

CROSBY: Check it out, folks, as I show our good Mr. Silvers some tough love out back. In a word from our sponsors, I proudly present, Mr. Ken Carpenter, Purloiner of Pennies in Payment for Products, both Perfunctory and Passable.

SILVERS: Tough love, eh? You got anything with studs?

(*Mr. Carpenter, Kraft's Product Announcer, begins his usual 40 second advertising slot. However, His breathing is heavy and labored; he audibly struggles to keep his usual pacing and significantly overruns the slot. Mild dropout impedes entire monologue*)

CARPENTER: Folks, the good…the good people of Kraft have, have always tried to bring the best tastes of American dining straight to the kitchen in the home. Into your home. And with Christmas near over… That is why, why we think you'll love (*A pause, possibly wiping his brow*) Kraft's All American…all American burger patties, retailing for no more…than a dime. A dime for six. (*He stifles a cough*) Made from 100% Texas' Finest, you'll save on both…both time, money and effort…for your efforts. That's Kraft's All American Burger Patties. The…kids will thank you. For it, for the patties.

CROSBY: (*An awkward moment passes*) Golly-gee, Ken, you're all wet and just fit to drop, aren't ya? I haven't seen a face that sallow since the Pirates lost Honus.

CARPENTER: Must be the weather.

CROSBY: I'll bet. Maybe keep your lamps open for a Kraft's…All American…Miracle Cure or something

SILVERS: So anyway, Bing, how much are they paying ya to be here on Christmas day? What's the color of your kale?

CROSBY: Let's just say I'm covered now until I die or retire.

SILVERS: Then why don't you do either?"

CROSBY: Well, I'm under contract till the first and my wife expressly forbids the latter. (*Snare drum lick, audience chuckle. Mr. Carpenter is heard coughing*)

SILVERS: Says, how is the wife anyway?

CROSBY: Happy as she's ever been.

SILVERS: Oh *dear*. (*Much laughter*)

CROSBY: I'll pass on your concerns.

SILVERS: And assure her they are my deepest concerns. (*Much laughter, applause. Mr. Carpenter continues coughing*)

CROSBY: So why are you keeping an old jacksnipe like me company on this festive day? No wife? Or did she see your movie, too?

SILVERS: Who, little old me? Why, I've just got a big heart and a noble Christian spirit

CROSBY: How terrible for you.

SILVERS: I know, I'm taking tablets six times a day.

CROSBY: Well, you know what they—Christ Ken, what's the matter?

(*A commotion has started to build. The coughing has turned into a severe, painful-sounding retching. A series of crashes are heard, as Mr. Carpenter stumbles from his stool and into the orchestral section, causing an odd, discordant wail. Mr. Crosby and Mr. Silvers are heard rushing over to his aid. Booming, guttural sounds emanate from the stricken man*)

SILVERS: Mother Mary, Bing! There's blood everywhere! He's puked it all over himself. It's disgusting, I can't look!

CROSBY: Shut your mouth before I bust your chops Phil! Help me get him up (*Mr. Crosby speaks directly to Mr. Carpenter*) Ken? Ken? Can you hear me, friend? (*Rapid shaking is heard: it appears Mr. Carpenter is having a seizure*)

SILVERS: What do I do, Bing? What'll I do?

CROSBY: Get on the ringer and call him a doctor!

SILVERS: Urgh, it's on my shoes!

CROSBY: Act like a goddamn man, Phil, and call a doctor!

SILVERS: I can't stand the sight of it…oh, I feel kinda woozy. (*The shaking starts to subside*)

CROSBY: Ken?

(*The shaking has stopped. Silence*)

CROSBY: Ken?

(*Mr. Silvers throws up and sobs. The audience and technical staff are speechless. Eventually they break into distressed chatter. Tape too damaged to transcribe accurately, approx. 90 seconds missing audio. When we resume, Mr. Crosby is about to address the listeners at home*)

CROSBY: (*Aside, possibly to staff*) What do you mean the lines are down? Try the next building. Try the whole block if you have to! (*He switches focus*) Well, folks, as much as I'd like to be able to continue the Christmas cheer, a great tragedy has befallen us here at the Kraft Music Hall. I'm afraid a dear old friend of mine, Mr. Ken Carpenters, who has been with this show as long as I remember, has suffered some kind of sudden illness and tragically passed away. Now we've been having some difficulties with the phone lines, so if anyone at the General Practice can hear this broadcast, we…

SILVERS: (*Interrupting, his voice shrill*) Bing! Look! Look! It's Ken!

(*A soft scraping is heard. Slowly, Mr. Carpenter is heard getting to his feet. He grunts twice, and is heard shuffling towards the hosts*)

SILVERS: My God, it's a miracle!

(*Mr. Carpenter then emits an awful, piercing shriek*)

SILVERS: My God, it's a nightmare!

(*Further commotion ensues. Thunderous footsteps are heard as Mr. Carpenter races towards the audience. Shill female screams are heard and the assembled mass scatters, screaming and running off in every direction. Another shriek is heard, as he turns his attention to the orchestra and Charioteers. He tries grabbing at them, and they are forced to fight him off with instruments: first, a heavy bass instrument clunks several times off him; then the strings of a harp are heard twanging and snapping, and finally piano keys are struck with great force as the vast man falls against them. An unknown voice shouts that he's 'been bitten', as does a woman. Mr. Carpenter sounds more labored now. He goes after Mr. Silvers, who has taken refuge behind a Christmas tree. Ornaments are heard jingling, and the branches rustle as Mr. Carpenter tries in vain to reach him*)

SILVERS: You gotta help me, Bing, this ain't the rocking around the Christmas tree I expected!

(*Mr. Crosby approaches his old friend hesitantly*)

CROSBY: Ken, I don't know if you can hear me, but I'm gonna have to ask you to step away from Phil.

(*The scream that follows tells us he's ignored*)

CROSBY: Last chance, now.

(*The crazed man leaves the Christmas tree and turns his attentions towards Mr. Crosby, and leaps at him, but his body crashes to the floor as Mr. Crosby breaks a guitar over the assailant's skull. A final, bubbling sigh is heard before silence falls once more. Mr. Silvers slaps his hat down off the lifeless body*)

SILVERS: Advertise that, ya freaky ghoul!

CROSBY: That's not an appropriate comment to make at this time, Phil.

(*Tape too damaged to transcribe accurately. Approx. five minutes missing audio*)

SILVERS: But I don't wanna be left on my own.

CROSBY: Phil, there's about thirty people in here with you.

SILVERS: I mean with the mic. I get stage fright.

CROSBY: The way that storm is out there, I doubt a thing's getting put out anyway. Describe the weather or something.

SILVERS: What if Ken gets up again?

CROSBY: You knock him down again.

SILVERS: But…where are you going?

CROSBY: Where am I going? I'm gonna light up a Louie Armstrong special and get as high as a kite. I'll see you in fifteen minutes.

(*Mr. Crosby leaves. Mr. Silvers is left with the microphone. He hesitantly begins his monologue*)

SILVERS: Okay, people, the man says describe the weather, so I'm gonna describe the weather to ya. Hopefully no one is actually listening to this or else the ratings are gonna fall through the floor. Okay, folks, live from the second floor… Well, that the streets are covered in snow you already know, I ain't gonna win no broadcast of the year for saying that…come to think of it there's a lot of people out there, unusual for the weather…oh hey, carol singers!

Well, would ya think it! Just down by Garth's Hardware Store on the corner of Jefferson St., not two blocks down: In the middle of a snowstorm, carol singers. 'Tis the season to be jolly,' I suppose. I wish I could open this window and hear what they're saying for themselves. That's kinda screwy though…it looks like they're singing to a pick-up truck?

(*The studio door is heard crashing open*)

SILVERS: Hey, Bing! Clamp your peepers on that! A couple of whack-job carol singers! More like singing snowmen in that weather.

CROSBY: (*Out of breath*) You ham head, Phil. That ain't the local choir. Look at them!

(*Mr. Crosby starts searching for something. Mr. Silvers looks out the window once more and falters*)

SILVERS: Aw jeez-Louise.

CROSBY: What did I tell you?

SILVERS: The way they're moving. They ain't singing, they're attacking that truck. Every one of them is crazed, Bing, just like Ken! But…what about the people inside it?

CROSBY: That's why I need these.

(*He hoists up something heavy. Metallic clicking is heard*)

SILVERS: Your five irons? Great, I never realized we stopped Ken with a game of Texas Scramble. Are you that hopped up?

(*The studio porter, 'John' now enters, breathing heavily*)

JOHN: Mista Bing, suh! We got to help them people!

CROSBY: I'm on it, John. Let's go.

SILVERS: Sheesh, and I thought THEY were the whack jobs.

(*Mr. Crosby and the porter leave quickly. Heavy tape warping renders the next few seconds inaudible, until Mr. Silvers resumes his narration*)

SILVERS: I don't believe it; they are actually going out there! The two of them have just appeared below me, and they're heading straight for the trouble on Jefferson St. I'm gonna describe this as best I can to y'all, as it might just be the Nutcase Formerly Known as Bing Crosby's last few moments on Earth. He's got his bag of golf clubs on his back, and he's swinging his putter over his head like a mace. Boy, he means business…Uh, the negro from the desk downstairs, he's got that little Billy club with him, though it looks like he could eat six of them before they eat him, if you know what I mean…and they've been spotted! They're twenty feet away from the truck, and two of the ghouls have broken off from the main group; they're charging straight for Bing…wham! He does a full 360, swings it low and takes the legs out from underneath it. Urgh…urgh, he's LITERALLY taken the legs out from underneath it.

(*He lowers the microphone, and throws up. He unscrews a cap from a bottle and takes a long swig, before continuing*)

SILVERS: As I was saying…the porter, he's taking care of the other ghoul. He's sitting on its chest, smacking away at it… Bing's up at the truck: he's going through clubs like crackers now…two ghouls are flat out, hitter's sticking out of their skulls… Bing's trying to pull the guy out of the pick-up. As far as I can make out, it looks like he's the only person in it… Yikes! This is playing havoc with my stomach. The porter just pulled a ghoul's head clean of its shoulders! The ghoul might have taken a handful of his moustache as it was going, but I'd say our man was winning on points… It looks like they've got a clear run now to get the fella out of there…Oh no. Oh no…another five of those things have seen them…wait, ten…oh no! Twenty ghouls, they're comin' from every direction. Bing's surrounded! Our two intrepid heroes are climbing up, climbing up onto the back of the pickup…the guy from inside has joined them…one of them got his leg! Oh Christ, it's…it's biting him! Look at that three ghouls have got his leg, they're tearing at it and trying to pull him down… Bing's fighting the others off, old John's trying desperately to save our civilian…he's gone. They got him. Mother Mary.

(*The cap is unscrewed again, and he takes another long swig*)

SILVERS: This is…horrible. Those monsters have broken him up like a gingerbread man. Our two are surrounded now. They're swinging, they're fighting…but they're not gonna get out of this. It's a busted flush. Only a miracle could save them now.

(*Tape too damaged to transcribe accurately. Approx. 20 seconds missing audio*)

SILVERS: Should continue with this…don't even want to witness…

(*He lapses into silence. He takes another drink. Suddenly, something catches his attention*)

SILVERS: What is that?

(*A faint jingling is heard. Mr. Silvers jumps up, knock his chair to the floor, and whoops with joy*)

SILVERS: I can't believe it! There's a vehicle coming towards them. It's stopping! The falling snow is making it hard to see, but it looks like it….wait a minute, that's a sled. It's a goddamn sled, reindeers and all! If they can just get to it…well now the driver—I guess that what you'd call him—he's waving at Bing, motioning for them to get in. He's wearing…oh, of course he is. I'm not making this up, folks. I thought they were a couple of goners, but it looks like renowned musician and actor Bing Crosby is about to be saved from a troupe of flesh-eating ghouls but none other than Santa Claus himself.

(*Gunshots are heard*)

SILVERS: Ah. Except this Santa just pulled a pair of six-shooters out of his longjohns, and is blasting a path clear for them to get to the sled. Ya know in my day, if you were a bad boy you just got a lump of coal. Now they're making a jump for it…oh!… It looks like Bing twisted his ankle there, but he's made a recovery, and…they're safe! Both of them are on the sled…there's a someone else in there, too, a chick by the looks of it…with gams like that, she can't be anything else! Now the sled has started moving, our gun totin' gift-giver is cracking the whip, he's trying to build up some speed as it looks like their being pursued… Wait, are those kids? No, it's elves. Bloodthirsty elves are chasing them as they head right for us…oh lord, they're heading right for us! They ain't stopping! Ahh!

(*A huge crash is heard from downstairs. Building plans from the time show us that the studio had large glass double doors leading into the small reception area. Best scenario is that the reindeer-pulled sled smashed through these doors at full speed, before up-turning against the front desk and door leading into the building, later restricting the 'ghouls' ability to pursue Mr. Crosby and his friends*)

SILVERS: Eeep.

(*He drops the microphone, and for a few minutes little can be heard. Section missing from the tape, unknown amount of audio missing. We pick up again as the four people from the crash return to the studio, wounded but alive*)

JOHN: I'm goin' to make sure the devils don't get past the door. You fellas come with, all hands on deck!

(*The porter leaves to secure a barricade. The Charioteers, male choir of the show, go with him*)

CROSBY: I'm going to need the entire contents of your hip flask, Phil.

SILVERS: Santa Claus! You okay?

ZAROFF: (*Carrying a thick German accent*) Please… I'm quite all right. I just need a moment to catch my breath.

SILVERS: Hey, that ain't no Santa Claus! He's a stinkin' Kraut!

MARY: Don't you talk about Mista Zaroff like that or I'll knock ya teeth out!

CROSBY: I'd say she's stuck on you, Phil.

SILVERS: Bearcat.

MARY: Mashed potato brains!

CROSBY: I don't think your reindeer made it, but that was a hell of a save, mister…?

ZAROFF: Zaroff. Professor Zaroff. And it's of no… consequence. We're safe.

SILVERS: So much for animal rights.

MARY: What'd I tell you about disrespecting Mr. Zaroff, wise guy?

SILVERS: And who do we have here; Mary Motormouth?

MARY: Mrs. Claus, actually. Ain't cha got peepers?

ZAROFF: Mary, schweigan! I apologize for my…associate. She…'has spunk.'

CROSBY: Professor huh? I didn't realize they did qualifications in gift-wrapping.

ZAROFF: Biomedical sciences…if you must know.

CROSBY: And what are ya doing here?

ZAROFF: In Brooklyn? Working. In a grotto.

SILVERS: So the axis are spying on kids now, too?

ZAROFF: I have my…reasons.

(*The porter and Charioteers return*)

JOHN: Oh lord, it's the rapture, make no mistake.

CROSBY: We water tight, John?

JOHN: Ain't nothin' getting' in here anytime soon, suh.

ZAROFF: Interesting. You think this ze work of ze Gods?

JOHN: No suh. Of Jesus Christ. He gonna punish all men for what you Europeans are doin', all killin' and ignorin' His Word. That's why He raises the dead, bring devils to our streets.

CROSBY: Interesting. It sounds like you know different from our honest friend here.

MARY: Want me ta shut him up, Mista Zaroff?

ZAROFF: Nien, Mary. We came for their help, remember? Zis is ze man we spoke of.

MARY: Oh! Oh my, so it is! Mr. Cosby, what big eyes you have! Let me tell ya, the pictures just don't cover how… *tall* you are.

SILVERS: Horsefeathers! Whaddaya want with Bing? You'll have to get through me first I tell ya, you especially, Little Miss Muffet!

MARY: (*She punches into the palm of her hand*) With pleasure.

CROSBY: As fun as it is watching the little lady giving Phil the old hi-hat, I agree I'd much like to know the reason for your visit, Professor. I'll guess with those crazy cats out there it's not my autograph?

ZAROFF: Nein, nein. Although I…would like one, at some point. But first! I will need manpower, to recover some things from ze sled, and I will require use of your transition equipment. Then I will explain…everything.

(*Prof. Zaroff walks away from the hosts and is heard returning to the wreckage of his sledge. Tape too damaged to transcribe properly, approx. 300 seconds missing*)

ZAROFF: My appearance may suggest otherwise, I'm not merely a…'Jolly St. Nick.' It is true that I own ze local grotto, and indeed I…derive simple pleasure in dispensing candies and treats to ze needy children. White, negro…a happy child is one of life's few graces.

MARY: And let me tell ya, he's the best damn Santa this side of Greenland!

ZAROFF: Schweigan, Mary!

SILVERS: Yeah, Mary, schweigan.

JOHN: (*Aside*) You carryin' a torch for her, suh?

SILVERS: Not in a million years, pal. She's as ritzy as a two cent steak.

CROSBY: So there's a twist to this heart-warming tale of a Jerry gone good in the US of A?

ZAROFF: 'Got it in one,' Bing. I…foresaw the current, terrible conflict, and new ze Nazis would take my work if I did not flee. They would wish to use it for evil: I…I only wish to use it…for good.

CROSBY: I don't think I like where this is going.

(*Tape too damaged to transcribe accurately: approx. 120 seconds missing audio*)

JOHN: That ain't holy! That's blasphemous!

ZAROFF: Many thought as you did. Your…government disagreed.

CROSBY: So Uncle Sam knows about this crazy scheme?

ZAROFF: Know of it?! They *welcomed* it, Bing. Welcomed it. They…they provide ze funds for my secret laboratory, hidden in plain sight under ze grotto!

CROSBY: This is unbelievable.

ZAROFF: As all science of ze future is…to men without vision.

SILVERS: So those ghouls running around, banging on the doors ta get at our blood; that's your vision?

ZAROFF: Nein, Phil Silvers. No…as I had feared the Nazis would misuse my work…your government has done ze same.

SILVERS: You watch who's country your badmouthing there, Adolf.

CROSBY: Let the man speak, Phil.

ZAROFF: Thank you. Yes…I wished only to reunite parents…with children. Lovers…torn apart in their prime. Give back…ze seconds taken by fate herself. Unfortunately, your government, they see soldiers…men who never disobey orders. Who need no sustenance. A warrior who never dies. An army that needs not bullets, only saliva and blood to kill!

CROSBY: And you gave it to them on a platter.

SILVERS: (*Looking out the window*) And now it's our turn to be on the platter. There's over a hundred of them out there now.

MARY: He's right, Zaroff baby, they're coming for us.

JOHN: I'll make sure they ain't tryin' to get up here.

SILVERS: But what do they want with us?

ZAROFF: They will attack without prejudice. However, within their minds resides a…protocol, to search me out should I seek to end their existence, as I do this day. Please believe me, Bing. I fight this with my every breath. It is…an abhorrence to me. To my work. So I work against it.

CROSBY: So my good friend Ken fell to this disease. What a way for a man to go.

SILVERS: Wait a minute, you mean folks change through biting and stuff?

ZAROFF: Ya, Phil Silvers.

(*Quiet shuffling, which started some time ago, is now noticed by everyone*)

SILVERS: Like all those people Ken took with him?

(*Loud, awful screams fill the studio*)

SILVERS: Save me, Bing! Save me!

(*Chaos ensures. Three, perhaps four 'ghouls' attack the assembled cast. Mr. Crosby, still carrying his golf clubs, has drawn one and the dull thuds tell us he's battling them fiercely. Mr. Silvers, not renowned for his displays of courage so far, yelps and runs aimlessly around. At several points he yells warning to the others, but doesn't seem to interject. Professor Zaroff and Mary struggle with the same assailant. Eventually Mary fells him, yelling for it to 'have a taste' of her 'size fives'*)

MARY: Phil, will you get involved and start looking like a man?

SILVERS: I'll start looking like a man when you start looking like a woman, sweetheart!

(*Finally, with the crunch of a club through a skull, the last 'ghoul' is dispensed with. Relative peace ensures. The porter re-enters the studio*)

JOHN: They goin' ta get through! That barricade ain't holdin'!

CROSBY: Professor, this would be a swell time to tell us how to stop this thing.

SILVERS: Ah nuts, look at him, Bing.

(*A bubbling, hissing noise is heard. The professor has been bitten on the neck*)

ZAROFF: I'm…not done yet. My case…the one from ze wreckage: Bring it to me, Phil Silvers.

SILVERS: Soitenly.

ZAROFF: There is a…signal…that can be sent to ze brain. Shuts down their regeneration. This is my…Electric Signal Amplifier. I'll set it up, Bing…but I must have time.

JOHN: It's them little people, the elves! They're leadin' the charge. I should go fight them off, buy the professor the time he needs to save us.

CROSBY: Not alone, you won't.

(*He draws a golf club, and 'swooshes' it through the air*)

CROSBY: You know what? I'm sick and tired of these damn ghouls in my radio station! You've got ten minutes, Professor, and then I'm comin' swinging.

(*Mr. Crosby and the porter leave in an attempt to stall the 'ghouls' and give Professor Zaroff enough time to set up his equipment. For the next ten minutes little can be heard. Mary aids the professor in setting up his equipment. Mr. Silvers throws up again. After a few minutes, Zaroff requests a marker pen. It squeaks as he writes on the wall*)

ZAROFF: Phil Silvers…these are the frequencies. The signal must be broadcast as close as…possible to them.

SILVERS: Don't look at me, it's all French as far as a can tell.

ZAROFF: I expect so. But if I go…Bing will know.

MARY: Save your strength, Zaroff baby, you ain't goin' anywhere yet!

(*They continue on. Finally, once the ten minutes have passed, Zaroff has finished. He stumbles and collapses against the wall*)

MARY: Zaroff, don't go! I need ya!

ZAROFF: Schweigan, Mary, schweigan. Phil Silvers…will take care of you.

SILVERS: Baloney!

ZAROFF: Remember…the frequency, it must be exact.

SILVERS: But Bing ain't no scientist! Can't ya just say it straight?

(*A door bursts open. Dozens of the 'ghouls' enter the studio*)

SILVERS: Oh no, they're comin' through the Green Room! I guess the canapés are done for, too.

MARY: Don't you ever shut up?

(*Professor Zaroff expires. The 'ghouls' surround Mr. Silvers and Mary, cutting them off from any escape*)

SILVERS: This would be a good time for Bing to come back with his whatever-it-is, mumbo jumbo.

MARY: I don't think he's coming back at all, Phil.

SILVERS: Nah, don't looks like it eh?

MARY: Oh cripes, Mista Zaroff!

(*A new roar, much closer and most likely belonging to Professor Zaroff, is heard*)

SILVERS: So, Mary, cash or check?

MARY: Get futzed.

SILVERS: Worth a try.

MARY: We go down fighting, yeah? Ya know what they say, ya gotta try everythin' once before ya die, Mr. Lilly-liver.

SILVERS: Hey! I resemble that remark!

MARY: You don't say!

SILVERS! Oh! Why didn't Herr Hitler teach you how to work the machine?

MARY: I'm the looks of the operation, sweetie: I can't even spell 'frequency.'

(*The situation is hopeless. Until over the shrieking, a few, tiny notes are played on the piano*)

CROSBY: Mumbo jumbo, huh? Looks to me more like a scale: G Major, to be precise.

(*The 'ghouls' turn their attention to Mr. Crosby, but he continues playing the baby grand. The porter has started playing on the drums. Mr. Crosby takes a deep breath, and starts to sing*)

> *I'm dreaming of a white Christmas,*
> *Just like the ones I used to know.*

CROSBY: Get your hands on your clarinet, Phil, and tootle for your ticket out of here.

> *Where the treetops glisten,*
> *And children listen,*
> *To hear sleigh bells in the snow.*

(*The noise level in the room has fallen dramatically. All the 'ghouls' screaming and snarling has stopped, and now they stand lamely around, entranced by the music. The piano, clarinet and drums wash over them*)

CROSBY: Apparently our friend Mr. Clay here plays drums at his local Sunday sermon. And very well too, I must say.

JOHN: Thank ya, Mr. Crosby.

CROSBY: So you see, friends, a frequency is just a sound. Now I can't make heads nor tails of how that contraption works, but that there writing tells me a certain sound will take all our troubles away. And if there's a man in here who knows how to make a sound, well, no offence Phil, but it's me.

JOHN: And such a sound you make.

CROSBY: Say, Mary, you ever played? We sure could use a string section here.

MARY: I can double bass, sure.

(*Yawning can now be heard. One at a time the 'ghouls' fall down to the floor with a heavy thump, as they are overwhelmed by Zaroff's machine. Mr. Crosby, Mr. Silvers and the rest continue to play until none are left*)

I'm dreaming of a white Christmas
Just like the once I used to know.
Where the tree tops glisten
And children listen
To hear sleigh bells in the snow

Yes I'm dreaming of a white Christmas,
With every Christmas card I write.
May all your days be merry, and bright,
And all your Christmases, be well.

(*Remainder of tape completely degraded, impossible to transcribe accurately. Unknown amount of audio lost. Only one last exchange remains audible*)

CROSBY: Well, fellas, that was one hell of a game of golf.

SILVERS: They're all dead. Every last one of them, dead as a stone.

MARY: Poor Mista Zaroff.

SILVERS: So what now, Bing?

JOHN: Yeah, Mr. Crosby, what now?

CROSBY: I think...I think I need a drink.

MIDNIGHT SERVICE

CHRISTOPHER NADEAU

If John had broken free of the ropes binding his wrists five minutes earlier, he might have bolted for the church's main entrance and run like hell all the way home. But when the supposedly dead body started moaning, he knew he had no choice but to stay.

That was what he got for volunteering to work on Christmas Eve. Reverend Linklater was insane. That was the only explanation for what he was planning.

John's mind raced back to the moment he realized he was being held prisoner.

John swore to himself that, should he break free of the ropes currently binding him to this chair, he would strangle the pious bastard on the floor of his own church. And if he didn't stop that horrible, off-key singing, the reverend would soon discover just how willing John was to snap his own wrist bone in order to reach him.

"No use struggling, son," Linklater said. "The glory of Jesus will not be denied by one such as you."

One such as him? What was so bad about him? He wasn't a scumbag or anything, just an honest, hardworking family man. In fact, it was his hardworking nature that helped place him in his current predicament. If he got out of this, never again would he volunteer to cover a co-worker's shift.

And that fucker Gerry would get an earful, that was for sure! Lazy son of…

"I'll bet you don't even believe, do you?"

John blinked and realized Linklater was still staring at him with those pale blue eyes that were devoid of anything except blind, unquestioning faith. "Here we are on Christmas Eve, and it means nothing to you, does it?"

"It usually means being with family," John said.

Rev. Linklater shook his head. "Such selfishness. Leaving God out of the equation."

"I'm not an atheist." John gazed about the tiny church. "Maybe I don't go to church as often as I should, but I believe in God."

Rev. Linklater rubbed the jaw of his gaunt face and sighed. "So many have said that to me, John. So many have lied."

"I'm not really interested in convincing you."

Rev. Linklater smiled; his eyes still far away. "Finally, an honest moment. Perhaps you will be the witness after all."

John grunted; there he was with that 'witness' crap again. Like all men of the cloth in charge of tiny churches, Rev. Linklater had a need to be seen and acknowledged by others that rivaled a two-year-old's. Maybe a few appeals to his ego would turn the tide in John's direction.

"I'm honored you chose me," John said.

Rev. Linklater, in the middle of downing a glass of what appeared to be water, halted in mid-gulp and turned to look at John. "You feel it, don't you?"

All conditioning to avoid encouraging the delusions of a crazy man flew right out the window of John's mind. "Sure do," he said.

Rev. Linklater broke into a wide grin. "Praise God!"

"Praise him," John said.

"Glory be unto the Lord!"

"Amen."

Rev. Linklater turned and stared at John with glassy eyes. "*He* sent you to me, didn't *He*?"

John shrugged. "Probably."

"No *probably* about it, son!" The reverend clapped his hands twice. "This fallen man is not worthy."

"Sure you are. Don't be so hard on yourself."

Rev. Linklater shook his head violently, his smile now gone as if wiped from his face. "None of us are, son. Know why?"

John smiled. "I'll bet *you* do."

Rev. Linklater trotted over to the area John refused to follow with his eyes, that little corner of dementedness only a zealot could manage to create. Earlier, he'd only glimpsed what the reverend had going on over there before something had struck him in the back of the head and he'd lost consciousness. And what he'd seen was enough to last several lifetimes.

"This is where it starts," the reverend said.

Reluctant as he was, John knew he had to keep the obviously insane man talking no matter what. He needed more time to come up with some type of escape plan. "Where what starts, Reverend?" He didn't need to see him to know Rev. Linklater stood a bit straighter at the sound of his proper title. These guys were so transparent they never needed Windex.

"The New Times." The hushed awe in Rev. Linklater's voice was equal parts disturbing and soothing, much like how John imagined his weekly Sunday sermons would be. "We must prove to God that we are serious!"

John wondered why an all-knowing God who sits outside of time needed humans to *prove* anything, but questions like that inevitably lead to deeper theological ponderances a man who made deliveries for a living wasn't supposed to entertain. John had a good idea that's why Rev. Linklater had chosen him, assuming a delivery man would be an easily controlled moron.

You got another thing coming, Bible-boy, John thought.

"For the entire six-thousand years of Earth's existence, we have told God we worship Him and then turned our heads to look at naked bodies and piles of gold!"

John hung his head and thought, *I guess I asked for it.*

"We, His favored creation, held above even the angels, have been a source of constant disappointment to Him!"

John couldn't argue with that. Surely God wasn't pleased with how we'd turned out. But that included loonies like this who thought they could know God's mind and act accordingly with nothing more than their own certainty as a qualifier.

Rev. Linklater went on, his Biblical diatribe growing less coherent with each wheezy pause. He said something about Man living in the Age of Grace and squandering our second chance at salvation. He disagreed with the common assertion that Christ was supposed to be killed and that it was always the plan. In his theology, Christ was sent to save us back then at that time and we screwed up, causing God to have to resort to Plan B.

Never mind the constraints and box he was wrapping around an omnipotent supreme being, Rev. Linklater's beliefs had led him to a conclusion that was, for want of a better word, unique.

"Jesus needs a second chance."

Now John forced his head to the right and did indeed look at the monstrosity the reverend had in the corner of his little church.

"No way." John whispered.

Rev. Linklater threw his head back and howled. "He's coming back! Like he said he would!" He did a little dance, some uncoordinated mirror universe version of a soft shoe, and skipped back over to where John sat with a look of pure dejection on his face.

"I always knew I had a special purpose."

John nodded, decided not to share with Rev. Linklater how *special purpose* was the name given by Steve Martin in the movie *The Jerk* for his penis. John had a feeling the mere mention of that happy organ could cause the reverend to go into a blind and violent rage.

"You have no idea how many churches I've been kicked out of," Rev. Linklater said. "No one understood me. No one!"

John recoiled from the snarl in the reverend's voice. This was the real Rev. Linklater coming out, the man who had repressed his true rage for decades, biding his time until some synapse in his brain misfired and provided him with the 'divine' knowledge he required for self-validation. Getting a man like this to talk wasn't the grandest notion, but it was the only one that made sense. Somewhere in there had to be a reasonable man who could still hear logic.

Rev. Linklater checked his watch and frowned. "Goodness, it's getting late."

John tried to get a glimpse of the watch and thought it was somewhere around ten o' clock. Christmas Eve would be over in two hours and here he sat bound to a chair with a nutjob.

The reverend sighed and sat down across from John. "You might not know it to look at me, but I've been all over the world. It took a long time for me to find myself."

Great, John thought, *a history lesson*. He looked away, down at the floor, anywhere that wasn't the crazy eyes of the loony reverend…

The stinging slap across his face was so sharp and quick, the sound came a moment later. John blinked, his eyes filling with tears, and looked up in time for a second, even harder slap.

"This is God-talk, boy! You pay attention!"

Rev. Linklater once again checked his watch. His demeanor grew more agitated, his face covered in sweat. "There are secrets out there, John. Crazy ways of doing things. So much evil you wouldn't believe it." He snapped his fingers at that last part. "Then it hit me, like an anvil from a tall building."

An abrupt banging on the door to the church's main entrance caused Rev. Linklater to thrust his pelvis forward in a comical attempt to maintain his balance. He stumbled further forward, his ankles wrapped around either chair leg, coming cheek-to-cheek with John.

"Pardon me," he said. "I'm a little anxious."

Eyes widened to the breaking point, John told him it was perfectly understandable. Rev. Linklater patted him on the shoulder, disentangled himself from the chair, and trotted out into the main area.

While he was gone, John worked at his bonds. The ropes holding him in place were thick and old, making them difficult to grab onto long enough to try and untie.

John sighed and stomped his foot on the floor, freezing as the sound of something high-pitched and metallic filled the quiet room.

Slowly, he forced his head down and noticed a tiny nail clipper that must have slipped out of the reverend's pocket when he'd lurched forward. Without hesitation, John placed his foot over the tiny metal symbol of freedom and pulled it closer.

"Thank you so much!" Rev. Linklater said from the front of the church. "God bless you!"

When he returned to John, he was a much happier reverend carrying a large cloth bag. "That was my friend the voodoo priest. Nice fella."

John's jaw dropped. "Did you say…"

Rev. Linklater nodded. "Hard to believe he's going to Hell, but maybe after tonight he'll see the truth of the Lord's word." He plunked the bag on the nearest table and started rifling through it. "Paid a pretty penny for this stuff."

John said nothing; he didn't want to know what was in the bag. Whatever was in it was bad news and he'd experienced enough of that already. Now that he had the nail clipper, he needed to focus on escaping. Let the crazy old fucker do whatever he was planning to do. Aside from kidnapping John, it didn't look like the reverend was hurting anyone.

And was it any of his business if John was wrong about that? He had a family to protect, let the rest of the world deal with its own shit.

"Oh, that idiot!" Rev. Linklater dug around inside the bag. "He forgot to bring the…never mind. It's here. We're fine." He buried his head inside the bag.

Shaking his head, John removed his right shoe and wrapped his toes around the nail clipper. He slowly brought his leg up to a crossing position, simultaneously twisting in his seat so that his left hand was within grabbing distance of the small clipper. Once he was sure he had it, John lowered his foot and slipped it back into his shoe.

Please have a nail file, please have a… Yes!

John opened the nail file and began to saw at his bonds.

He'd nearly cut all the way through the ropes when Rev. Linklater trotted over to the dark corner and started fooling around with some unseen object.

John squinted into the darkness and noticed for the first time that something large was covered by a sheet.

Without a word, the reverend yanked the sheet away, exposing the cadaver of what appeared to be a young male hanging from a gigantic crucifix.

"No way," John said.

Rev. Linklater whirled and broke into a ridiculously wide grin. "Yes, indeed! And you shall bear witness. It is no coincidence that your name is John."

"Did…did you kill that man?"

Rev. Linklater glared at him. "Who do you think I am?"

John bit not only his tongue, but also his bottom lip and the inside of his cheek.

Rev. Linklater glared at John a moment longer before pulling something out of the cloth bag given to him by his voodoo practitioner friend. John turned away and began furiously sawing at the ropes.

He tried to ignore the bizarre chanting coming from the crazy old coot. Somehow, pointing out the lack of logic in indulging so-called black magic as a method for proving to God we still respect Him seemed pointless.

Rev. Linklater, like all great heedless zealots before him, had embarked upon a path of his own devising which no logic could ever deter.

The moment John felt the ropes loosen, the room seemed to spin madly out of control. He swooned and fell over onto his left side, the chair coming with him.

He heard a harsh wind but felt no air, followed by the floor beneath him shaking.

John remained on his side for a moment, wondering if more tremors were coming, when the sound of something screaming provided the necessary jolt for him to get to his feet.

He immediately wished he'd stayed on the floor.

Whatever was under the sheet was in pain, the kind of agony that was indescribable. It writhed, moaning and yelling as if something at its very core was being ripped out. Rev. Linklater laughed and clapped and jumped up and down as if watching a Fourth of July fireworks display.

"What have you done?" John yelled. "Have you lost your fucking mind?"

Rev. Linklater halted in mid-clap and looked at him as if remembering John was there. "The Lord freed you?"

"Not unless he uses a nail clipper."

Rev. Linklater shrugged. "Doesn't matter now. We're almost there!"

Almost where? John wondered. What insanity was this? Surely the person under that sheet wasn't actually dead a few moments ago?

Rev. Linklater pulled back the sheet like some demented circus ringleader and yelled, "Behold!"

John couldn't stop the bile from rising in his throat. The decaying body moved its head blindly on the large crucifix to which its wrists and ankles had been nailed.

"Jesus Christ!"

"That's right! He's back!"

He'd really done it. The old lunatic had actually brought a dead body back to…maybe *life* was too strong a term, but there it was moving and making noises. It said something John couldn't quite make out but he could swear it sounded like, "Release!"

"You have no idea what came back with that…thing!" John yelled. "The dead should stay dead!"

Rev. Linklater made a *tsk* sound and wagged a stern index finger in John's direction. "If that were true, we'd all be Jews right now. I've been patient with you so far, son, but those that bear witness should also shut their *fucking* mouths!"

Shocked into momentary silence, John watched as the reverend approached the dead man and began singing hymns.

If the poor creature on the cross could hear him, it gave no indication. Instead, it continued moaning and saying, "Release!"

What didn't make sense was how exactly the old man thought this was going to prove anything. One witness these days was not enough to justify mass acceptance. As crazy as he was, Rev. Linklater wasn't so far gone that he didn't have a plan. He checked his watch. "Nearly midnight. The congregation should start arriving soon."

John glanced from Linklater to the man on the cross. "I won't bear witness for this. No friggin' way."

"I'm afraid you don't have a choice." Rev. Linklater raised his right hand to reveal a small caliber revolver. "God has already chosen you, so man up."

It was one of those moments you read about but never experience.

One of those instant reaction deals where one moment you're standing with a gun pointed at you and the next you're dropping to the floor with superhero speed and grabbing the nearest weapon you can find.

Moviemakers spend wads of cash making scenes like this work and somehow it happens for real in the blink of an eye.

The first shot from the reverend's gun filled John's ears as he grabbed the nail clipper and rolled under a table. The second shot hit the table and caused splinters to fly.

John didn't wait for the third shot. He stood up, lifting the table over his shoulders and charged the old man, whose screams were louder than John's, who kept running until he felt the table connect, followed by one more gunshot.

Shaking from adrenalin overload, John dropped the table and stepped back, surveying the carnage before him.

It only took a moment for him to realize that Rev. Linklater had fired just as the table struck him, causing the gun to be shoved under his chin when it went off.

Somehow the sight of his blasted-out brains paled next to the moaning tragedy to John's left; a being the reverend probably planned to kill and resurrect over and over until he'd made his 'point.'

Slowly, John walked up to the creature and gazed into its blank eyes.

"*Releasssse,*" it said.

"Okay," John said.

The fire engulfed the little church so quickly, John found himself hurrying outside before it got him, too.

A pair of headlights bathed him momentarily as he ran outside, followed by an older couple wearing befuddled facial expressions.

Behind John, the first stained glass window exploded to reveal orange and red flames.

"Service is cancelled," John said. He glanced up at the digital clock across the street and saw it was now midnight. "Merry Christmas."

He limped away into the night.

KEEPING WARM

JAMES JEFFREY PAUL

Karen promised Matthew she would give him a very special present for Christmas. Furthermore, she promised to deliver it to his door personally at nine o' clock on Christmas Eve. Now it was Christmas Eve, and while it normally took her only fifteen minutes to walk to Matthew's house, it was only thirteen minutes to nine according to her watch, so she had to hurry.

She flung open the door to her apartment building and was gently assaulted by the mild chill in the air. It was a notably mild Christmas; it hadn't snowed for over a week and for the last few days the temperature had persistently hovered around forty degrees. So on this night she was lightly clad considering the season, in tight-fitting jeans and a red knit sweater with the design of a snowman on the front. Her long blonde hair, which extended almost to her waist, waved from side to side as she bounced along in her walking shoes. The breeze idly lifted up clumps of it and made them dance half-heartedly.

Her smile, preternaturally cheery on normal occasions, was transcendent now, and her dark-blue eyes sparkled as she recited over and over again the words she was going to say to Matthew as soon as he opened the door: "Your Christmas present is ME! I'm moving in with you on New Year's Day and we're getting married this summer, and there's nothing that you can do about it!"

Karen tossed back her head and laughed. She knew Matthew wanted them to live together and get married, but was too shy to broach the subject. He was such a sweetheart, though, and she would do anything for him. She would just have to give him a little push to get their life together started.

She walked three suburban blocks that were empty save for herself, and silent except for her constant repetition of: "Your Christmas present is ME!" and her gales of merry laughter. Nothing ever happened in this dreary part of town, even at Christmas. Oh well, she and Matthew had each other, and needed nothing else. They'd be moving to an apartment downtown soon, where the action was, if she had anything to do with it.

Karen reached an intersection and was miffed when the walking signal changed to red. She glanced at her watch—only five minutes left, and six more blocks to go. She could run there in nothing flat, of course, but she didn't want to arrive at Matthew's and make her big announcement when she was all breathless and sweaty. She was deciding if she should jaywalk when she heard the skidding of tires.

She looked around. Where was the sound coming from? The empty streets made such a good echo chamber that it was impossible to tell. Then the sound died down, and contrary to her imperturbable nature, she gave a little sigh of relief. She decided to wait for the light to change to green, though.

Suddenly, there was a bang and a crash right behind her. Then once more, but terribly close and insistent now, the skidding of tires.

Karen gave a little start—bounced up and down like a puppet on a string—and was turning her head when the car's right front fender crashed into her backside and sent her flying through the air. She soared in an arc across the narrow street and crashed face-first into a telephone pole.

For a moment, it was as if her dead body was glued to the telephone pole; then it slowly slid down and came gently to rest on the curb. Most of her face and a sizable portion of her scalp remained stuck to the pole.

The car skidded to a stop in the middle of the intersection and the drunken driver stumbled out.

"Jesus Christ!" he yelled as coherently as his condition would allow.

His equally drunken companion also stumbled out of the car, fell to his knees, and quickly raised himself on shaky legs.

"What'll we do?" his companion slurred.

"We gotta get outta here!" the driver cried.

"Do ya…do ya think anyone saw us?" his companion mumbled.

The drunken driver looked around quickly. "Naw. I don't think so. Come on."

"Ya think we should call the…" his companion began.

"The cops? No way!"

"No. Just call…the hospital…on your cell phone. Don't give your name, just tell 'em to come here…after we've gotten away."

"There ain't nothin' they can do for her now. Come on. We gotta get downtown to celebrate!"

The driver got back into the car. His companion, his eyes riveted on Karen's demolished body, hesitated.

"Come on," the driver ordered. "It's too late for her. We don't wanna spoil our Christmas, now do we?"

"Naw," his companion agreed quietly, and got back in the car. The tires squealed on the pavement and the car sped away.

The car was two blocks away when Karen's dead body began to move, and after a pause, struggled to her feet. She had five more blocks to go, not counting this one. Her dead eyes could only make out basic shapes and primary colors. There was no way they could have read the dial and hands of her watch, even if the watch hadn't been smashed and fallen off her wrist. She staggered forward, stopped, staggered forward a few more steps, stopped again, and then began to move without stopping, with a jagged, weaving stride.

Nine o' clock had certainly already come and gone. Her dead brain could still form that thought, and stilled nerves could still tremble with the dream of anxiety at it. She must hurry. Not only was it late now—when she had been a human being, she had never been late a day in her life—but it was only a few moments before her body began to grow cold, and then she would have no more residual memory, no more powers of volition. Karen would truly become the corpse she already was.

She wove her way onward for half a block before stopping to rest. What remained of her brain urged it on. Already, deep down in her dead husk, she could feel with dead nerves the stirring of the eternal chill. To make matters worse, a cold front had just blown in, speeding up the process.

How could she keep warm? *How* could she? But first off, she must keep moving. She staggered and wove forward, still moving steadily, but at a slightly slower pace than before.

She could barely feel the cold air, but felt the vague chill within as if it were a blizzard. There was no escaping the chill within; which was more final than death. A dead body with unfinished business could overcome death for a short while, if its dead heart and brain felt a strong enough urge to finish said business; but that miracle couldn't last, for it fed on the warmth remaining in a dead body, and once that feeble supply of warmth was exhausted, the heart and brain were helpless.

Something tugged at her left arm. It was the strap of a purse, sliding down her arm and coming to rest in a nerveless left hand, soon to fall from stiffening fingers.

A cigarette lighter. The dead brain could still allow that memory to flicker within it. She had a lighter in her pocketbook. When she was alive she had scorned smoking, but Matthew smoked, and a good girlfriend must always be ready to light her boyfriend's cigarettes, and so she had bought a cheap, ninety-nine cents lighter and always carried it in her purse. She needed that lighter now.

She stopped, and with her dead, clumsy right hand and stiffening fingers, poked around in her purse until she found the lighter. Slowly, wasting precious seconds, feeling the eternal cold within growing slightly colder, she pulled the lighter out of her purse and dropped it onto the sidewalk. The index finger of her left hand was the most elastic, the most functional of her fingers, and with it she grasped the lighter. But now she had to flick it on. And although she was right-handed, the fingers of her right hand were now all but useless. What could she do?

Some of the feeble warmth remaining within her body raged up like a blast from a furnace, robbing that body of the precious fuel of locomotion, but giving her the strength to set her thumb against the tiny wheel that set the lighter's sparks in motion, and tried to rotate the wheel fast, so that the destructive life-giving flame would shoot up.

She failed, but her left hand, arm and fingers now had renewed vigor. She flicked the wheel again, and this time was successful. The flame blazed up and roared like the warmth inside a living thing, a warmth that would seemingly never dwindle down or be extinguished.

Holding the lit cigarette lighter in her left hand, she began to shamble and weave forward again. As Karen did, she held the flame against her right wrist.

It took a while for her dead skin to feel the fire burning into it, but eventually she could feel her wrist begin to blacken and blister. The growing coldness within her raged forth, outraged that its advance was being checked, its primacy threatened; but eventually it yielded a little to this encroachment from the outside, and its advance slowed a precious little.

The thing that had been Karen reached another intersection. By force of habit, her head and eyes bobbed from side to side, looking for oncoming cars. Her glazed eyes could just register the fact there were none. She stepped down off the curb and began to hobble across the street.

When she was halfway across the street, the lighter went out. She needed to light it again, but then realized she had just a little extra internal energy remaining to get across the street, so she did, and just managed to step up onto the opposite curb. Then a cold exterior wind began to blow, giving the cold within added force, and the animated corpse despaired of ever reaching its goal. She had four more blocks to go.

She stopped and tried to spark the lighter again. It took longer this time, but the rage within kept her going. Again she held the flame to her right wrist, and awakened memories of pain in her dead nerves, which made her shuffle ahead a trifle faster. On and on it went, and the flame burned through layer after layer of skin and muscle. This time the flame didn't go out until she reached the next intersection.

The pain still lingered, but the cold within and without began to increase as well. The rage flared up again, keeping her going—going—across the street and up onto the next curb. Three more blocks to go. How, she wondered, could she hurt herself to keep warm and moving until she reached Matthew's house and spoke the words she'd promised?

The nose, she remembered. When you were alive, the nasal passages were very sensitive. She flicked the lighter once more and held the flame to her nostrils. This time the memory of pain was much, much greater.

She actually shuffled along a little faster this time, and the longer her nose burned, the keener the memories of pain became, and held the cold within her at bay.

Outside, as darkness fell, the cold grew.

By the time Karen reached the next intersection, her nose had become a blackened and twisted nub of burnt flesh and cartilage, and the memories of pain were growing dimmer. The flame went out again, but this time she ignored it. She had to make it, she needed to make it. Her will burned within, and fought the cold, giving her enough energy to cross the street. Two more blocks to go.

What else was sensitive enough to awaken the memory of pain? Then she remembered the base of her throat, and how in life she'd loved to be kissed and caressed there. She tried to summon forth the flame again, failed, then tried and failed again, then tried once more and succeeded.

She held the flame to the base of her throat, and for the first time the memories of pain almost became more than memories, as the flames blistered and bubbled and crackled what, in life, had almost been the most important part of her body.

Memories of another feeling, another state of mind and being, more precious than life and locomotion, teased the dead wiring of what had been a human mind.

Sometimes something else, more potent and living than flame, had kissed and caressed her there, and blessed her with so much strength that it seemed it would take several lifetimes to exhaust it. But now flame was destroying that precious part of her body, and had she been able to, she would have rejoiced.

Long after the inner layers of the skin at the base of her throat had blackened and begun to crackle and flake off, the pain and the shards of remembered love kept a small but steady fire burning within, burning the probing fingers of the cold without that kept trying to burrow inside the dead body, to extinguish all warmth from it, and rob it forever of the power of locomotion. The dead didn't deserve to be walking around, the cold outside seemed to say; they must leave the streets and paths of this world to the living.

Karen crossed the next intersection without stopping or even pretending to look for oncoming cars. Her powers of hearing had almost entirely died out, so she barely heard the squeal of tires, the scream of a horrified and disbelieving driver, and the roar of an engine as the car screeched around her and sped away, far away from the horrible sight of a mangled and bloody woman.

She had only one more block to go.

Karen took a dozen or more steps down the new block before the flame from the lighter gave out, and she stopped, realizing that this most sensitive spot of her anatomy had been burned down to the bone, and that its destruction could no longer awaken memories of pain. As her dead mind struggled to think of what to do next, the outward cold encroached on her dead body, and the cold within, no longer kept at bay, increased as well. The thing that had been Karen longed—if a dead thing could be said to feel such a clear emotion—to lie down on the cold pavement and admit that it was dead.

But no. She must go on. She must keep her promise. Her determination to keep her promise no longer raged or even flickered within it; rather it jerked about automatically within it like the limbs of a hanged man. And so, slower now and much more wasted effort, she managed to get the lighter burning again. But what should she hold the flame against this time?

Of course. The other sensitive part—or rather, parts—of her body, the stimulation of which had given her such pleasure in life, made her burn with such inner heat.

She looked down and with her dead eyes could barely make out the jagged rent that had torn her sweater nearly in half, and had completely sundered the top beneath it. Still managing to clutch the lighter in her left hand, she reached out and laboriously moved the left halves of her torn sweater and top aside, exposing her left breast. Then, with her right hand, she held the flame to her left nipple.

The flame seared Karen's left nipple, awakening even more fragmented but even more powerful memories of the joy that the stimulation of that part of her anatomy had brought her in life — specifically, the memories of Matthew stimulating it with his lips, tongue and teeth.

She managed to walk most of the next block in nothing flat, albeit in a jagged, shambling fashion. When at last the memories of pain and joy died down, she managed to move the lighter and its flame to the nipple of her other breast.

The memories of pain flared up again, holding the growing cold within at bay, although by now the dead woman's skin was as cold as ice, and the jagged memories of the pleasures this part of her anatomy had brought her in life were becoming ever more fragmented, and growing ever dimmer.

The thing that had been Karen plodded and shambled ahead, faster than ever, and soon she was crossing the final intersection and standing at the edge of the final sidewalk, the one along which her goal lay.

The darkness had almost completely descended now, and with it came biting cold, dark cold, cold that nearly made her teeth chatter. And the cold within, the vital inner cold, was growing within her, and she knew this time there would be no stopping it. She would fall upon the sidewalk, less than a block from Matthew's house, on Christmas Eve, dead truly and forever.

Then the last glimmering fragment of memory that would ever flicker in her dead brain gleamed forth. Once, when she had been a human being, and had been running along the beach with Matthew, he had exclaimed over the sight of her hair spreading out and bouncing and gleaming in the sun. "It looks like fire!" he'd laughed.

"Really?" she'd asked in that time when such things mattered to her, amused and touched.

"Yeah!" he'd replied. "It looks like the sun!"

She'd giggled. "I've got the sun on my head!"

"Yeah, you do." He'd stopped running and tackled her, rolling around on the sand with her, and then, overcome with desire, they'd raced back to their hotel room and spent the rest of the afternoon making love.

With stiffening fingers, she tried to ignite the cigarette lighter again. She failed once, twice, three times. But on the fourth try, she succeeded, and the flame rose from the lighter like a final beacon of hope in a dark world.

Karen forced her stiff arm to raise its numb fingers, and the burning lighter, to her hair, still long, blonde and beautiful, if a bit tangled, although now it crowned the head of a corpse.

The flame immediately set fire to a clump of the hair, and the thing that had been Karen held the match flame to her head for another moment, until the flames began to spread throughout its crown of glory, the hairspray within helping the hair to burn.

She no longer felt the memory of pain—for there were no nerves in strands of hair—but the fact that her hair was aflame, and what had been said of it during life had now literally come true, set her moving faster than ever before. She didn't run, but took longer, faster strides than before, and the pauses between each stride were shorter.

The fire had now spread to every strand of hair, and as she hurried along, her hair and then the scalp blazed like a golden halo, as if she were a creature born of fire. She took several moments for the memory of pain to be reawakened within her dead brain, for it took the fire several moments to spread from her hair and scalp to her tattered clothes, and to the rest of her body.

But for those few moments, while the cold within and without advanced, never to retreat again, the animated corpse that was once Karen still moved ahead, her brain stimulated, her nerves thrilled, her veins pumping with something that warmed her body and animated her limbs in a way that the warmth of life never could.

As she moved down the block, she became more and more engulfed in flame, which consumed her head, clothing, flesh and sinews.

She let go of the lighter and let it fall to the sidewalk, no longer needing it. Now she burned inside and out as she had never burned in life, and the heat and wind of the flames sped her along a little faster.

Ahead on the right, three houses ahead, was a home that Karen no longer recognized, but knew she must go to. Colorful red and green lights blinked on the bushes outside the house and a plastic Santa Claus sat on the front lawn.

She no longer resembled the human being she'd once been, or the corpse she still was; she looked like a stick figure made out of charcoal, from which tiny dark pieces were continually breaking off. She stopped stumbling forward and seemed to dance on the wind raised by the flames, an orange and red butterfly with a tiny black armature at its center.

She flew and danced past one house, then another, until she reached her goal.

She turned her around to face the house, like a dancer executing half a pirouette. Her memory was gone—she couldn't have spoken the words she wanted to say even if she was able to remember them—but nevertheless the flames led her down the driveway in slow motion.

As Karen advanced, she drifted from side to side, bringing herself into contact with the shrubs and flowers lining the walkway and setting them ablaze.

When she reached the front door, she bumped against first one and then another of the wooden pillars supporting the front porch roof, making the garland wrapped around them catch fire as well.

The flames licked at a hanging flower pot, making it burst into flame like a torch to light the burning corpse's way.

She raised the burning stump that had been her right hand and pressed it against the doorbell, melting the button as she pushed it.

She stood there, unknowing, uncaring, as the flames enveloping her spread further and further, enveloping her in an ever larger pyrrhic ball.

There was a pause, and then the door opened to reveal a living being whose name the burning corpse could no longer remember. Matthew stood there, eyes and mouth agape, a strangled cry choked off in his throat.

Karen reached out her flaming arms toward him, and he let out another strangled cry and backed away. She floated into the house, setting the Oriental rug in the entrance hall ablaze.

Matthew backed away from the woman he still loved but could no longer recognize, until he backed up against the wall, and yelped that his escape route was blocked.

Karen floated toward him like a burning moth extending its fiery wings. His face was transformed by fear, bafflement and disgust as he pressed against the wall, hoping to vanish into it.

The heat from the burning form began to burn his flesh before the flames had even touched it, causing the terrified man to rediscover his voice, or at least his ability to scream at the top of his lungs.

Karen didn't hear her beloved's screams, for although she was a blazing inferno inside and out, all of the warmth that had animated her in life and death, and that extra indefinable something that had spurred her along the last steps toward her goal, had left her forever.

She might have been a block of ice. As her flaming body slowly fell against the wall and the living being she still loved but could no longer recognize.

She engulfed Matthew in her inferno and drowned out his screams.

He tried to run, but the pressure she exerted upon him made Mathew fall to the floor, never to rise again.

The Christmas tree in the corner of the room was now aflame, the fire sizzling and hissing as it reached the ceiling and began to spread, the curtains of the nearby window already aflame.

The house and the grounds surrounding it were slowly eaten by the spreading flames, and as the two corpses lay entwined together, like two lovers sleeping in each other's arms before a Christmas fire, the flames slowly burned them to ashes.

A CHRISTMAS CARD FOR KATHY

KEN L. JONES

As far as I know, I might be the only one still alive in the teeming metropolis that I live in. When I was young, my father called Long Beach, California the 'city of the living dead.' He owned a business there and repaired people's refrigerators in their homes. Most of these people were elderly and shuffling, hence the derogatory nickname. I heard him say it often when I helped him make his service rounds. But there are far worse things than being old and there are far, far worse things than being dead.

I ought to know because I live in the midst of thousands of things worse than death and the smell of it all is more than enough to rob a man of his very sanity. I've been shacked up in this high rise building, where I had long rented an apartment for the last three months. I've turned the entire place into a fortress. It has become a universe unto itself for me. It has most of what I need and I've never needed much. The canned goods down below in the grocery store on the first level have been like manna to me. The variety and plenty of its now-dusty shelves have provided me with many a suitable meal. The cupboards and the larders of the various apartments in my building have also yielded treasure after treasure.

Mr. Ditko, the mystery man who used to live in unit 333, has done better than that by me. According to his diary, he was some kind of a mystic visionary who believed in all the ancient prophecies about the year 2012. He was such a firm adherent of this point of view that he turned his penthouse into a survivalist's paradise.

It's full of weapons, medical supplies and a most handy water treatment system. It's too bad the old fellow couldn't take the reality of everything he so strongly believed in. The first month, he jumped off our roof, hoping to die…he did.

Now I never had much use for people back when all of them were so-called living and I have even less use for them now that they are the so-called dead. The remodeling job that was taking place in my building's bar and grill was a boon. It provided me with more than enough material to seal myself in my place good and proper. I've long been the only one here, and unless the things in the street learn to scale the wall like Spiderman, I'm safe as the fabled master of the assassins Hassan-I-Sabbah was in his high mountain fortress Alamut.

The analogy is apt, for I too, take great delight in exterminating the creatures that fill the teeming streets below me. Occasionally I do this with the various guns I've found in my building. Though just as often I accomplish these petty acts of extermination with heavy objects I have no other use for.

The other day I dropped a full oak dresser from one of the upper level windows and took out five of the reeking retches on the tarmac below. I have to admit that I obtain a certain sadistic glee whenever I do something like this that goes well beyond the obvious. When the world was as it used to be, I often longed to murder most of the people in it just because their very existence annoyed me. Now that things are as they are, I no longer have any excuse not to and so I act out as I please.

Now I would be remiss if I portrayed all the last few months as nothing but survival and slaughter, for such is not the case. The building is rife with DVDs, which I live to watch on a battery-powered portable laptop computer. These discs contain everything from Shakespeare to pornography. There is also much to read and lots of candlelight to do it by. When the few batteries I've found for the laptop are depleted…well, I don't want to think about that.

I've found particular diversion in the comic books and graphic novels I've unearthed in many of the apartments. And in odd moments I've amused myself for hours by playing an acoustical guitar I came across. I'm now actually once again in good voice and of sufficient skill to sing loudly enough to overpower the hungry cussing and the growling that echoes throughout the concrete canyons below me.

Still, the holiday season has been very hard for me to endure. Halloween seemed appropriately filled with monsters, which was okay in a strange, ironic sort of way, but Thanksgiving was the loneliest one I'd ever known and the onslaught of the Christmas season has proven unbearable. I never realized exactly how much I loved this most magical season of the year until I had no one to share it with. That is, no one who doesn't want to have me for lunch.

To the best of my knowledge there might still be a few other people in the world alive besides me, and I'll very soon head out into the unknown world around me to search for a certain some-one I once knew.

Before the internet went down for good, she was still amongst the living, still holed up in an air raid shelter in the office building she works in. It's only blocks away from here.

Kathy and I were in love long ago but marriage never hap-pened. She had her career and I had my duties as a poet and a professor at Cal State University, which always got in the way.

We hadn't spoken in decades, but then, about a year ago, I published an epic poem written about her back when we were still dating. By chance she came across it and contacted my publisher and then she and I began exchanging emails and twitters and texts, even though we were not quite bold enough to see each other in person.

Then civilization ended just like the Mayans predicted and the few blocks that had always separated us became an unnavigatable galaxy.

But there was something in our last few electronic exchanges that was both poignant and beautiful. She confessed her love and need for me and I did the same. I was moved by all, and shed tears for all that might have been.

Thus today, I will take a well preserved Humvee that I've beefed up to be somewhat combat ready. It's in the parking garage, and like all three hundred of the fabled Spartans, it will traverse the distance between here and the object of my most burning desire. With any luck at all I will once more by nightfall lay gently in her arms.

But before I set forth upon this most difficult of errands, I plan on visiting an apartment I have sometimes gone to in the darkest hours of my lowest ebbs.

The old woman who once lived there was a devout catholic and her living room is filled with religious icons and a very elaborate altar. I will go there once more to pray.

When I arrived at the old woman's apartment, I could barely summon up little more beyond the obvious.

Despite all that I've been through, I still believe in God and accept that all of this is His doing. But why exactly He willed it to be like this is what troubles me the most. Back when things were still normal, I used to enjoy a speculative TV series on the History Channel called *Life After People*.

The show ran down various scenarios whereby men vanished from the Earth and then speculated on what would happen after that.

Being basically misanthropic, I used to smile and hope something like that might come into being. I often felt a peaceful contentment as I mediated on such matters.

But now, here I am living in a post-apocalyptic world and am very unhappy with it indeed. That puzzled me until yesterday when it dawned on me that man hasn't really gone anywhere at all and that ugly fact has made everything even worse than it was before.

At least in the old days, when someone died, especially a jerk like Hitler or Nixon, they would finally be out of your hair. But now, when any member of so-called mankind bites the big one, they continue to stumble around town, groaning that they want your brains as they attempt to valiantly do something about it.

Okay so I know the score already going into the game…so what. I've always been a tilter at windmills. The Don Quixote of Long Beach, that's me, and anyway what do I have to lose? I've been looking down into the streets for the last sixty days and not one living person is moving around down there.

Last I heard, Kathy was still alive even if it was a month and a half ago. I have no other way of even attempting to find her if I don't go to the last place she was, so really what choice do I have?

She's the only woman I've truly ever loved and something like that will make you do some stupid and dangerous things.

There's still one more thing I need to get. By lucky chance I came across a sample case in one of the apartments back when all this started.

He or she must have been a greeting card designer because there were many different samples of the various seasonal-type cards as well as drawing boards and drawing instruments…even an easel. It's dumb and sentimental of me but I go up there once in a while. I spent an hour rifling through the place one time until I came across exactly what I was looking for.

It's almost a dead ringer for the Christmas card I gave her back on our first Christmas Day together so many years ago. I spent another twenty minutes composing an original poem for her on the back of it just the way she used to like me to, I'll be bringing it along with me.

I worked my way down to the basement garage one last time, saying a fond goodbye to my well-fortified fortress. The Humvee is stocked with canned goods, basic medical supplies, and the best of my arsenal with an emphasis on handguns and rifles. I also brought along a machete I found in the janitor's closet.

It took a while to get the engine to kick over but kick over it did. The Humvee is filled to the brim with siphoned gas from the other vehicles parked around it.

Good thing they kept the keys to it and all the other vehicles in the attendant's office. It's a real nice set of wheels and I guess worth every dime that someone paid for it. Back when life was normal. I could never have afforded it…but now, it's all mine.

The garage has a remote controlled door that is quite stout, so getting out isn't a problem. I deliberately picked high noon because I've observed that those things hate direct sunlight. I guess it makes them decompose faster and they know it.

During the heat of the day they keep to the shadows or stay indoors. Not unexpectedly, several of them are huddled in the murky depths of my path out leading to the street.

It doesn't matter; I floor the gas pedal and exit the garage, taking down several of them as I leave. They're better off. As I'd hoped, the streets are pretty empty and the few shamblers I can see look angry at how easily I'm getting past them. I think at some level they know that it's Christmas Day and they want me to spend it with me.

I guess you could say they want my heart for their Christmas dinner. Well, they aren't going to get anything resembling me.

Since the roads are still pretty navigable, I do fifty miles per hour all the way. Minutes later, I arrived at the building where Kathy worked in a heart specialist's office.

I quickly secured the Humvee as best I could in the street in front of it. Then I used the fire escape to work my way to the top of the building. I've got a rifle, extra ammunition, my special pistol, a Kel-lite, the machete, and her Christmas card. The most sensible way in is through the skylight of the building. Once inside, I did a floor by floor search with my Kel-lite, but nada. Luckily,

I didn't encounter any of the hungry, hungry dead who rule Long Beach currently. An hour later and still no Kathy. I'm about to give up and leave the building but there's still one last place to check: the basement air raid shelter.

I follow the signs to it and notice a strange noise coming from down there. It's definitely a female voice but I can't understand what she's trying to say.

There are other weird noises, too, but I have no idea what they might be exactly. With the Kel-lite in one hand, my machete in the other, I cautiously enter the room.

My heart shrivels up and dies at what I see. It's my Kathy, but now she's an ugly, drooling zombie, swinging from a noose she made out of her own clothes. She's dangling from one of the overhead plumbing pipes and she's very angry and hungry-looking. I drop to my knees and wonder what to do next.

I don't know how long I sat there but I soon realized I no longer had anything to live for without her.

I know exactly what I need to do next but I'm unsure of the best way to do it.

Looking around, I formulated a plan. First I shot Kathy in the head to put her out of her misery, then I cut her down and placed her on my jacket with the Christmas card I brought for her tucked gently under her head as kind of a pillow.

Now, as I sit here, I contemplate how to kill myself. At first I considered death by overdose from the morphine shots that are sure to be somewhere amongst the civil defense supplies, but then I remember if I do that, I will immediately come back to life as one of them. There's only one sure way to make sure that won't ever happen so I take it.

I lay next to Kathy one last time and for all of eternity. I cradle her in my arms just like we used to, then I kiss her tenderly on what is left of her lips. I ask God to forgive us both and to accept us into whatever Heaven might be waiting.

Then I write one final Christmas poem for her, one written with a Police Special that I found in my former apartment building that used to belong to a cop I played pool with back when there was still a world.

As I squeeze the trigger, I hear the shot, and my head snaps back.

Death comes easier than I thought it would even though it's scarier and more painful than I'd hoped it would be.

"Hi, honey, I found you. Merry Christmas."

AXE TO GRIND

REBECCA SNOW

"Dad, you know the chainsaw is quicker," Paul Duncan said, shaking the machine until the fuel inside sloshed. "A single cut and it's done, just like butter."

"You're right, boy." Norman stilled the sharpening stone in his hand and smiled up at his son. "But the axe is what we've always used. It's a tradition. It's the same one my daddy used, and it's quieter than your contraption. And as long as I'm alive, swinging this axe is how we'll keep doing it."

Norman focused his attention back to the tool and drew the whetstone along one side of its double blade. Paul flopped onto a kitchen chair. A few flakes of green paint fluttered from one of its peeling legs as its feet scraped across the scarred wooden floor. Norman's eyes flicked up from under a single raised eyebrow.

"Hush," Norman hissed. "You don't want to wake your mother, do you?"

Paul shook his head as hinges creaked at the back of the cabin. He stared at the box of glittering tinsel nestled on the sagging couch. Fuzzy slippered feet shuffled across the floorboards.

"Too late," Paul mumbled. He stood as his mother stumbled into the circle of light cast by the single bare bulb.

"What are you boys chattering about out here?" Mira eased into the seat her son had vacated.

"Don't you worry about it, Mira." Shoving a dirty rag out of the way, Norman reached for her hand across the tabletop. "You should be resting."

Mira blew out a quick breath and leaned across the wooden surface to grip his open palm. "I've rested enough. Lesley isn't coming back this time. I need to move on. We all do." She dragged a sleeve across her cheek to soak up escaping tears. "So, what needs doing?"

Norman twisted in his chair to find Paul leaning back on the counter with his arms crossed over his chest. The younger man shrugged and twisted his face into an uncertain half-grin. Turning back to his wife, Norman tilted his head back and forth, examining the woman from different angles.

"You think you're up for the dishes?" he asked.

Norman nudged her gaze with his chin toward the piled sink. Dishes that hadn't fit inside the basin leaned in a precarious tower on the counter. Mira slid her fingers from Norman's grasp and pressed her hands onto the tabletop, pushing herself to her feet. Norman leaned back in the worn wooden chair. When Mira stepped toward the sink, the table bobbled back to balance.

"I guess it's as good a place as any to start cleaning up your mess." She shoved her sleeves up to her elbows. "Don't you boys have something better to do than watch me scrub down the place?"

The two men locked eyes. Norman winked. Paul's lips formed a tight-lipped grin before he lowered his gaze to the toe of his scuffed combat boot.

"We do have an errand to run," Norman said.

He stood and held the axe behind his back. With an awkward, hobbling stride, he stepped to the sink and kissed Mira on the cheek as she reached to turn the knob for the hot water.

"You boys be careful," she said over her shoulder. "It looks like we might be in for at least a few more inches of the white stuff." She dunked her hands in the mountain of rising foam and pulled out a droopy sponge. "Get another scrubber if you're anywhere near a store."

Norman nodded and zipped up his coveralls. "We'll be back soon." He still hid the axe from his wife. "Come on, Paul."

She raised a mound of bubbles and waved without turning away from her work. Her tuneless hum filled the room, making the two men smile.

Paul wriggled his hands into a pair of fingerless gloves and lifted the chainsaw from where it sat beside the table.

"Leave it," Norman said under his breath. "We won't need it."

Paul hefted the chainsaw to get a better grip on the handle and shook his head. He stepped over a battered box of glass ornaments. "I'll take it anyway. Just in case your tradition breaks."

"Just don't start whining for me to carry that monster as soon as we get halfway down the driveway." Norman chuckled. "I'm not going through that again."

"Geez, we had to bury the dog somewhere," Paul said as they stepped onto the porch. "And I was seven. Can't you just let it go?"

The porch floor creaked with their combined weight. Norman wiggled the knob to make sure the door was locked.

"Nope. Not a chance." Breaking a path through the snow, Norman continued, "Let's get going. We don't have a lot of time to get this done."

Without a word, they wound through the forest grove surrounding the empty yard. When the two men reached the secured gate, Norman slid a silver key from his glove and drove it into the padlock. He twisted his wrist, and the lock opened with a clank.

The world beyond the high stone wall was covered in a snowy blanket. Body-sized lumps in the smooth whiteness were the only indications of the decimated corpses that littered the area.

Paul inhaled, stretching his lungs to capacity. "At least the cold cuts down on the smell."

"Keep your eyes open, boy." Norman raised a hand to shelter his eyes from the flurries. "The quicker we get this done, the quicker we go home."

"Dad, I'm twenty-four. I'm not a kid."

The two men shuffled through the unmarked snow toward the brook. In the spring and summer, water slid past the length of the stone fence and disappeared into the woods. The water froze to a sheet of ice when the winter weather came.

"Hey, Dad," Paul said when they reached the sloping bank. "Do you remember when we used to skate out here?"

"Nope." Norman held the axe under his arm for a moment as he blew hot air into his gloves.

"Are you serious?" Paul shot his father a sideways glance and slid to the slick surface of the ice. "Lesley broke her arm, and I had to go back to the house so you could carry her home."

Norman took a tentative step onto the solid white ice. He shuffled aside the snow as he slid his boots across the frozen water.

"You were down here skating?" Norman asked, paying most of his attention to his footing. "Well, I'll be. I thought you were out here causing trouble."

The older man wobbled and threw out his arms for balance. The axe in his hand threw his equilibrium in the opposite direction, and he collapsed onto his back. He stared at the falling flurries for a moment before rolling to his knees. The ice beneath him creaked in protest.

"When did we ever cause trouble?" Paul asked and took a final nimble step onto the far side.

"I'd say dragging me out in the cold to carry home my broken daughter was trouble," Norman said. He crawled across the remaining few yards of frosted ice.

Rising to his feet, the frozen surface gave way under his work boot. A slight chill seeped around his ankle before he pulled his foot from the frigid water and onto the hardened mud. The hole he'd left behind had spread and reached halfway across the stream.

"It'll freeze over again in no time," Paul said. He grabbed his father's arm and helped him over the crusted lip of soil.

Portions of ancient barbed wire trailed the stream in patches. Cows had been pastured beyond the rusted remnants years ago when the land had been part of a farm. Lumps of snow topped the few remaining posts. Paul shrieked as he stepped through a break in the fence line. Up ahead, Norman whirled to see his son thrashing at the ground with the quiet blade of the chainsaw.

"What's wrong, boy?"

"Something's got me. I can't get loose." Paul threw a quick look at his father and continued to whip his leg back and forth. "I think it's one of them."

Paul lashed at the ground with the saw tip as he tried to pull himself free. The leg of his pants snagged on an unseen object. The younger man grunted and squealed. When he jerked his foot, the nearest fencepost lurched. The post's hat of snow scattered through the thin weed stalks that poked through the frozen crystal crust at its base.

Norman jogged to his son and put a steadying hand on his shoulder. "Hold still, boy." He tugged off a glove and leaned over to examine Paul's leg.

"There's got to be a hand down there." Paul wriggled. "I felt the fingernail scrape against my boot."

Norman froze, then his face twisted into a smirk as he reached out with a rigid fingertip and plucked a buried barb from Paul's wool sock. The bouncing post sprang straight as Paul lost his balance and tumbled to the frozen ground.

"I didn't know the virus could make metal come to life," Norman chuckled.

"What do you mean by metal?" Paul propped himself up on his elbows. "I felt a finger."

Norman gave a slow shake of his head and extended his gloveless hand to his son.

"Look for yourself," he said and pulled Paul to his feet. "Worst you could get from that is tetanus."

Paul scowled. He squatted next to the fingers of wire blooming from the scattered snow and plucked a stray thread from the rust.

"Come on, boy. We've got a job to do." Norman huffed out a hearty laugh and replaced his glove.

Paul scanned the copse of shaped pines in the distance. Two indistinct shadows skirted around the branches before breaking into the clearing.

"Do you know which one you want?" Paul asked.

Norman looked from one cadaver to the other and lifted his axe. "I'll take the little one on the left."

"Figures," Paul mumbled. He abandoned the chainsaw and removed a long screwdriver from a loop on his pants.

"What was that?" Norman asked and took a step toward the shambling walker, then swung his axe into the zombie's skull. Brain matter exploded through the air and landed in a random pattern on the snow. The bones crumbled as the body fell, marring the white powder with dark stains.

"Nothing," Paul mumbled. He pressed his hand to the approaching figure's chest, drew back his arm, and plunged the screwdriver deep into the zombie's left eye socket. After several upward thrusts, the decomposing form dropped into its footprints.

"Did you decide which one we're taking home?" Paul motioned toward the group of triangle trees. A small clump of snowflakes clung to his eyelashes.

"We're taking the one your sister marked." Norman stepped into the glade and lifted branches until he found a weatherworn red ribbon tied around a trunk. "Here's her hair bow. Now stand back."

"Are you sure Mom can handle it?" Paul asked. "This tree is the reason Lesley didn't make it to her last birthday."

"We won't tell your mother this is 'the' tree," Norman said, raising the axe to swing. "But this is what Lesley would have wanted. This is the one she picked. She always knew the right thing to do."

"She would have wanted me to use the chainsaw, too, but we aren't doing that," Paul said under his breath.

Norman lowered the brain-covered axe blade to the ground and leaned against the butt of the handle. "If you've got something to say, boy, then say it."

Stuffing his hands deep into his pockets, Paul widened his eyes, poked out his bottom lip, and shook his head.

"That's what I thought." He repositioned the axe and began to chip away at the bark. His assault echoed into the valley and back. After fifteen minutes of steady chopping, the tree snapped and swooshed onto the snow-covered ground. As Paul lifted the evergreen over his shoulder, he saw a dozen walkers crest the hill beyond the grove.

"We'd better go," he told his father.

"I gotta rest." Norman's breath chugged like a locomotive, and he was sweating like a bag of frozen peas in the summer.

Paul pointed to the incoming threat. "No time. Let's go." He strode toward the closed gate in the distance. "As long as we keep walking, they'll never catch us."

Norman dragged his beloved axe through the snow as he trudged behind his son. His legs felt as if he'd run a marathon in lead shoes, but he kept pace with Paul until they reached the stream. Paul lurched into the shallow water and sloshed through to where it met the remaining ice. At its deepest, the stream only reached a few inches below his knees. He turned to see his father struggling down the trampled far bank. The dead were gaining ground.

"Come on, Dad!" Paul shouted over the approaching moans. "Just jump in. The water isn't very deep."

Using the axe as a walking stick, Norman tottered down the small incline. He slogged through the icy stream and cast a glance over his shoulder in time to see the first of the walkers tumble down the bank. Norman waded to the ice and dragged himself to the surface as the tide of dead wallowed to their feet.

"Hurry!" Paul yelled. He stood next to the open gate, his arms relieved of both the tree and the chainsaw.

Norman tripped twice, but stumbled through the opening before being caught. When the padlock clicked shut, he leaned against the cold stones and gasped for breath. Dead hands smacked against the heavy wooden door.

"That was closer than it should have been," Norman wheezed.

"If you'd let me use the chainsaw, we would've been home by now."

The sky glowed a dull gray as the two men made their way through the woods toward the cabin. Paul hauled the tree in a fireman's carry, the unused chainsaw dangling from his other hand. The rhythmic crunch of their footsteps was the only sound penetrating the hushed silence of the snowy afternoon. It seemed as though the entire world held a collective breath. Their earlier tracks had been flaked over, smoothing the edges.

"Hey," Paul said after Norman had pushed a branch out of the way and let it go before the younger man had gotten past. "Watch it. I'm walking back here."

Norman grunted and continued to follow the indent of the snow-covered path. His head snapped up when a thrashing sounded in the bushes beside him. He retreated a few steps and held the axe at the ready. A stand of evergreen shrubbery shook as if it were dancing to an unheard techno drummer, but nothing emerged from the shadows.

"What do you think it is?" Paul asked. He held the silent chainsaw as a barrier between himself and what lurked within the twigs.

As his adrenaline dissolved, Norman took a cautious step toward the wiggling bushes. "Don't know," he said, poking the greenery with the blade of the axe. "Doesn't look like it's coming out to greet us. Guess we'll have to drag it into the light to find out."

Paul shied away from the trembling foliage. "Do you think it's safe?"

Throwing a glance to his cringing son, Norman raised an eyebrow. "Nope. I don't reckon it is." He parted a few branches and squinted into the dim shade. "But no one else is gonna do it."

Without warning, a rotted hand erupted from the undergrowth and fumbled at the front of Norman's canvas coveralls. Stumbling backwards, the man tumbled over a root and landed on a small holly tree, bending it double. The dead, crusted fingernails grasped empty air as a deep-throated moan crept through the limbs.

Norman sprang to his feet and circled the tangle of greenery. The festering fingers clawed at the empty space.

"Dad," Paul said, his voice quaking. "What's it doing? Why hasn't it attacked?"

"That thing tried to grab me." Norman brushed the snow from the back of his pants. "I'd call that an attack."

"Yeah, but why is it still in the bushes?" Paul stood on his toes and craned his neck to peer around the evergreen at his father.

A patch of snow jumped as the body in the brush tried to turn toward the older man's voice. Norman used the head of the axe to clear a patch of soil.

"Well, I'll be," Norman said, adjusting his frayed knit cap with a gloved hand.

"What is it?" Paul jumped higher hoping to see around the leafy obstacle.

"You remember the bear trap we set last year?" Norman jingled a rusted chain with the toe of his boot.

"The one we didn't think would work?" Paul asked. "Yeah, I remember it."

"Well," Norman said as he returned to where his son bounced in anticipation. "Looks like it worked. We caught one."

"A bear?" Paul shuffled his feet so that his father was between him and the quivering mound of foliage.

"No, boy. Bears are extinct in these parts." Norman thrust a thumb at the thing trapped inside the shivering shrub. "*They* ate them all."

A wide grin spread over Paul's face like a spring sunrise, and he turned on the chainsaw's choke. Before he could yank the pull cord, his father pressed a hand on his arm.

"Not so fast," Norman said. "If it's been traveling in a pack, the rest will hear you start that thing. Then we'll be in real trouble."

"But it's inside the fence. We've never had a pack inside the fence." Paul tilted his head as if he were listening to a distant bird.

"There's a first time for everything." Norman shook the sharpened blade at his son. "Now put that thing away."

"Then why did I bring it?" Paul asked. He let the chainsaw's weight straighten his arm.

"Search me. I tried to tell you we didn't need it." Norman lifted his axe. "Now, yank that walker out of there so I can bash its head in."

Paul left the chainsaw in the snow and trudged around the mound of evergreens. He found the end of the rusted chain staked into the frozen ground. When he pulled, a decomposing leg emerged from the underbrush. The foot was clad in a worn red hiking boot. Some ink pen scribbles were still visible on one side of the rubber sole. Paul yanked again, and the torso slid free. Frozen blood and pus caked its skin and shredded clothing. One more tug brought the entire rotting shape onto the open ground. What was left of its blonde hair hid half of its decayed features.

Norman lowered the axe.

"What are you waiting for?" Paul pulled the chain tight. "Brain the thing."

"I can't." Norman tore off a glove and reached into the back pocket of his coveralls. He removed a red bandana and wiped his face before crumpling the cloth and returning it to his pocket.

"Why not?" Paul squealed as he struggled with the tethered carcass.

Norman stared at his son. Then his gaze shifted to the squirming form before easing back to Paul. "Don't you recognize your sister?" Norman gritted his teeth as he examined the bits of torn flesh hanging from his once beautiful child. "I don't know how she made it back inside the fence."

Norman turned away and searched the woods while Paul dropped the chain and took three halting steps back. The dead girl, released from the restraining pressure, toppled into the brush. Righting herself, she jerked toward the two men until she reached the length of her chain. Her body wrenched sideways and she fell to the ground.

"What do we do?" Paul asked. "We can't let Mom see her like this."

Norman nodded once before his knees gave out on him, leaving him sitting on a snow-covered log.

"Mom just said Lesley wasn't coming back." Paul lifted his arms and dropped his hands on his fleece cap. "We can't let her get back to the cabin like this."

Norman blew out a long stream of air. It condensed into a cloud that lingered for a moment before dissipating. His lips were tinged a slight shade of whitish pink. "We could just leave her. Looks like she's been here a while." He scratched the back of his neck. "That bear trap won't open on its own."

"You're kidding, right?" Paul shook a chapped finger at the snapped jaws of the trap. "What happens when her leg finally gives way and her foot comes off? What then?" He walked to his father and grabbed him by the shoulders. "I'll tell you what happens then." He stepped behind Norman. Placing his palms on his father's tear-stained cheeks, he raised Norman's face to his dead daughter. "She drags herself home and Mom has another breakdown."

Norman shook off Paul's grip, pressed his face into his hands, and sobbed. Lesley's flailing arms stretched toward him but couldn't reach.

"If you can't do it, I will," Paul said. "She won't feel a thing." In a quieter tone, he added, "You don't have to watch."

The older man shook his head as if clearing away a lifetime of cobwebs and then stood up, his joints cracking with each movement. "No, I can't ask you to shoulder my responsibility." His voice was unsteady.

"You didn't ask." Paul stepped between his sister and his father and bent his knees to look into Norman's eyes. "I offered. Consider it a gift."

The two men stared at one another as the dead girl tried to right herself. The chain securing the trap in the ground clanked and jangled as weak moans rose from Lesley's collapsing throat. The sky cast a pinkish haze through the naked branches as the sun burst through a break in the clouds. Flakes still trembled through the air.

"Okay," Norman said, looking as though he'd aged twenty years in twenty seconds. "You do it, and we'll never breathe a word of this to your mother."

Paul gave a quick nod and retrieved the chainsaw.

"Not with that." Norman raised the axe's smooth handle toward his son. "She'll hear the motor."

Paul sighed and reached for the handle. His hands slid into position along the polished wood. He stood over his sister's scrabbling shape and felt the weight of the axe balance in his grasp. His sister's dead eyes flicked from side to side as Paul raised the sharpened blade above his head.

"Goodbye, Lesley," he whispered.

Norman's gaze shifted to the distant pillar of smoke wafting from the cabin's chimney, not wanting to look. The girl's already torn forehead shattered when Paul's single swing found its mark. Lesley's body relaxed. Norman sniffled in the lingering stillness.

"What should we do with her body?" Paul asked, his fingers still wrapped around the wood axe handle.

"I reckon we can just leave her here. I don't think your mom will be leaving the house before spring." Norman slid his hands back into his gloves, fingering the torn lining as it passed. "Anyway, the ground's frozen. We can't bury her yet."

Paul handed the axe to his father and gathered some fallen branches to cover his sister's still form. "Well, at least this'll keep her a little hidden." He wiped the small pieces of bark from his hands. "If Mom goes for a walk, she'll have to get pretty close to find the body."

Norman nodded and lifted the chainsaw and Paul reached for his father's arm.

"I can carry it, Dad."

Norman swung the chainsaw out of reach. "No, it's the least I can do. You get the tree. Your mom's waiting for us."

As the two men plodded through the dark yard toward the shining porch light, Norman asked, "What do you want for Christmas, boy?"

Paul scratched his chin and searched the sky for an answer. Swinging the tree around, he almost knocked over his father. He smirked as the other man caught his balance.

"I'd really like it if you'd stop calling me 'boy.' "

"You got it." Norman grinned, showing off a broken crown. "Merry Christmas, son."

A ZOMBIE FOR XMAS

ASH HARTWELL

Stephen, like most teenage boys, had left his Christmas shopping until absolutely the last available moment. So while his younger twin sisters were enjoying a Christmas Eve visit to Santa's grotto, followed up by a burger in one of the many fast food outlets scattered around the shopping mall, Stephen was trudging from one store to another searching for inspiration.

Having finally made his choices, he hurried through the crowds of last minute bargain hunters, heading for the fountain where he was due to meet his mother and two sisters.

The mall was full of little stalls selling seasonal items such as decorations, gift wrap and roasted chestnuts. The air had a spicy seasonal aroma.

Taking a shortcut through a department store, he stepped sideways to pass an old couple and crashed straight into one of the shop's mannequins. The mannequin looked as if it was going to topple over, and without thinking, Stephen dropped his shopping bags and reached out to grab it before it fell. His hands grabbed the scantily clad doll by her red, satin-covered breasts as he slid to the floor, pulling the garment free.

As he untangled himself from the mannequin and got back to his feet, a very severe-looking sales assistant came towards him, cutting through the crowds like a war galleon in full sail. "Get out! You boys are all the same," she shouted as Stephen made a hasty exit with his shopping bags and a very red face.

When he was almost out of earshot, he heard her shout, "Pervert!" Stephen was glad that as soon as he rounded the corner into the main plaza, where the fountain was, he could see his mother and sisters waiting by the giant Christmas tree.

When he reached them, he hurried them towards the exit to the car park and was relieved when his mother was soon steering the car carefully through the snow and out into the traffic heading for the suburbs.

The journey home was spent exchanging small talk with his mother, and teasing his sisters that he'd completely forgotten about them and had therefore not bought them a present. Occasionally, one of them would point out a brightly-lit house decked out with festive decorations or statues of Santa Clause standing on the roof, and before long they were pulling up into their driveway.

Stephen rushed upstairs to wrap his recently purchased presents. After a few minutes, he heard the doorbell ring and his father's voice telling them to leave it in the garage.

A few moments later his father called up to him. "Stephen, can you come down for a minute? I need a hand with something."

"Sure, Dad. I'm on my way." Stephen hid the unwrapped presents in his cupboard, then went back downstairs. "Where's Dad?" he asked his mother, who was in the midst of preparing vegetables. She pointed towards the door that led out into the garage and workshop area.

Stephen walked into the freezing cold garage and saw his father standing next to a large crate. He had a childish grin spread across his face. In Stephen's experience that could only mean trouble. The sort of trouble that charged into view in pursuit of one of his father's stupid ideas.

"Ta dah!" his father said with a grand gesture towards the crate.

Stephen looked at the crate then back at his father, who was now just grinning inanely.

"Okay, Dad, because it's Christmas I'm going to be polite and pretend I'm interested in your crate," Stephen said.

"Take a closer look, son. Read what it says on the lid." He was almost jumping up and down with excitement.

Stephen walked over to the crate. It was constructed of wood screwed onto a sturdy metal frame. The suppliers name and logo were stenciled on the lid and a clear plastic wallet, containing a shipping address and a small booklet marked **INSTRUCTIONS**, was taped to the lid using yellow tape that was printed with the words **EXTREME CARE: BIOHAZARD** in black lettering. He read the company name to himself again, letting the pieces fall into place in his head, then when he was sure, he read it again, this time out loud. "The Dead Helpful Company."

He looked at his father who was by now nodding so violently that Stephen thought his head was going to fall off. "You bought a zombie for Christmas. That's so cool!"

"I know!" But his father didn't stop smiling or nodding. "Your Uncle Richard is coming over to help get it set up so we can have it working tonight."

"Oh great! Uncle Dick's coming!" Stephen liked to emphasize the name to make his feelings about his uncle clear. He'd never liked Uncle Richard. The man had no sense of responsibility and generally acted like a complete idiot.

Ignoring Stephen's barbed comment about his brother, his father took a powered screwdriver from his toolbox and stood over the eight foot long crate. "Let's get started." Without waiting for a reply, he began to undo the series of screws holding the lid on.

Stephen stood in silence, watching as each screw rose up out of the wooden lid. He could sense his anticipation rising with each screw his father let drop to the floor. After the first five, Stephen was beginning to shift his weight from one foot to the other, and by the time the seventh had bounced across the floor, he could bear it no longer. He walked over to the toolbox and retrieved a retractable knife with which he proceeded to cut open the plastic wallet.

Placing the shipping note to one side, he began to read the instructions. After the usual blurb about the company congratulating the purchaser on their decision to buy this particular model, he came to the page explaining the installation and setup process.

"Hey, Dad, we need to follow this set of instructions." He waved the instruction booklet at his father who was undoing the last screw. As it fell to the floor, his father stood upright, the huge inane grin having reappeared. He sat on top of the crate and gestured for Stephen to join him.

Sitting down, Stephen offered the booklet to him, but his father waved it away.

"You read it, son. Then we'll crack this cadaver's coffin open and let him tidy up. Why buy a zombie, and moan yourself." He laughed at his joke.

Stephen cleared his throat, then began to read aloud from the booklet. "Dead Helpful is unable to accept responsibility for any damage to property or loss of life, either directly or indirectly, caused by the purchaser's or operator's failure to comply with the guidelines and instructions set out in this manual."

"Yeah, yeah, yeah. Let's get to the important part, son."

Just as Stephen was about to start reading again, Uncle Richard opened the door from the main house and entered the garage. He was wearing a set of flashing antlers and a long scarf with large woolen snowballs on each end.

"Wow, it's cold in here. Is that so the stiff still thinks it's in the mortuary?" Richard removed the antlers and stuffed them in his coat pocket.

"No that's 'cause it's the middle of winter and it's snowing out," Stephen said, slowly making sure that Richard knew he thought his uncle was stupid.

Richard looked at Stephen, then laughed out loud. "Little Stevie has mastered sarcasm. I'm so proud." He leaned closer to Stephen and ruffled his hair, then went over to his brother and hugged him.

"Stephen is just about to read the set up guidelines," Stephen's father said.

"Wow! Little Stevie can read as well," Richard said with a look of mock surprise on his face.

Stephen tried to ignore him, to not let the comments upset him. His uncle was an idiot that thought he was cool. Clearing his throat, Stephen said, "Right. The crate contains not only the zombie, although they prefer to call them 'reclaimed bodies,' but also the clothes that you ordered at the same time. It's also provided with a generic white boiler suit for general day to day use."

"There's a huge range of costumes and accessories in the catalogue. Some of it's quite disturbing. Who'd want their zombie to look like Rob Patterson, complete with 'Team Edward' t-shirt?" Stephen's father said, looking genuinely perplexed.

Richard shook his head in disbelief. "There are some sick, sick people out there."

"What's next? Zombie Ken and Barbie, complete with pink sports car and interchangeable heads?" Stephen said and all three of them started to laugh.

"One Christmas when we were kids, your dad and I ripped the head off your aunt's doll and stuck a dinosaur head on it. Then we tried to sell it back to her as 'Reptile Barbie.' She went mental, it was so funny," Richard laughed.

After a few moments for the laughter to subside, Stephen continued. "The crate also contains a care pack which contains a supply of everything you need to maintain the zombie." He fell silent as he quickly read to himself, then said, "Okay. I get it now. Inside the care pack there's a smaller box containing a set of pre-filled syringes, a year's supply of what they refer to as 'Appetite Suppressants,' which are patches that you stick onto the zombie's skin."

While Stephen was talking, his father and uncle stood on either side of him, and without warning lifted the crate lid up, and tipped Stephen still sitting on the crate onto the garage floor. Stephen jumped up and joined the two older men, who were staring down into the open crate.

"It looks a bit on the blue side," Richard said.

Stephen looked at the dead man lying in front of him. The corpse was encased in molded polystyrene so that only his front was visible. The discarded lid had the rest of the mold attached to its inside. The cadaver's eyes were closed and there was a pull-out plastic stopper wedging the mouth slightly open. The body was completely naked and the pale skin did indeed have a blue tinge to it, particularly around the mouth and extremities.

Around the wrists, ankles and neck there was white plastic strapping which held the body in place during transit. By the feet there was an inner box with a clear plastic lid. Stephen's father crouched down cautiously next to the open crate and removed this box. Under that there was a cardboard box which Richard removed.

Standing back up, Stephen's father said, "I thought it would come wearing something, maybe that white boiler suit or even a loin cloth."

Richard pointed at the dead figure's groin. "Don't let your Claire see that. Or you might end up being the one that ends up sleeping in a crate in the garage." Stephen tried desperately not to laugh. His father made a silent sarcastic laughing face towards Richard but his eyes betrayed him by showing genuine mirth.

Stephen picked up the manual he'd dropped when his father and uncle had tipped him onto the floor. He read some more, "The care pack also contains a special moisturizer that stops the skin from drying out and slows down the decomposition process." As he said this, his father was opening the wooden care pack box and laying its contents out on the floor.

"What's that for?" Richard was pointing to the inside of the crate lid where there was a long-handled axe strapped into the polystyrene.

Stephen flicked over a page in the manual and continued to read for a few more seconds, then he looked directly at Richard. "Emergencies." All three stared silently down at the zombie lying before them, suddenly aware of the cadaver's lethal natural desires.

"That's cool," Richard said, getting a knife. He cut the axe free of the polystyrene and took up a baseball stance. He took a few practice swings before placing the axe on the work bench.

Stephen's father finished laying out the contents of the smaller care pack box. Richard pointed at the plastic container containing the syringes. "What do we do with those?" he asked Stephen.

The plastic container had six blue vials and one bright green one. Each had a snub nose with a screw thread connection and a red plastic guard covering the plunger.

Stephen didn't need to consult the manual. "The green one kick starts the system, then you give one blue one every eight weeks to act as a preservative. You have to inject them through a special port in the neck."

Richard picked up the small packet of patches, studying them intently. "If these are appetite suppressant patches, then what appetite does a zombie have that needs suppressing? It's dead!"

Stephen looked at his uncle for a moment, and then speaking with deliberate slowness as if speaking to a child, said, "Well, I'm no expert, but as I understand it they're partial to feasting on human brains. Although I suspect that if they crack *your* skull they'd be sadly disappointed." Stephen accepted his father's offered high five upon hearing the jibe.

Richard had a wry smile on his face. "Okay, smartass, I deserved that. So what do we do now?"

Stephen began to read through the instruction manual again, making sure he understood the process correctly. He was aware that his father was entrusting him with an important job and he wanted to be absolutely sure he got it right. The consequences of making a mistake were almost too awful to contemplate.

While Stephen was busy reading, Richard looked into the cardboard box he'd taken from the crate. He smiled as he took out a Santa Suit complete with black boots and belt. "Is this what you didn't want to tell me about on the phone 'cause the girls were with you?" he asked Stephen's father.

"Yeah. I thought it would be a nice surprise for the girls. It's not often you can get Santa to deliver to their rooms and hand out presents on Christmas Morning," Stephen's father said.

"It's not often that a kid wakes up to see a skinny blue stiff roaming around her bedroom in the middle of the night masquerading as Santa Clause either. You're gonna scare the crap out of them," Richard said.

"Yeah, you could be right there. I didn't really think the whole costume thing through. Maybe I should order a more sensible set of clothes after Christmas." Stephen's father took the Santa Suit from his brother and folded it up, then put it back in the box.

"I think that would be a wise move," Richard agreed, still shaking his head in disbelief.

Stephen began to speak, regaining the two men's attention. "Right, here we go." He put the manual down. "First we need to completely unpack the zombie. Apparently the crate comes apart to make this easier." He watched as his uncle and father struggled to free the zombie from the polystyrene mold. Finally the figure was lying face up on the cold floor.

"Look, there's a tattoo on the left arm." Richard was peering at the naked man's arm. "There's the name 'Christian' and a bar code."

"Maybe that was his religion so his body can be disposed of correctly," Stephen suggested.

"No, they've already had their religious ceremony after they died. The company comes and collects the remains at the appropriate time, and arranges for their disposal," his father said. "It is a name given to them by Dead Helpful to make them a little more personal. No one knows what their name was during life; it's so their living relatives can't trace them. The barcode is the registration, it means they can be returned to their owners if they get lost and it also contains their bio metric information. That means we can order clothes and accessories in the correct sizes. The next thing we need to do is slap a patch on the back of the neck. This must be done prior to re-starting them. According to the manual they wake up hungry." Stephen watched Richard peel the backing off one of the patches and then, with the help of Stephen's father, roll Christian onto his side. Richard placed the patch and then they let Christian roll onto his back.

"Just like a nicotine patch. This bad boy's a twenty brains a day corpse," Richard joked, doing a passable Groucho Marx impression.

"This is so weird," Stephen said. "I've never even seen a dead body before and the only zombies I've seen have been from a distance, like the ones that fix the roads. But now I'm standing here in my garage looking at a dead body and I'm perfectly fine with it."

"That's because all you teenagers are freaks! Brought up on a diet of sick horror movies," Richard said. Picking up the box of vials, he took the green one out and handed it to Stephen. "Which is why you can do the honors and bring our friend here back to the land of the living. Or whatever it is they come back to."

Stephen took the syringe from his uncle and looked at his father for confirmation. His father nodded and Stephen took a few faltering steps towards the dead man on the floor. All of a sudden he was decidedly less fine with this. Taking a deep breath, he crouched down by the body's head. He slowly stretched out a hand, and summoning up all the courage he could muster, touched the cold blue skin. He was desperate to turn around and run away, but he was more desperate not to let his father see his fear.

With tentative fingers, he felt the back of the zombie's neck. His fingers explored the cold skin, searching for the small injection port. Locating it, he rolled the heavy head onto its side and connected the syringe to the port. Again he was aware that he took a deep breath, then snapped the red plastic safety guard off and carefully pressed the plunger down, forcing the bright green fluid into the zombie's system.

Having emptied the syringe, he shuffled back across the floor before staggering to his feet and standing next to his father. The three of them just stood and watched as the zombie known as Christian did nothing.

The body didn't even twitch, but just remained motionless on the cold floor. After a full minute of Christian doing nothing, Richard crept up to the body and placed a foot on either side of the zombie's hips, then bent down to look into the pale face.

At that exact moment, Christian opened his eyes wide and Richard let out a little scream. He moved out of the zombie's way as it tried to get to its feet. It sat upright with slow deliberate movements until it was on its knees, then came to a standing position.

It stood in front of them swaying slightly. It was becoming aware of its body again. It flexed its fingers and moved its arms and legs about as if discovering them for the first time.

Stephen looked at the walking dead man with a bizarre combination of gut-wrenching terror and childish curiosity. The eyes were sunken into the skull and showed no emotion, no life. He didn't quite know what he expected but this wasn't it.

Hearing his father's voice as if it were from a great distance, Stephen forced himself to pull his eyes away from the shuffling wreck that had once been a human being. He watched his father retrieve the Santa suit from the workbench and throw it on the floor in front of Christian.

No. In front of the *zombie*. To give this thing a name was abhorrent. No amount of names or costumes would make this thing human again. Stephen had always thought owning a zombie would be cool but now realized it was just inhumane.

His father spoke directly to the zombie. "Christian, could you please get dressed in those clothes on the floor in front of you."

Stephen watched as the zombie struggled to pick up the bright red suit. His father laughed as the zombie got tangled up in the strange clothes.

Richard joined in with the laughter. "Don't you think that this is just a little disturbing?" Stephen looked at Richard, hopeful that common sense was about to prevail. That his annoying uncle was about to put a stop to this once and for all. But then Richard said, "Us three watching a naked guy get dressed."

Stephen watched his uncle and father laugh at the zombie as it struggled to get dressed in the bright red Santa suit, complete with long gray beard.

After a while his father said to Richard, "Let's tidy up a bit while Stephen goes and gets some of the girls' presents for Santa's visit."

The two men turned their attention to the dismantled crate and polystyrene packaging that littered the floor. While they were busy cleaning up, Stephen casually walked past the workbench and picked up the axe. The bewildered zombie was just standing still, watching him, as if it were awaiting instructions. Walking with a newfound purpose, Stephen moved around behind the zombie, and reaching up, tore the patch away from the back of its neck. This would teach his father and uncle to laugh at zombies. To laugh at him. Then he hurried through the door into the warm and welcoming house, bolting it behind him.

After a few seconds passed, he heard sounds of a struggle and a muffled scream come from the garage. He left the axe by the door and rushed to gather some presents from under the over-decorated tree. He needed to look as if he were on an errand. He shouted a greeting to his mother who was in the kitchen cooking and got himself a piece of mincemeat pie before returning to the garage door.

He put his ear to the door and listened intently. He could hear nothing but the sound of his own heart beat. He slid the bolt back as quietly as he could and pushed the door open, then lifted the axe up and crept into the cold December air in the garage.

He could see Uncle Richard lying on the floor next to the broken crate. A large pool of blood had spread out around him. Moving closer, Stephen could see that he had a large wound on the top of his head. Richard's dead eyes stared up accusingly at Stephen as he tiptoed past.

Stephen could hear a strange sound coming from the far end of the garage, behind the workbench. He renewed his grip on the axe and edged around the end of the workbench. In the corner, he could see his father's legs sticking out from behind a toolbox. They were motionless. When he took another step, he saw the zombie sitting on his father's body, and the strange sound he'd heard was the zombie tearing the brains from his father's exposed skull.

Stephen took another step, and zombie Santa looked up. Its gray beard was now streaked with various shades of red and brown as fresh blood mixed with old. The zombie's eyes were now more alive, as if rejuvenated by the kill.

Stephen quickened his pace forward, swinging the axe down at Santa's head.

He missed. The axe tore into the upper arm of the zombie. He struggled to free it as the zombie Santa used its other hand to pull at the axe. After what seemed like an eternity, the axe came loose, the tip banging onto the concrete floor.

Stephen took another swing, and this time it severed the head from the zombie's shoulders. The head, complete with fake gray beard, bounced across the concrete floor. The body continued to kneel on top of his father's body and Stephen prodded it with the axe. It toppled over.

Stephen took out his mobile phone and picked up the instruction manual he'd been reading earlier. He turned to the advertisement he'd seen earlier and dialed the number.

After a conversation lasting just a few minutes, he dragged the three bodies out of the garage and into the snow, then went back into the house in search of his mother. At almost a hundred thousand a body, he wanted to cash in. The snow would keep them fresh until The Dead Helpful Company would collect them.

A CHRISTMAS DINNER

VINCENZO BILOF

Tommy 'Bats' hated the idea of celebrating Christmas down in Florida. He always suffered under the heat because of his large body, and the uncomfortable humidity put him in a sour mood. It was bad enough that he had to supply the hooker—he was the professional muscle, not an errand boy—but Christmas away from Queens without the cold and the snow didn't feel like Christmas at all. He was out of his element.

He grumbled and wiped at his forehead with the sleeve of his gray suit jacket while sitting in the villa's massive guest bedroom. The hooker was a slight, rat-faced girl who chewed gum at a machine-gun rate and scratched incessantly at a large, stained bandage that was wrapped around her thigh. Her red lingerie hung loosely, and the bells on the Santa hat jangled with her awkward, constant shifting of one leg over a thigh, and then the other leg over the other thigh.

"What the hell happened to you?" he pointed at the bandage. It was bad enough that she was pencil-thin with a protruding rib cage and flat chest; she was damaged goods.

"Got bit by some crazy john," she wiped at her nose and sniffled. "You said you got some coke around here?"

Tommy wrung his thick hands. He'd earned his nickname because the swing of his arm could break a man's skull with a baseball-bat crunch. He identified with the name, but he didn't identify with Angelo Scarlotti's idea of a good time. What would Angelo say when he walked into the room to inspect the gift that was supposed to go to his nephew, Dean the Jew?

Laughter and loud music from the party reached his ears, and his eyes once again flickered to the worn bandage that seemed about to slip from her thin flesh. She shifted again in the lavish, paisley-patterned armchair.

"Ain't nothin' for you." Tommy rubbed his stubby fingers through his thin, well-greased hair. "Don't touch nothin'." He closed the door to the room. He regretted leaving her in a room with silk sheets and hand-carved, mahogany-stained furniture, but the girl's scratching had stretched his patience to the limit. Even in the air-conditioned room, the Florida heat seemed to get beneath his suit and provoke an outpouring of sweat.

It was no secret that Angelo had been mulling retirement and thinking about settling down. Angelo had been coming more frequently to his home in Florida, where he often visited with his shy, socially-dysfunctional nephew, Dean the Jew. The kid wasn't even half-Jewish, but he was damn good with numbers.

Angelo had a lot of friends and well-wishers. Small groups of well-dressed mistresses smiling over lipstick-stained wine glasses moved out of the way before Tommy had to excuse himself. He searched the faces of the assembled revelers for signs of his boss, and wished he had ice cubes to put into his mouth to chew on. The sparkling blond women with their bright-white teeth only reminded him of his failure to find a girl worthy of Angelo's nephew.

With his thick eyebrows arching over a high forehead, Angelo appeared with a larger-than life smile on his face. He wore a yellow suit with violet pinstripes. This was normal for the outlandish whoremonger and gambling aficionado. He didn't care if he appeared to be flashy—Angelo believed that he earned his money and should enjoy it.

"Bats, where you been? Did you hear that we were havin' a party?" He threw his arm around Tommy's broad shoulders.

"What's the matter? Huh? The Feds are chasin' terrorists; they ain't got time for us. Besides, they know me here. What is it? Huh? Look at you; you're getting sweat all over my carpet." Angelo withdrew his arm.

"I got that broad for the Jew," Tommy said. He was in no mood to have to explain himself.

"Good, that's good," Angelo said. "As long as we make him happy tonight. Cheer up, Bats. It's Christmas! The party's in full swing. You need a drink. You call your wife? What's your problem?"

"Why do we need to be down here? We coulda done all this back home. Business is good back home. You know I ain't got no problem comin' down here, but this ain't ours."

Angelo shook his head. "I wouldn't worry about it. Listen, why do you need to bust my balls about this right now? I'm hosting a fuckin' party. This is for my nephew, you know he's a good kid. He don't like to come north. Now why am I explainin' this to you? Huh? Quit your damn cryin' and get yourself a drink."

Tommy clenched his meaty hands into thick fists. There'd been plenty of arguments between him and Angelo before, but his old friend seemed to be holding something back. The party was unnecessary, and Tommy had never been included in its plans. Years on the street together had brought the two of them close; they trusted one another, and anything big like the party would be discussed at length, even if Angelo had every intention of going ahead with it, no matter what Tommy said.

There were too many people that Tommy didn't recognize. With each step he took toward the wet bar, he couldn't help but fume over the idea that he'd been asked to fetch a hooker. He didn't like that the party was crawling with girls who could have been bought or would have likely been willing to pay on a favor that was owed to Angelo.

When Tommy saw his old friend 'Vito the Cheese' at the wet bar, the evening's future immediately brightened; Vito had been in the crew almost as long as Tommy, and he was far more ruthless. Vito had the uncanny ability to make every shit-storm of a day smell like roses with his dry sense of humor, but Vito was un-flinchingly ruthless.

Vito always looked good in a suit. Unlike Angelo, whose tastes bordered between flashy and ridiculous, Vito's tailored look included pinstripes and power ties. Even when he was on the job, he preferred to wear a business suit over a jumpsuit. When Tommy stood next to him at the bar, Vito was playing with his smartphone. He smiled widely but kept his attention on the device.

"Shit, Tommy, you're sweating so damn much I ain't gonna recognize you when the party's over! You'll be skinny. Mother Mary, jump in the fuckin' pool, Bats."

Tommy grinned. He ordered his drink and said, "You've been playing with that thing for hours. You'll get us all pinched playing with that GPS and shit."

"Naw, I'll just get *you* pinched. This has been one memorable Christmas. There's a riot in Miami, there's one in New York...look at this: there's one in fucking Utah. I forgot that was a state. People are actin' like it's the end of the goddamn world."

"Back home?" Tommy was semi-interested, but his own thoughts kept him distracted.

"You can power a spaceship with this thing but you can't get the straight news. The stories on this thing! Last-minute shoppers gotta cause hell. This one joker working for the *Times* is sayin' there's some kind of epidemic that's makin' people crazy."

"So you haven't heard from nobody?"

Vito's well-manicured eyebrows dipped between his eyes. "You think I'm gonna make business calls on this thing? Do I gotta slap you upside your head like your mother used to? Shit, Bats, the Feds can touch anything that goes through this. I ain't callin' nobody. I use the pre-pay-and-go, and only for incoming calls. I figured they'd get in touch with Angelo if it was that serious. You seen the old *fanoik*?"

Tommy shook his head. He'd been half-ashamed to complain to Angelo about his disinterest in the party, but his embarrassment would have only been enhanced if he'd continued to rant about his long-time boss and friend to Vito. Tommy was a loyal soldier, and he hated that he'd started to feel uneasy about his status with Angelo. They didn't owe each other anything except for loyalty, and Tommy didn't want to think about that word in a negative light. It meant too much to him.

Vito the Cheese continued. "So anyway I get this call from back home. Jimmy Hangover's got this bite on his arm. Guy's on the street mindin' his own business when this little kid starts fucking with him. Just kinda pushing into him I guess, and you know Jimmy, he gets wise with the kid. Fucking kid bit him on the arm. He says there's people running all over the streets, and there's shit on fire, you know? Ain't seen nothin' like it. I mean, I know the economy is bad and all but... hey, Bats, that reminds me of that one job we pulled..."

Angelo appeared again, a pair of dark shades over his eyes. Vito looked him up and down and said, "Hey, Ange, Nigeria called, they want their bananas back. I'm talkin' about the ones they used to make that fucking suit. You hear anythin' from back home?"

Angelo frowned. "Listen, my nephew's been waiting to open his Christmas present."

Vito looked at Tommy, then back to Angelo. The three of them stood there for a long moment. Angelo finally shrugged his shoulders and said, "Did I just stutter? You're both looking at me like I'm speakin' some Canadian-French bullshit."

"Let him have his fun," Tommy finally said. "What do we have to do with it?" He felt like he sounded more annoyed than he wanted to, but it was becoming difficult not to hide his disappointment in Angelo's scheme.

"What's your problem?" Angelo asked him. "I'm doin' you a favor by bringin' you out in this heat. Christ, Bats, you hungry or somethin'? Remember when you almost ate that whole ham last year? Cheese, you remember that? So much for Christmas dinner. I made sure I had some extra ham for tonight in case you get hungry."

Vito laughed but Tommy wasn't in the mood. He stood up suddenly, spilling Crown Royal on his sweat-soaked jacket. He smoothed his hair. "You're tellin' me you want us to come up there with you? You're out of your mind. I didn't come here for this. I got better shit to do. You want the Jew to pop his cherry? He don't need me to help him. You want to show him how to do it or somethin'?"

Angelo put his hands up. "What the fuck's your problem, Bats? I'm just bustin' your balls a little! This is a special moment. You comin' upstairs or what? You got somethin' better to do? It's the Jew! He's like family to you guys! Huh?"

Vito shrugged. "Take it easy. Take a Viagra or somethin', will ya? That's the most popular poison on the market now. You know how much of that shit we moved last week?"

Angelo turned his back to them. It was the one thing that irked Tommy the most about his flashy friend; when he seemed to be asking for something, he was really demanding it, and he often curtailed any further argument by walking away. There was no arguing with Angelo.

The party was becoming a bit unruly. More and more guests were playing with their phones, each of them relaying rumors of the chaos that was supposedly erupting in the world outside of the party. Tommy thought he heard, "...Yeah, but it says here that the cat was already dead..."

Dean the Jew was waiting outside of the bedroom door. His hands were buried in his pockets, and his big glasses were perched atop his nose. He stared at the floor and muttered broken sentences that were comprehensible to him alone. Tommy had heard once that the Jew had once been called 'Rain Man' by an old friend of Angelo's. The nickname didn't stick because that old friend had his skull broken into pieces. The Jew's affliction was similar to the movie character's; a form of autism that made him socially inept but incredibly magical when it came to understanding numbers. He was Angelo's secret weapon when it came to sports betting.

Tommy stepped inside the bedroom with his comrades, and Dean followed them in. Off on the corner, a Christmas tree sat, blinking silently in reds and blues. Silver garland was draped across the branches.

The girl lay slumped in the chair, semi-conscious and drooling. The smell that emanated from the half-ripped bandage was a combination of sewage and old milk. Tommy cursed his luck and was prepared to defend himself against Angelo's accusations. With all of the women that'd been invited to the party and could have been coerced into this room after a few drinks, why had he been stuck with getting this coke-head of a girl?

"Perfect. Get her on the bed," Angelo said.

Tommy exchanged a look with Vito.

"What the fuck you doin'?" Angelo asked. "Get her on the damn bed!"

After running his hand through his hair, Tommy picked the girl up and tossed her onto the bed. Her body felt like dead weight and was heavier than he anticipated.

"Shit, she looks sick," Angelo said. "I hear there's a bunch of these broads that are comin' down with the sickness. You see, Dean don't need any sass or back talk. He's sensitive. She got a name?"

Tommy thought for a long time. He was often forgetful and he wasn't as clever as Vito, but he thought about it for only a moment. "Barbara."

The girl moaned and her eyelids fluttered. The Santa hat hung limply over her half-open, liquid-filled eyes.

Dean shuffled his feet. "Uhm, can I, uhm, can I, uhm, do you think she likes me?"

Angelo slapped him on the back. " 'Course she likes you! Now get those clothes off! We'll show you how it's done! Tonight, you become a man!"

Vito chuckled. "Merry Christmas. She looks dead tired, though. Wake her up, Dean."

The Jew slowly eased out of his clothes and approached the bed apprehensively.

"Bats, make sure she's ready," Angelo said.

Tommy shook his head. He muttered under his breath and removed the girl's tiny string thong. Vito the Cheese started to egg him on while his index finger slid down her flat stomach to the juncture of her thighs. He slid his finger into the placid hooker, then another finger, until he could fit four fingers in her cold, damp pit. He'd never felt anything like it. Vito started to suggest a strategy of approach to Dean. Tommy withdrew his hand and wiped it off quickly with a handkerchief, while the girl on the bed lay with her arms splayed out, unmoving.

Dean mounted her and began thrusting away recklessly. Drool dripped from his chin, and Tommy couldn't help but watch the entire thing go down with amazement. It dawned on him that Angelo had recommended a pimp to him so that he could find the girl—he'd known all along that the girl might be sick. Did that bite have anything to do with it? He stared at the slipping bandage and tried to remember something the Cheese had said at the bar.

Arching his back, Dean screamed...and not in a good way. The sick girl suddenly shot up and grabbed his shoulders with both of her hands. She bit into his throat and thick red blood gushed into her mouth and down her chin. She'd been too fast for Tommy, but he moved quickly enough to push the Jew off her and get her down on the bed again. Then, he proceeded to do what he did best. He rained his fists down on her face. She tried to sit up, but he ended each attempt with a blow to her bloody face. She eventually stopped moving, her face pulped beyond recognition.

Angelo held on to his bleeding nephew. "What the fuck was that? Look at this blood! You know how much this suit cost me? Bats, clean up your mess. Don't get no blood on the carpet. You hear me? You fucked up, Bats. The bitch ate his neck! There's a fucking hole in it!"

Angelo didn't bother to clothe Dean, but instead left the room quickly. Tommy dripped sweat on the dead girl's face. The Cheese was still in the room.

"Shit, Tommy, that girl survived you sitting on her," Vito quipped.

In the corner of the room, the Christmas tree still blinked silently.

On the floor, the dead hooker was wrapped up in the silk sheets, while Vito helped clean the blood off the wall from the beating. They made sure that no more blood touched the expensive carpet.

Tommy couldn't help but complain. "You heard what he said? He set this whole thing up. He was hoping that the girl would be sick like that."

"He's got somethin' cooking," Vito said. "She looked like the people they've been talkin' about in the news."

"What people?"

"The people that've been causin' the riots. The sick people. Listen to me, Bats. It ain't no secret that Angelo's settin' up shop down here. He's not retirin'. Did he already talk to you about it?"

Tommy didn't answer. He stared at Vito, and it was clear that the Cheese had already been asked to join Angelo in Florida, while Tommy was going to be left out in the cold. Fresh anger boiled his blood, and a rush of heat flushed his face.

"Angelo knows somethin' though," Vito said. "About this whole damn mess."

Wringing his hands, Tommy had to ask, "You didn't hear anythin' else?"

Vito shrugged. "He wouldn't have you clipped. We know the guy. I mean, come on, right? Why are we even talkin' about it?"

Tommy clenched his teeth and opened his fists to flex his fingers. "I'll have to straighten him out. I've done it before."

"These things have to happen every now and then. Hey, listen, you won't mind if I take care of business myself, will you?" The Cheese had already unzipped his fly. He opened his palm to reveal a blue pill, then tossed it into his mouth and swallowed.

"Be careful, she bites," Tommy said while opening the door. He glanced at his depraved associate once more.

"Close the door already! I gotta test the product that we're puttin' out on the street! See if it works!"

Closing the door behind him, Tommy left Vito to his perverse lust and purposefully walked through the party, on the hunt for Angelo. The crowd had thinned considerably since the Jew had unwrapped his 'gift,' with more discussion centering around the distorted news stories that were filtering through the Associated Press's rumor-mill. He had no time to listen; he had to find Angelo to set the record straight. He couldn't bear the thought that after so many years together, he was about to be betrayed.

Suddenly, someone grabbed his arm and he was turned around sharply. He almost brought his fist right into the face of Young Paulie, a tan, half-Cuban, half-Italian who hung around with Angelo in Florida.

"Bats, we've been lookin' all over for you. We need you at the door. We got this crazy bastard tryin' to get in. Damn drunk stirrin' it up at the door."

"Take care of it," Tommy growled at him.

"But the guy ain't goin' down. Angelo don't want no mess, see..."

Instead of waiting for the kid to sputter out his story, Tommy pushed past him through the front door, where a drunken Santa Claus was being held by two members of Paulie's crew.

"We ain't just gonna clip the guy," one of them said.

Tommy's patience had worn thin. Another opportunity to wreck someone's face was attractive to him. The wavering Santa tried to hold himself upright, and he moaned in the same way as the dead hooker. Tommy hesitated; he couldn't smell any alcohol on the man's breath.

"Santa's taken a beating, and he won't go down," one of Paulie's boys said.

Storm clouds obscured the stars overhead, and in the humid darkness, Tommy couldn't see anything but a bright white beard. He figured that the time had passed for conversation, so he straightened his shoulders and leveled Santa with his massive fist. Santa reeled but remained upright, so Tommy introduced him to his left fist. Santa collapsed in a heap, and Paulie's boys let him go.

Santa sat up.

Tommy had delivered some heavy beatings before, but he'd never seen anyone get back up with so much ease after experiencing the kind of force that he'd delivered.

Tommy spat on the ground. "Here's for that lump of coal you put in my stocking." ¬He kicked Santa in the chin.

Santa fell back but a second later was sitting up again.

"Shit," Paulie said from behind Tommy. "Look at this guy. Let's get him a job!"

Tommy was a professional and had been one of the best muscle guys on the street. His ego was severely bruised, and the confidence that made him feel both invincible and untouchable weakened just enough for doubt to creep in. Angelo wanted to replace him, to cut him out. Was Paulie the new muscle? He'd picked up the hooker that nearly got the Jew killed, and now he couldn't even lay out a drunk Santa.

A fury unlike any that Tommy had ever known filled him; his fists felt heavier and he took a deep breath, filling his lungs with air as if he were jumping into an ocean of blood and violence. In that familiar ocean, he was the best swimmer. He picked Santa up by his shirt and brought his fists down like pistons, until the face began to feel soft. He couldn't stop. To experience the pleasure of destroying another man's likeness was not unlike enjoying a hard drug for the first time. He loved every second of it.

When he finally ceased, he panted and wiped the sweat from his lip.

"I can't even see his face no more..." someone said.

Tommy wanted to say, "He doesn't have one anymore," but he labored to catch his breath. Paulie stood next to him, and when

Santa's arm grabbed his potential replacement's ankle, Tommy couldn't react. No man could have survived such a beating. A glimpse of light from the house behind them revealed a Santa face that was a mask of dark, syrupy blood. Santa had Paulie's ankle in a tight grip as he opened a blood-encrusted mouth to bite down hard.

Paulie yelped, and Tommy stood upright. The adrenaline that had guided his actions cooled instantly. His heavy breathing seized him, and he felt his hands shake. He'd stared death in the face before, but fear was new and unwelcome. He took a step backward while one of Paulie's men drew a gun and pumped two rounds into Santa's skull.

"He was already dead," Tommy said. "He had to be, no one coulda took that kinda abuse and lived." He looked around quickly for the Feds, who would have been watching the party from an unmarked van out in the street; the sound of gunfire should have brought them running.

An eerie silence fell over them while Paulie, clutching his ankle, bled onto the ground. "He ain't movin' no more now," one of them said. "Santa ain't deliverin' presents this fucking year."

Tommy turned back to the house and went inside. He had to find Angelo and take care of business. The entire night had gone wrong. Where were the Feds?

The same hush that had fallen over the scene outside followed him inside the house. The suited men and plastic-chest blondes stared up from the top of the staircase, where 'Barbara' and the Cheese ambled awkwardly over the steps on their way down. The Santa hat had nearly fallen over the hooker's eyes while she stumbled over the steps without her underwear; her chest and face were covered in blood. Vito the Cheese tried one step and then toppled down the staircase.

A partygoer rushed to Vito and turned him over. Tommy could see there was a massive hole in his stomach; his insides had been ripped out.

But that didn't stop Vito from reaching up and grabbing Angelo's associate and taking a bite out of the man's bottom lip, ripping chin flesh as if he were pulling melting cheese away from a hot slice of pizza. The entire room erupted into a frenzy of screams and terror.

Tommy stood and allowed them all to rush past him and out the door. He had one thing on his mind: Angelo.

There was no time for Tommy to fear, nor was there time for him to think about the situation in which he found himself. Thinking was far from his specialty, and whatever was happening would have to wait for him to finish his business with Angelo.

He didn't want to know what Vito and the hooker had become. His fists were raw from the beatings he gave to Santa and the hooker, but there were other ways of dealing with his old friend.

"Hey, Dean, quit it! You're gettin' blood all over the rug!" Angelo had changed his suit to something simpler, but he still wore the shades over his eyes. He had a phone up to his ear while his nephew scooped organs out of a dead man's stomach into his mouth. Angelo shouted something nearly incomprehensible into the phone while the Jew continued to eat.

"Bats!" Angelo said. "I've been lookin' for you! Will you look at this? You know how much I paid for this rug?"

It felt good to wrap his hands around Angelo's neck.

The phone dropped from his hands; he hadn't anticipated that Tommy would attack, and he'd been too slow to draw the piece hidden in his jacket.

"You were gonna cut me out," Tommy said and drew Angelo's gun.

"No!" Angelo breathed, choking. He watched as Tommy dropped his gun to the floor. The feasting nephew looked up, his hands fool of gore.

Tommy eased off Angelo's throat just enough for him to talk. He still hoped he was wrong, because he was afraid how much his heart might break if Angelo had really planned to betray him.

"Listen! I made a deal! The Feds were supposed to help us out! Everything's goin' to hell. Don't you see what's happening?"

"You made a deal with the Feds? You didn't tell me? What was supposed to happen to me? Was that bitch supposed to eat me, too?"

He squeezed Angelo's throat again. Dean the Jew slowly rose from his meal and stood up, blood running out of his mouth and staining his thin, nude body. He hadn't dressed after his escapade with the hooker.

"You love your nephew, don't you?" Tommy asked. "He looks hungry. He looks like he could eat a whole Christmas dinner by himself. Think you can help him out?"

Angelo kicked wildly while Tommy lifted him off the floor. He turned and found that the hooker and Vito had found them. Tommy was starting to feel better about the situation.

"We ain't got a crew no more," Tommy said. "But I gotta say, Ange, you can throw one hell of a party. I bet Vito and the bitch are hungry, too. Why don't you share with them?"

He pushed Angelo to the floor and stood behind him, holding him down by the shoulders.

The trio of walking corpses groaned in unison, and they knelt next to Angelo; Tommy was serenaded with Angelo's screams.

They began to dig in with their fingers, then their mouths, and Tommy couldn't help but laugh. He was still a damn good killer, after all.

When the feast was over, Tommy figured that he still hated Florida, even in the winter time.

He made sure that the villa wouldn't survive the holiday. While he watched it burn, he couldn't help but think of melting snow, and of home, where the snow would be.

RED CHRISTMAS

SUZANNE ROBB

D r. Conrad Jenkins opened the cabinet as his hands shook. He'd been working on the serum for almost three years and had nothing to show for it except an ulcer and the beginnings of a bald spot. The company he worked for had originally hired him to work with a team of the world's top scientists in order to cure cancer.

Conrad had been chosen because of his radical approach to things and his lack of morals when it came to human trials. At first he'd tried to cooperate with the others, but they were taking too long and he wanted to do something now.

So he worked on his own, taking bits and pieces from all of their formulas. A dash of something to help regenerate dead cells, a bit of something to stabilize brain function, a pinch of something meant to mutate cells so the cancer wouldn't know where to go after, and last but not least, a certain chemical no one wanted to talk about.

Compound 19 was something the government had worked on years before. They were told it didn't work, that it changed people, made them different. The compound altered DNA on a basic level, turning the host into mindless fools.

When Conrad asked why they'd developed it in the first place, looks and murmurs went around the room. The response was subdued and he didn't buy it. Why would the military work on something to make people psychic?

Now he was convinced the compound needed to be part of the cure. The government had left it there, within his reach. There had to be a reason. Of course the others disagreed.

His colleagues laughed at him, his assistants threw darts at his picture. To top it all off, he'd just gotten sacked, and three days before Christmas! How he'd tell his wife was a mystery, but he wasn't worried about it right now.

He needed to think about where he'd gone wrong in his calculations. Somehow, when he'd tested on people with Compound 19, they all died, re-animated, and then died again. For a moment he felt like Frankenstein; he was only missing the lightning to make everything work together.

Conrad sighed and shredded his files, though he had duplicates at home. They were sending up a security escort for him; the lab was full of all sorts of pathogens and diseases no one wanted unleashed by a vindictive employee. Thank God he remembered to keep an extra vial of his cocktail in his office cabinet. Since it was not a Level 5 biohazard, security was a bit more lax.

The vial was placed with care into his briefcase. There was a knock at the door, and a second later it swung open. Two men with no necks, square shoulders, and biceps the size of tree trunks entered.

"Dr. Jenkins, you need to come with us now."

Conrad smiled and picked up his things, but the one on the right stopped him with a beefy hand. "We'll need to see what's in there." He pointed to the leather briefcase.

Conrad stood back and allowed them to look through everything. The vial wasn't a concern since it looked plain and harmless. No stickers or warnings were attached screaming, *Toxic substance known to mutate people into carnivorous things!*

"What's this?" One of the men held something up for him to identify.

"It's a lighter."

The one holding it tried to use it, and the childproof switch frustrated him until he tossed it away.

Great, Conrad thought. *Now I need to get a new one.*

"Everything looks fine here, let's go," the man said.

Conrad walked out of the building between the two men. The other workers watched him; he heard the snickers and a few whispered comments. He smiled coldly at them. He'd show them. He would make things better for the world; he would cure cancer all on his own.

He reached his car and waited patiently as they scraped off his security decal from inside his windshield, then ripped off his identification tag from his jacket.

Once inside his vehicle, he turned on the ignition to get the heat going. The briefcase was placed on the seat and spent a moment waiting for the wipers to clear his windshield. His cell phone chirped and the ring tone gave it away. It was his wife, Mary.

Damn it, he didn't want to talk to her right now. Flipping it open, he inserted as much enthusiasm into his voice as possible. "Hello, dear, I was just thinking about you."

"Conrad, I need you to get some milk on the way home and Tommy needs some string cheese for snacks."

"Of course, honey. Anything else?"

"No, that's all for now."

She hung up abruptly. He shook his head, sometimes he hated his life. With slumped shoulders, he put the car into gear and started the drive home, with the obligatory stop at the bar to kill a few hours first. He'd tell Mary he was fired after New Years.

"I'm serious, man, there's a secret government facility a few blocks from here. It's disguised to look like a rundown warehouse, but it's full of all sorts of scary stuff." Conrad belched.

The bar was a dive, but decorated in a festive manner. Red and green garland hung from the ceiling, a slightly stale smell emanating from them. A sprig of mistletoe hung over the bartender, but Conrad wasn't that drunk yet. A twelve inch Christmas tree sat on the bar a few feet from Conrad and on the muted television, a commercial for Gillette ran, complete with Santa Claus riding a razor through the snow.

The music playing from the worn-out speakers mounted in the wall was a tune you could only hum the words to because they were so stupid no grown man would say them aloud.

"Buddy, you're drunk. Only morons believe in government facilities," the bartender said while wiping the counter with a dirty rag.

"Well, I may be drunk, but I'm no liar. Hey, you got a light? Those bastards threw my lighter away."

"There's no smoking in here."

"Whatever. Get me another one of these barkeep. I'll be back." Conrad held up his mug, the time slipping by faster than he realized.

Dick Henderson and Mark Whitmore had been watching the nice car for over an hour. Whoever owned it was most likely in the bar, and therefore not coming out for a while.

"Let's do it. There might be something in there worth while, and if not, we'll just take the whole damn car."

Dick walked up to the driver's side door and reached into his pocket, pretending to reach for keys as he eyed the interior. A briefcase and a small bag were in the back. He saw a small blinking light on the dashboard, signifying that the car was alarmed.

He was about to turn to his friend and tell him they needed to break into the car and hotwire it, and do it quickly before people realized that the alarm wasn't turning off, which Dick knew would sound the instant he broke the window.

One of the wonderful things about people, especially around Christmas time, was their total and complete obsession with themselves. Too concerned with shopping, and making assumptions that the wind made car alarms go off, or simply not caring, made his livelihood that much easier.

Mark smashed the window without having to be told, reached in to unlock the door, and made quick work of the alarm. Seconds later, Mark drove out of the parking lot, while Dick rifled through the contents of the briefcase in the passenger seat. He found a cell phone, some papers, and then a vial of something clear. The car was cold because of the broken window, but the chop-shop was only a few blocks away. He had seconds to decide what to do with the vial before they reached their boss.

Vinny the Meat Grinder would take all their findings and offer them a flat fee. Dick rolled the vial around in his hand as he considered what to do. Finally, he shoved it into his pocket and hoped Mark didn't notice.

"Anything good?" Mark asked.

"Nah, must've been some geeky type guy."

"Okay. Then let's get this over with, should get a few grand for the car at least."

Conrad walked outside to have a cigarette. He planned to use his car lighter, but noticed the spot was empty. His beer-soaked brain worked in slow motion, bits and pieces of what happened falling into place.

"Someone stole my car; are you serious?" He stumbled back into the bar yelling to anyone who would listen, which wasn't many.

"Hey, my car's been stolen. I need to call the police or something." As he said it, he realized what was in the car and his panic rose. He grabbed a mug of beer and downed it, ignoring the cry of the man it belonged to.

"Huh, bet it was those government people you were talking about. Take me to that place and I'll help you get it back," someone said from behind.

Conrad perked up at the words. The man might be right. This would be just the kind of kick to the ass they would give a guy who was already down. He tossed a few bills on the table and stumbled out of the bar with his new friend, Bob. Or was it Brian?

"Thanks, Bob."

"No problem, Connor."

Conrad looked at him and decided not to correct him. Bob had most likely screwed up his name as well. He really hoped he was right about who had taken his car, for that vial getting into the wrong hands would be a disaster.

Dick watched as the rolling door opened and Mark pulled the car in. He stepped out of the car and walked towards the head of the operation, Kyle. He was the mouthpiece for Vinny.

"My man, Kyle. What's up? We got a car for you," Dick said.

Kyle glanced up from the line of coke on his desk with an annoyed expression. Then he looked over towards the car. "You brought me a piece of crap, at least four years old by the looks of it, and with a busted window."

Dick watched as Kyle opened a drawer and pulled out a wad of bills. He counted off a few and tossed them on the table. Dick reached down and counted them—two thousand.

"Merry Christmas, now get the hell out of here," Kyle muttered.

Dick handed half to Mark and they left, knowing better than to argue with a mafia henchman.

"Well, that sucked. What do we do now?" Mark asked once they were outside and alone.

Dick shook his head. "I'm going to the mall. My kid wants some Barbie doll for Christmas. If I get it for her, then maybe there'll be one person I don't let down this year."

He opened the creaky door of his '85 Honda and slipped into the cracked leather seat. The car had almost 300,000 miles on it, but it still ran, sort of.

"Give me a ride? I need to pick up some stuff for my girlfriend. Otherwise she's gonna withhold sex for the holidays."

Dick chuckled, then reached over to unlock the passenger door.

They made their way to the mall, having to park almost a quarter mile away due to the last minute shopping crowd taking up every available spot.

They separated as they entered the mall and Dick watched his friend until he was out of sight. Then he turned and walked up to a coffee stand, and pulled out the vial of clear liquid as he waited in line to inspect it some more.

Just before he got his coffee, there was a tap on his shoulder, and when he turned around, he saw it was Mark, with a very unhappy look on his face.

Conrad rubbed his shoulders to keep warm. He'd just hung up on Mary. He thought he sounded sober enough, and his story about being car-jacked and fighting off the imaginary three men with guns sounded promising and exciting. The fact that she'd laughed and hung up on him did nothing to deter his mission.

"All right, Bob, this is the place. We just need to sneak up the driveway and avoid all the security cameras. Then we can break in through the three foot thick steel door on the side. Then things might get tough." He didn't wonder why Bob was helping him, he just took it at face value.

He looked over at Bob and saw a strange look on his face. "Are you crazy?"

Conrad stared back him, wondering how to answer the question.

"And my damn name is Carl. Try and remember that, will you please?"

Conrad nodded, and began to sidle along the exterior wall of the garage ramp. He hoped the new falling snow would cover their entry to a degree, or at least obscure them on the camera.

Mark looked at his buddy of ten years, then shoved him against a back wall of the mall, and out of sight. He'd moved them out of the main shopping area and they were now in some sort of service hall.

"So, you've been holding out on me. I saw you put that thing in your pocket. What the hell is it?" Mark punctuated each statement with a poke to Dick's chest, each one getting harder and harder.

Dick opened his mouth a few times and then sighed. "I don't know what it is. Things are so tough, ya know? And the holidays are kicking my ass. I have no idea what it is. It's just a stupid clear vial. For all I know its melted snow."

Mark went to reach for the vial and Dick attempted to block him. They began to scuffle and knocked each other to the floor. Rolling around and taking punches when possible, they didn't realize they had ended up in a small conference room.

"Hey, what the hell are you two doing in here? This is for employees only," a deep voice said in anger.

Mark glanced over at the group of people and jerked back in shock. From his angle, he saw a group of kids, their feet dangling off the chairs they were seated on, and a few adults. He straightened himself up, and with his peripheral vision, kept track of Dick.

When he got a better look at the people in the room, he realized they weren't kids at all. The room was full of midgets, or was *dwarf* the proper name for little people? Mark couldn't keep up with the politically correct terms nowadays. 'Vertically challenged' maybe?

"Uh, sorry we'll get out of here now," Mark said and motioned to Dick to move. Mark's lower lip was split open and blood dribbled out of his nose. He debated apologizing, but was still too pissed off that his friend had tried to screw him over.

As soon as they were out of the room, Mark grabbed Dick and said, "Give me that vial."

"Screw you."

There was more fighting, but this time the vial went flying through the air when it was knocked from Dick's hand in the scuffle. They both watched as it went flying back into the employee meeting room to land in a punch bowl. When it landed, it struck the side of the bowl and cracked, then slipped into the dark red liquid. A few seconds later, the punch began to fizz and smoke.

Hank Willis pushed himself further up on the chair as the two strangers left the room, then started to hand out the assignments to the others in the room. They were the malls hired elves for the next few days and would be responsible for taking kids' pictures on Santa's lap, hanging around a shoddy version of the North Pole, and stopping—or preventing—the little brats from crying.

He never understood why parents needed to have a picture of their eight month old taken with Santa. He had yet to see a single child who didn't break into hysterics at the sight of the man in red.

Finished with papers, his crew suited up with a few grumbles about the stupid pointy shoes and floppy hats they had to wear.

"Hey, why are we always dressed in this puke-green color?" a voice in the crowd asked.

Hank ignored the question and went over to the refreshment table. He didn't see something drop into the punchbowl but did notice the smoke rising out of it. Ah, the dry ice thing, usually they only did that on Halloween when they dressed up as pumpkins and black cats. Still, nice touch from the management.

"All right, guys, come have some chow before we go out and do our thing."

Each newly dressed elf took a ladleful of the punch as well as some finger sandwiches and other random goodies.

Conrad and Carl made it to the back door of the building. Without his security card, Conrad knew they would have a problem getting inside, though back in the bar, talking about hacking into an electrical system didn't seem too daunting. Now he understood the error of his thinking. He turned to Carl and shrugged his shoulders.

"No way, man, you got me all the way out here, we're going in," Carl said.

A second later, the door opened as one of Conrad's ex co-workers stepped out. Conrad attacked the man, but soon found himself flat on his back from a blow to the jaw. Carl stepped in to save him and punched the man in the side of the head. A tooth fell out of his mouth and made a strange tinkling sound when it hit the ground. The man dropped to the ground a second later.

"We need to hide the body. I'll get his security pass," Conrad said, trying to regain control of the situation. He grabbed the card that would grant him access and opened the door with it. Carl helped him pull the body inside and they found a storage closet to hide it.

"Okay, Carl, just walk around like you belong here and they won't say a thing."

A janitor rounded the corner and Conrad let out a small shriek and began to examine a plant in the corner. He could see Carl shaking his head, and tried to muster as much dignity as he could before turning around. The janitor barely paid him any attention and was gone in no time.

"Now we need to get to the upper level where they keep all the nasty bio-hazard stuff. I'll grab something there to leverage for my car."

Carl looked around, an uneasy look on his face. "You were really being serious about this place? You sounded like some drunk jerk. I ain't about to grab anything from here." Carl turned to leave, but Conrad grabbed his arm.

"You can't leave without me. I have the pass card." Conrad waved it in the air to make his point.

"I could grab it and take your ass down, but I think that would attract too much attention. What with you screaming like a little girl and all."

Conrad shrugged his shoulders, not disputing the truth of the other man's statement. He started towards an elevator. The reception desk was empty at this hour. The guard from earlier walked out of the elevator when the ding sounded to signal its arrival.

One look at Conrad and it was over. The guard took out his gun and shot him point blank in the face. Carl looked down at Conrad, the man's face a bloody ruin. When he looked back up it was into the muzzle of the guard's gun.

He never heard the report from the bullet that blew out the back of his head.

The guard searched the area for more intruders. When he was satisfied the two men had been alone, he spoke into the two-way radio mic clipped to his shoulder. "We got a clean-up in the lobby.

Two intruders, both down. One of then was Dr. Jenkins. Lock this place down and do a sweep to make sure there's no one else."

Dick watched as the little people drank up the smoking punch. A few minutes later they began to twitch and grab at their heads. They fell the short distance to the floor with a groan.

He entered the room and reached out to the closest one to see if there was a pulse. Nothing. He stood up and backed into Mark.

"What the hell happened?" Mark asked.

"I have no idea, but I think it's a good thing we got rid of that vial. That could be us laying on the floor."

Mark nodded and they slowly backed out of the room. A few seconds later, one of the bodies jerked and blood gushed out of its mouth. The two men stood there, scared stiff. Then the rest of the bodies began moving around and expelling nasty fluids.

"I think we should get the hell out of here," Dick said as he tried to turn and run.

But when he was fully turned and about to take off, he found there was an elf facing him and blocking his path. Blood frothed the elf's mouth and tiny teeth snapped at him.

Suddenly, a flurry of motion and then a searing pain radiated out from Dick's groin. He fell to the floor screaming in agony. Leaving his friend to fend for himself, Mark ran from the room, a stampede of little feet trailing after him.

Mark ran into the main area of the mall with two dozen zombified elves chasing after him. Most of the shoppers, stuck in their own hellish nightmare of last minute shopping, thought it was some sort of holiday show.

Mark grabbed at people, hoping his screams would break through to them. A few people glanced around at the invasion of blood-covered short people.

As shoppers were bowled over and gorged upon, kids ran screaming in all directions. Mark had no idea which elf to kick or pick up and throw, so he decided to run full tilt towards the exit.

He didn't make it five feet before something attached itself to his ass and he dropped to the floor in a tumble of snapping teeth and puke-green outfitted midgets.

Hal George watched the chaos around him with an inquisitive look. He'd been sitting in the North Pole for an hour waiting for the damn elves to get there. The little bastards had been on break for almost an hour and he was beginning to think they weren't going to show. Damn little people union.

He stroked his fake white beard and tried to ignore the bits of food left over from the people who'd previously worn it. Smoothing the front of his red suit, he was shocked out of his holiday stupor when one of his helpers approached him.

"Glen, that you?" he asked the elf.

The elf continued to move forward and Hal noticed Glen was chewing on a human hand, bloody strands of flesh and sinew flapping in the air.

"Hey, just take it easy, Glen. I really didn't mean all those things I said earlier."

The elf paid him no attention and Hal stood up and grabbed the man-size candy cane next to his seat and swung it at the little elf. He knocked Glen into the side of Santa's house and watched the dwarf slide down, but scramble to his feet unfazed a second later.

The zombie elf let out a disgruntled moan and launched himself towards Hal once more. Hal blocked the attack with his cane, noticing several more zombie elves appearing out of the woodwork. Glen fell to the floor at his feet and he stomped on the elf's head with his shiny black boot.

The head popped like a grape, and Hal stepped away when the crushed head began to smoke. He swung the candy cane to ward off the invading zombie elf army. He trampled over the back fence, and realized the shoppers had finally figured out that this wasn't some sort of demented show from holiday Hell.

People ran around screaming, trying to protect their kids, some shoving their presents into shopping bags and making a run for it. Hal continued to swing his candy cane in an attempt to fend off the undead elves, though there was a growing crowd of adult-sized zombies rambling around, too.

Hal stabbed one of the elves with the candy cane and watched as a full set of internal organs spilled out the back of the dwarf. He yanked out his weapon and smiled, then quickly screamed when the disemboweled elf continued to move towards him.

Using the candy cane like a baseball bat, Hal swung as hard as he could and separated the head from the body of the zombie elf. He watched as the headless body stood there gushing blood like a hellish fountain.

Glancing around the mall, he saw people screaming, blood-spattered window displays, and holiday decorations, which added a surreal quality to everything going on around him.

A huge zombie came after him, and as he aimed for the head with the candy cane, the zombie outwitted him and ducked to the side. Hal lost his balance and was grabbed, the giant candy cane pulled from his hands.

He was pushed to the floor, and as the zombie lowered onto the floor to eat him, Hal kicked out with his foot and heard a satisfying crunch. His foot had connected with the zombie's kneecap, dislocating it and popping it out of place. He raised himself to his feet and ran away, but the zombie kept after him, albeit a tad slower now.

Hal looked for another weapon of some kind. A sporting goods store caught his eye and he smiled. Heading straight for it, he clotheslined a few incoming zombies, and shoved a few shrieking women out of his way.

Once inside the store, he searched all the cabinets behind the counter for a gun of some kind, but a skeet shooter was the only thing he came across. He continued searching until he found an aluminum baseball bat and a helmet. Hal was gearing up and preparing to face the zombie infestation when he heard a few murmurs behind him. He peered over the counter and saw two teenage boys cowering. With their clerk vests, they were obviously employees.

"Hey, you two, grab a weapon and some protective gear and help me fight these damn things. Unless you want to die today."

"Are you crazy, mister? Have you seen those things?"

"The last person who called me crazy had to drink through a straw for six months, so you best watch what you say and get your butts in gear. Now move!"

Hal watched the two teens grab a couple of baseball bats and some protective gear: hockey masks and some catcher's chest gear.

"Follow behind me. We're gonna take out as many as we can."

Hal heard footsteps behind him as they followed him and he was glad the teens were listening. At least he would have a few things to throw at the elves should they come across one. As they made their way out into the main area of the shopping mall, Hal heard the two teens gag behind him.

The floor was covered in bits of gore and various appendages. People were on the floor, twitching, while others were being gnawed on. The store windows were smeared in palm prints of blood, and internal organs and viscera had been tossed around haphazardly.

One of the teens vomited. The sound echoes through the mall and in unison all of the zombies swiveled their heads towards Hal and his new friends.

"Get ready, you two, and for the love of God man up and stop losing your cookies over this."

As they were rushed, Hal swung his bat, kicked at heads, and in some cases picked up the smaller bodies of the elves and tossed them over the railing to the lower level. He smiled when one was impaled on the statue in the center of the fountain below, the water turning a dark brown color.

His two recruits held their own. He glanced back to see them decapitating a few bodies with their hockey sticks and smashing some skulls with cleats they'd grabbed at the last minute before leaving the sporting goods store. A growl off to Hal's left got his attention and he came face to face with a behemoth of a zombie.

The thing stood at least seven feet tall and resembled a body builder who had used steroids for breakfast, lunch, and dinner. The zombie reached out a hand and wrapped it around Hal's neck, then lifted.

Half felt the weight of his body strangling him as he was lifted off the floor. The mega-zombie brought him closer and opened its mouth. Hal clawed at the hand around his neck, and kicked at the torso in front of him. He stopped when he broke a toe, yelling out in pain.

Then, out of nowhere the end of a hockey stick protruded from its chest, a blackened heart on the tip. The giant zombie looked behind it to see one of the teens, and went to reach for him as well. Hal took the opportunity to try and free himself once more. He reached into his pocket and pulled out his flask, dumping a liberal amount of what remained onto the front of the zombie's chest.

He fumbled for his Zippo lighter, and as soon as he'd flipped open the cap and had it lit, he tossed it towards the zombie. He realized a second too late the thing felt no pain, and therefore was not likely to give a damn about being on fire. He'd just signed his own death warrant. Well, at least he wouldn't come back as a zombie.

The teen that had helped him pulled out the stick and ran around the front and swung it down on the arm holding Hal in place. The flames were burning Hal and he felt a few blisters pop on his face and neck from the heat.

As he fell to the floor, he crab-walked backwards out of the way. He saw the giant zombie reach for the teen that had saved him, but when he tried to yell out a warning, his throat was too damaged from inhaling smoke.

The large zombie reached out, oblivious of the flames devouring its body.

Hal shook his head. Why didn't the kid leave when he had the chance? That's when Hal noticed one of the zombie elves wrapped around the poor bastards leg, the teen never having a chance to escape.

The teen's screams echoed throughout the mall as his head was squeezed off his body. The zombie was proud of its work as it held the head to its face and tried to dig out the brains with a thick tongue. The elf below went to work on emptying the chest cavity of the kid.

Hal got to his feet, grabbing his bat as he did so. He looked around for the other teenager and found him behind a plastic shrub, one of many used to decorate the mall.

"They're gonna smell you, moron, this isn't the jungle. Come on, let's try and kill some more and make our way to the exit." Hal continued to swing his bat with amazing accuracy, and wondered idly if he'd missed out on a career in the big leagues.

Up ahead, the exit doors which led to the third level parking garage were blocked. In the chaos, a bottleneck had occurred and the result was a zombie free for all. Hal stopped and thought for a moment, but moved on when he realized a majority of the pile was jerking back to life.

"Time to go, kid. We need to find a different way outta here. We'll take the stairs down to the main level and see if we can exit into the open."

They walked to the elevator and realized it was stuck on a different floor. Looking up, Hal could see a body being squished every few seconds as the doors tried to close. They'd have to use the escalators, but when he glanced over at them, he cringed at what he saw.

Body parts rode up and down the blood stained metal stairs. But what truly worried him was the fact how easy they could be surrounded there.

He motioned the teen forward and moved towards the top of the escalator, only to find a group of zombies waiting. Hal threw himself into the mass of bodies, pushing and shoving. He swatted heads with his bat, and whenever possible stomped one into a red pulpy mess below his black boots.

"Get out of here, kid, there's too many of them!"

"I'm not going without you."

Hal spared a moment to look at the teen. What the hell was wrong with him? Why show loyalty to a complete stranger? Then he looked down and saw there was a horde of what looked like women power walkers riding the escalator towards them.

Right, so the kid wasn't loyal per se, he just had nowhere to go.

They'd just have to fight their way out.

"Explain to me again why you thought it was okay to shoot a former employee and a civilian." A man in a dark suit asked.

Lester Higgins didn't care what the bosses said, he'd been hired to do a job and he'd done it. His contract specifically stated to stop any unauthorized access to the facility with whatever force necessary. "I told you my answer, it's my job."

The man in the suit sighed, then grabbed his phone when it rang. He barked into it, and then his face went white.

"Are you sure?"

The man closed the phone with a snap, then regarded Lester with a critical eye.

"Mr. Higgins, just how good at your job are you? We've got a situation at a local mall and need someone with your skills to take care of it."

Lester stood taller. "Whatever you need, sir, just tell me what you want me to do."

"Go to *Hickory Point Mall*, and kill everything that moves."

Lester kept his face neutral, even though on the inside he was giggling with glee. He loved when he received orders like that. It was just like Christmas.

He nodded and left. He stopped by the weapons locker, selecting several items and tossing them into a backpack. He zipped it up and walked out of the building towards his car.

Ten minutes later, he pulled up to the main entrance of the shopping mall and watched people fleeing the scene. Getting out of his car, he pulled out his shotgun and began firing. Bodies stopped for a second, then flew backwards with the force of the impacts.

Police sirens could be heard, but Lester had orders to follow. He fired at anything that moved, finally making his way inside the mall. He was a bit shocked at what he saw. For a moment he thought someone had beaten him to it.

Bodies were strewn everywhere and there was a liberal coating of blood on almost every surface. Some holiday tune played in the background, but he ignored it and moved on. Upstairs, he heard a commotion and a woman landed a few feet in front of him, very dead by the looks of her.

Preparing to step over her, he was more than shocked when she began to get back up. He lowered the shotgun, gave it a pump, then blew her head clean off her shoulders. A rancid smell touched his nostrils, and a funny looking smoke rose from her neck stump.

With the shotgun empty, he reached into his backpack and grabbed a pistol as he made his way to the escalator. Outside, emergency personnel were most likely tending to the victims he'd gunned down and taking statements. They would enter the mall eventually, but he'd be done with his job by then.

At the top of the stairs was a man in a Santa suit and a teenager dressed in baseball gear. They were fighting off at least twenty zombies. Lester debated what to do.

Help them only to kill them, or let them do some of the work for him. He paused to watch, but was spurred into action when they saw him and backed up towards him, thinking he would help.

He reached into his backpack and he pulled out a special item. He pulled the pin and tossed it into the middle of the horde, then put a bullet between Santa's eyes.

As the zombies overtook the red-suited man, he shot the teenager in the leg so he couldn't run.

The grenade went off. Lester stared up at the ceiling as it was sprayed with gore, blood and guts raining down for a few seconds.

The giant Christmas tree centerpiece looked horrific. Bits of intestines, bloody bits, and a few eyeballs decorated it now, and the lights flickering on and off only added to the eeriness of the scene. He had to smile. He loved his work.

"Police! Don't move! Put your bag and weapon down, and raise your hands!"

Lester raised an eyebrow, but did as he was told. The rookie had come in alone and would soon be dinner for the zombies. A shocked look, a scream, and then silence as he was overwhelmed and fed upon.

Lester picked up his gun and backpack and examined the area with a critical eye. He needed to make sure everyone was dead.

Still…zombies, he hadn't counted on that. And the police were going to be all over him soon. He decided to just set the bricks of C-4 he'd brought and level the place.

He nearly jumped out of his skin when something wrapped around his neck and a sharp pain filled him as something bit onto his neck.

He stood up with a zombie latched onto him. He tried to stop the flow of blood with one hand, and toss the creature off with his other, but it was no use.

In the corner, he spotted a small boy huddling in fright. The boy looked at him.

"Help me, please," Lester begged the boy.

The boy only stared at him with tears streaking down his face. "You killed Santa! You're a bad man." Then he jumped up and ran away.

Lester watched the boy leave. Blood loss made him dizzy and weak. He didn't have long. He leaned over and flipped the zombie off him, a huge chunk of his throat going with the thing.

"Freeze!" one of the cops yelled.

Lester raised his hands, and the blood from his neck wound spurted out in rhythm with his heartbeat.

"That guy's hurt. He needs medical attention!" another cop yelled.

A few of the police officers approached Lester. The backpack fell off his shoulder to land before him on the floor. It was unzipped and the contents were clearly visible.

When the cops got a good look at what was in the bag, such as the blocks of C-4, they stopped moving in to help, their faces taking on a look of anger.

Realizing the jig was up, Lester reached around to his back and pulled a handgun, only he was far too slow thanks to blood loss.

He heard several shots, then nothing more.

Sergeant Rick Jones looked at the mess in front of him. Several civilians were shot outside, others trampled.

Those who could talk made no sense and the news vans were already set up in the parking lot.

"What the hell happened here?" Rick asked.

"No idea, but I think we better come up with some cover story. No one's gonna buy zombies," another police officer said.

Rick sighed, he hated the holidays. "But the evidence supports what the witnesses are saying."

"So what do we do?"

"Nothing," Rick said. "The press outside is already dubbing it *Red Christmas*. Maybe it's time for the truth to come out."

EVEN ZOMBIES LOVE CHRISTMAS

ANTHONY GIANGREGORIO

Santa leaned back in his stuffed red leather chair as he read over the wish list of children all across the globe.

"One white male arm, one black left hand, one Asian right foot, a kidney from a Mexican, a spleen from an albino." He paused. "An albino? Who the hell do these kids think I am?"

Herman the elf stopped writing and waited patiently for Santa to continue.

Santa kept mumbling to himself and then stopped, scratched his beard, and looked down at Herman.

"Ready when you are, Santa."

"I lost my train of thought. Where were we?"

"An albino spleen."

"Oh yes, A spleen. I tell you, Herman, things were so much easier back when there were living people and the dead didn't rule the Earth."

Herman shrugged. "Well, we did learn to adapt, right, Santa?"

Santa sighed. "I suppose, but you have to admit, things are a lot bloodier than they were before. So, how are the human pens coming?"

"Hang, on, I'll call Sherman and check." He reached into his pocket and pulled out his cell phone. Hitting the number one for speed dial, he paused a few seconds, humming a Christmas tune as he waited.

A voice came on the other end. "Go for Sherman."

"Cut it out, answer the phone right, you idiot," Herman snapped. "Listen, I'm here with Santa, and he wants to know how the human pens are doing."

"All good, fed and watered. We're ready to start chopping them up as soon as Santa gives us the list."

Herman covered the phone with his hand and said, "Just waiting on the list, Santa."

Santa nodded. "Then let's finish this up so I can go see Melvin."

Herman spoke into the phone quickly, telling Sherman what was going on, then snapped it closed and pocketed it. Santa nodded and continued reading off the list of items, and Herman kept writing them down.

An hour later, Santa was at Melvin's cottage at the end of Santa's Village. At one time Melvin had been the tailor, but due to the change in world events, the elf was now the armorer for the village.

As Santa entered the cottage, a small bell rang over his head.

Melvin looked up from the desk he was sitting behind, a strong white light illuminating the small red orb in his hand.

"Ah, Santa, just in time. Here, let me show you what I've been working on. Follow me outside, please."

Santa followed Melvin outside and around to the back of the cottage, where the snow was churned from what looked like explosions.

The two stopped by a four foot wall of ice and snow.

Melvin held up the orb so Santa could see it. "My new invention, an Ornament grenade." He handed it to Santa, who studied it.

"Well, I can see why you call it an Ornament. It looks just like the ones hung off of Christmas trees."

Melvin gestured to the top of the grenade, where there was the typical loop for where a hook would go for hanging. "Exactly. Now slide your finger in the loop and pull."

Santa did as he was told. "And?"

Melvin's eyes went wide. "And throw it, Santa! Throw it!"

"Whoops," Santa said and tossed the ornament downrange, where it landed and erupted a second later, sending a shower of ice and snow in all directions.

Melvin and Santa closed their eyes as the wave subsided, hiding behind the ice wall.

"Not bad, Melvin, not bad, but you know, you didn't need to make it look like an ornament. A simple grenade would have been fine."

Melvin shrugged. "Traditions die hard with me, Santa. I know things have changed for the worse, but we can still try to hold on to the old ways."

"If only that were true, Melvin," Santa agreed as the elf led him back inside, talking the entire time.

"I have a whole new arsenal for you to take with you this year, Santa," Melvin said as they entered the cottage and closed the door. Melvin waddled over to a bench stacked with what looked like harmless items. "Here, come take a look."

Santa shuffled over and examined the array of items. He spotted a few sugar cookies and he reached down and picked one up. It was in the shape of a star, and as he opened his mouth to take a bite, Melvin grabbed his arm and shouted, "No, don't eat that!"

"Why not? Melvin, I'm Santa, I love cookies."

"Yes, Santa, but that's not a real cookie. Here, give it to me, let me show you."

Santa handed him the sugar cookie and Melvin held it in his hand and turned to face the far wall, where Melvin then pointed. Santa let his eyes go to the wall and saw there were numerous indents in the plaster, like something sharp had been thrown into it; like a knife.

Melvin pulled back his arm and threw the cookie like it was a baseball. The cookie sliced through the air and ended up sticking in the wall by one of its points.

Melvin smiled. "See? It's modeled after a Ninja star. Perfectly balanced. You can throw it any which way and it always soars true and finds its target."

Santa frowned. "So you're saying there aren't any cookies to eat?"

Melvin looked at Santa like he was an idiot. "No, there aren't any cookies."

"Okay then, I'll have some of this cocoa," Santa said and reached for the open plastic thermos next to the sugar cookies/throwing stars. He picked the thermos up, and was about to take a sip when Melvin yelled, "No, wait, stop!"

Santa had the thermos half tipped back and all he had to do was move his arm a little bit more to pour out the chocolately goodness. He held his arm in place and looked at Melvin. "What now?"

"Santa, please, carefully hand me that hot cocoa and I'll show you. But be very careful you don't spill any on yourself."

"Why the hell not?"

"Santa, please just trust me, all right?"

Santa sighed and did as he was told, and a second later Melvin was holding the thermos of hot cocoa.

"There, good, wow, that was a close one. Here, let me show you what this really is." He walked over to a small statue of a snowman and poured some of the hot cocoa onto the top of its head. When the dark liquid hit the statue, the snowman began to hiss and melt.

Santa swallowed hard, imagining the liquid going down his throat. "What is that?"

"Hydrochloric acid that smells and looks like hot cocoa."

"Acid? Now why in all that's holy would you go and make it smell like…" Santa stopped and composed himself, realizing who he was dealing with. "You know what? Never mind, it doesn't matter."

Melvin smiled and walked over and put the cap on the acid, then handed Santa a large candy cane about the size of a walking stick.

"What's this, a throwing spear?" Santa asked sarcastically.

Melvin smiled. "You're getting the hang of it but no, it's not a spear." He gestured to the top where the cane curved. "Turn that and pull."

Santa did as he was told and a second later was holding a long sword the length of the cane.

"Now this I like," Santa said with a smile and waved it around.

"Toledo steel from Spain," Melvin bragged. "Will take a head off like…well, like a hot blade through butter."

Santa slid the sword back into the sheath and smiled. "What else do you have for me?"

Melvin showed Santa a few more clever items, such as smaller candy canes that worked as nun-chucks when they were attached or individually as daggers, the points sharp enough to pierce the skull of a human. He also had the standard firearms, such as pistols and revolvers, shotguns and machine guns and a few Uzis. Everything a Santa on the go would need as he made his rounds in an undead world.

"Good, good, it all looks wonderful. Melvin, my boy, you've outdone yourself this year."

"Thanks, Santa. I have to admit, this is a lot more fun than making your red and white suits."

"Well, it shows, it certainly does. Have all this stuff sent to the sleigh and I'll be ready come tomorrow night for Christmas Eve."

"Will do, Santa, you can count on me."

Santa left the elf amorer and headed across the village. Mrs. Claus was working on his suit and he was looking forward to what she'd done to it.

Mrs. Claus was busy working when Santa entered their home on the north side of the village. As he entered, she looked up, a wide smile on her face.

"There you are, and just in time, I'm about done with your new suit."

"And how's it coming?" he asked, joining her and giving her a kiss on the cheek.

"Very well, the leather was a bit tough to sew but I managed."

"Leather? On my suit? Really?"

"Of course, dear," she said. "Remember what happened last year? You were nearly bitten and it was sheer luck that old man had no teeth in his mouth. If he'd died with his dentures in, why, you wouldn't be here today!"

He had to admit she was right. He'd been in a nursing home delivering presents when an old man had come out of the shadows. The old zombie must have been in his eighties when he'd died and returned, and before Santa could react, the old man sank his teeth into his arm—or tried to. But the zombie was tooth-less, and other than leaving behind a trail of bloody spittle, Santa had been unharmed. He'd caved in the zombie's skull and got out of there before any others had seen him.

"That was a close one, wasn't it," he mused.

"It sure was. So I made sure something like that can never happen again. Here, have a look at what I've done to your suit."

He stepped closer to see his red and white suit was on a mannequin. He grunted a little in annoyance when he saw how *fat* the mannequin was. It made him uncomfortable. Though he'd always been rotund, he'd also always been sensitive about his weight. He played his eyes over the suit, admiring his wife's handiwork. She was an excellent seamstress and her skill showed in the fine stitching.

The suit was still red and white, only now it had touches of black leather as well. The arms and legs were completely encased in thick leather, as were the shoulders. A lightweight wire mesh surrounded the main torso and the belt was made of copper with a small, two inch knife hidden within the emblem of Santa on his sleigh. As he studied the suit, it reminded him of what gladiators in Greece wore when entering the arena in battle.

"Go on, dear, try it on for size. I just finished before you arrived."

"Okay, will you give me a hand?"

She nodded and helped him slide the suit off the mannequin, then helped him dress. Moments later he was wearing his new suit and he had to say it fit pretty well. It was heavier of course, but the leather was supple. As he walked around the room, he squeaked a little, the leather being broken in.

She frowned at the squeaking. "I'll see what I can do about it but I may not be able to stop it."

"I'll deal with it," was all he said as he waddled across the living room, bending and stretching to limber the leather.

"Did you see Melvin?" she asked.

"Yes, he has a full arsenal for me."

"Good, I want to know you can defend yourself if you have to," she said.

He walked over to her and kissed her again. "No worries there. One thing's for sure. Tomorrow night when I make my rounds, the living dead will find me a hard nut to crack."

The sun was just beginning to set as Santa Claus left the village behind and began his trek to the real world—or what was left of it.

Behind him, in his magic bag, were all the items from the wish list. The bottom of the bag was soaked with congealed blood and flies could be heard buzzing within it. Santa was just glad he was in the open air and the stench of body parts was lost in the wind.

For the thousandth time he wondered if what he was doing was right. Of course he knew it was wrong to kill the humans in the pens at the village, but he really had no choice. He was Santa Claus after all. His job was to fulfill the wish lists of children all over the world. Only now, the undead children didn't want bicycles, ponies or choo-choo trains. They wanted arms, legs and internal organs to feed on.

It was a new world and he either adapted to it or would die out. He may have been around for centuries but that was only because he was needed by the children. If they stopped needing him…why, for all he knew he would simply grow old and die. Or worse, fade away into nothingness. He'd really never thought about it much, and who would? Why contemplate your own existence and lack thereof?

No, better to do his job, no matter how macabre it might be now.

But that didn't mean he would let them use him as a human buffet. Oh no, he may have to deliver them body parts once a year but he'd be damned if he'd let them eat him too.

So where once he would simply drop down chimneys and leave presents under trees—the only danger that of being seen by some insomniac child—now he had to worry about being attacked by the undead homeowners, who were looking for a midnight snack.

Time passed and soon he arrived at his first home in the United States. He wanted to get the US over with first before going on to other countries. Out of all the places on Earth, the US was hit the worst when the dead began to rise. As far as Santa knew, there were no other human beings left alive in the world, with the exception of the ones at his village, and they were kept for only one very gruesome thing.

Luckily, if you took a man's leg or a woman's arm, it didn't mean they were dead, but could go on for years with the missing limb as long as they were cared for and the severed limb was taken correctly. For the limbs and organs had to be fresh or the dead wouldn't eat them.

Pulling on the reins of the reindeer, Santa steered for the first rooftop he came to. It was a ranch-style house with a three-car garage and a large swimming pool in the backyard. Of course, the pool now looked more like a swamp, with a few rotting bodies floating in the muck that was once clean water, and half the garage had been burned in a long-ago fire, and the grass of the front and rear lawn was more than three feet tall and had fallen over onto itself.

It had been years since the dead began to walk and the world collapsed, and in all that time, Santa had stayed at the North Pole, only coming out once a year like always. When he thought about the first year he'd gone out and found nothing but death…well, he tried not to think about it too much. It was too hard to bear.

As the sleigh settled on the roof, he climbed out and stretched. Then he checked his list for what this house had asked for. One white right arm and a black penis, complete with testicles. He blinked and took another look to make sure he'd read it right. Then with a shrug, opened the bag of parts and began digging.

Moments later he found what he needed and prepared to enter the home.

This was one of the tricks Santa used magic for, one of the few. There was only so much magic to go around so he had to use it sparingly. He used it for mainly three things. To go down and then up the chimney, and the third was too keep his gift bag bottomless. How else could he carry all the presents in one trip?

His nose wrinkled from the smell of rotting meat as he appeared in the living room. Though he was used to the odor enough that he didn't gag, it was still hard to accept fully.

There was a Christmas tree in the corner, a fresh pine by the looks of it, but instead of tinsel and ornaments made of glass or plastic, the tree was decorated with intestines and fingers, as well as a few eyeballs. On the top of the tree, instead of a star or an angel, a severed head looked out, only the eye sockets were empty, gaping black holes.

On the table near the chimney was a plate and a glass, but where once cookies and milk would be waiting for him, now the plate held a kidney and pieces of intestines; what the owners of the home thought Santa would like to eat.

Oh, how wrong they were.

Wanting to finish up and move on to the next house, he quickly laid the body parts under the tree and was about to leave when he heard footsteps come from behind him. He looked up to see two zombie children standing in the doorway.

With a hiss and a groan they were on him, small mouths biting and snapping as they tried to feed on Santa. Lucky for him, their teeth couldn't penetrate his new suit and it was simple to toss each child off him where they landed on the couch across the room.

"Merry Christmas," he said quickly and was gone before the children could attack again, back up the chimney in a flash. Once on the roof, he listened at the opening to the chimney as the two zombie kids gnashed and moaned from below. Santa shook his head at the thought of only a few million more homes to go before he could call it a night.

Climbing onto his sleigh, he flew off into the darkness, his destination the next house on his list.

Hours later he was still going strong. He'd had a few close calls but nothing he couldn't handle.

He was in the Midwest, in some town he would forget the second he left it. Landing on the roof, he slipped down the chimney, his mind already thinking of the next delivery.

As he appeared in the living room, he found he was surrounded by seven zombies, all with different rates of decay. One was so rotted it was nothing but skin and bones, the organs within its torso desiccated to the point they were useless.

The second Santa appeared, they lunged for him, teeth gnashing and fingers clawing at him, the tap sprung. One got a good grip on his long beard and only a punch to the face could get the ghoul off him.

Acting fast, Santa reached behind his back and pulled out a set of candy canes, each with a sharpened point. With one in each hand, he jabbed them into the eyes of two zombies, the points slicing into their brains and killing them instantly.

With a gap in the advancing line of zombies, he dashed through it and came up short at the opposite end of the room. Turning, he pulled out two ninja sugar cookie stars and threw them at another zombie. One cookie struck its face right below the left eye, but the second one hit paydirt, slicing through the skull and into the brain. The ghoul dropped to the blood-soaked carpet, dead.

Not having the patience for any more combat, Santa reached into his pocket and pulled out an Ornament grenade. Pulling the pin, he tossed it at the zombies with a, "Merry Christmas, assholes!"

The zombie in the center caught the grenade like it was a ball and looked at it with curiosity. It could see its reflection in the shiny red coating of the grenade and was fascinated.

Meanwhile, Santa dived behind a ratty couch and the entire home shook on its foundation. Bloody parts and gore flew in every direction, the walls becoming an original Jackson Pollock.

Poking his head up over the couch, he saw more than half the zombies were down. Taking his chance, he dashed to the chimney opening, and as the ghouls began climbing to their feet to renew the attack, Santa let out a laugh and yelled, "Sorry, fellas, but I'm not on the menu tonight. See you next year!" Then he was up the chimney and on the roof once more.

Later, with the United States finished, he landed on his first roof in London. It was an orphanage.

There was no chimney so he had to use the front door. It was locked but a little Christmas magic soon had him inside.

As he walked through the foyer and down a short hallway, he soon found himself in a wide open room similar to a hospital ward. Bunk-beds lined each side of the room, a thin walkway down the middle. At the end of the path was the Christmas tree. This one was old, the pine needles having fallen off years ago. The air was rank with death, but Santa swallowed the bad taste in his mouth and began walking to the tree.

When he was halfway there, he heard movement to his left, then his right, then from behind. Pulling a flashlight from his pocket, he shined it on the cause of the noise, and when he did, his heart lodged in his throat.

Undead children, more than two dozen, were coming out from under the beds and the shadows.

This had happened to him before, unfortunately, and so far he'd always managed to escape in one piece. Some zombies wouldn't settle for what he delivered them, but instead wanted to feast on his fat ass.

"Now, now, kids, let's not do this. I have some presents for you," he said and reached into his bag and tossed a few kids some bloody body parts. They grabbed them off the floor and began to feed on them, but the rest still kept coming for him.

He began to back away, but already his retreat was cut off by more undead cherubs.

He was trapped.

With a low hiss, a little blonde girl with sunken-in features charged at him and he kicked her in the chest, sending her sprawling away. Then more jumped into action, charging at him, their small hands curved into claws, their mouths open in anticipation of the kill.

A small boy tried to jump on his back. Santa pulled the thermos of hot cocoa from his pocket, and with lightning speed, whipped off the top. He splashed the hot cocoa smelling acid on the boy's face, who hissed in anger. The small zombie fell to the floor, his eyes melting, his face sloughing off, the flesh turning into a puddle of goo, the tongue dissolving, the teeth sliding out. The boy kept twitching until the acid finally ate into his brain and killed him.

Acting fast, Santa reached over his back and retrieved the Uzi he'd had hung there for just such an occurrence.

"Merry Christmas, you little dead bastards!" he screamed and squeezed the trigger, sending steel-jacketed rounds into the small bodies again and again.

Heads exploded, limbs were chewed off, and legs were crippled, blood and gore flying in all directions. The main line of children was quickly chewed up and it made a clear hole for Santa to use. Jumping over the first body, he ran for the door, shooting as he ran. More zombie kids were taken down as he fired.

His clip ran dry and there was no time to reload, so he let the Uzi fall from his hands to hang on its strap, then pulled a Glock from inside his suit. As a small boy came at him, he shot the kid at point blank range, blowing out the back of the boy's head in a spray of brown and yellow brain matter.

When he reached the door, Santa stopped and turned around. The children were crawling and limping towards him, some too wounded to move.

"There's a reason you little bastards didn't have parents before you died!" he yelled, angry at himself for even saying it but getting tired of always being the blue plate special.

In reply, the zombie kids hissed and growled at him.

Santa pushed through the door and locked it behind him, then made his way back to the roof.

Despite this and other setbacks, he still had a long night ahead of him.

That was okay; he also had a full load of ammunition as well.

By the time he was finished for the night and had returned to the North Pole, he was exhausted. He'd had countless battles with the dead as the night had progressed but his wits and weapons had seen him through unscathed. His new suit had a lot to do with it as well. There were many places where teeth marks could be seen on the leather and actual teeth were lodged in the metal mesh over his chest and back, but not one got through and touched his soft flesh beneath.

After making sure the elves in the stable were taking care of his reindeer, he made his way back home and his waiting wife.

When he entered, her eyes lit up with relief and Santa saw that she wasn't alone. Herman and Melvin were with her, no doubt keeping her company till he returned.

"I'm home," he said as he entered the house and she ran into his arms for a kiss. "Now, now, not too close or you'll get blood on you," he told her, his suit covered in zombie gore.

"I don't care, I'm just glad you're home and safe for another year."

He patted her shoulder and then extricated himself from her loving embrace. "I need to get out of this thing, it's killing me," he said and began to shrug out of the suit. "You two, give me a hand, will you please?"

Herman and Melvin did as requested and a few minutes later, Santa was standing in the middle of the living room in nothing but his red long-johns.

"How did the new suit work out?" Mrs. Claus asked.

"I have to tell you, the suit worked marvelously," he told his wife. "I can't imagine ever having done tonight without it."

"I'm so glad to hear it," she said. "In fact, I have a few more ideas for next year. How about a helmet and gauntlets and oh, what about a shield and…"

"Later, you can tell me later," he cut her off. "For now I just want to sit down and have something warm to drink."

"Here are your slippers, Santa," Herman said and slid the slippers on his feet as Santa dropped down in his favorite chair by the fire. To the right of him a beautiful pine Christmas tree brought back from the real world blinked with colorful lights. But only the standard red, blue and green ornaments on this one—no body parts at all.

Melvin went off to the kitchen and came back a minute later with a steaming mug. "Here, Santa, I made this just for you."

Santa took the mug and sniffed. It was hot cocoa. He gave Melvin a stern look and Melvin nodded and said, "Yes, Santa, it's real cocoa."

He hesitantly sipped it, and after he swallowed the first mouthful and his throat wasn't being eaten out from the inside, he began drinking it with gusto.

"How did my weapons work out, Santa?" Melvin asked eagerly.

Santa let out a hearty laugh and patted the small elf armorer on the shoulder. "They were excellent. Couldn't have been better. Thank you again, Melvin, you probably saved my life more than once because of your inventions." He winked. "And the guns didn't hurt either."

"That's so great to hear," Melvin said. "Because while you were gone, I was still working and I came up with even more great ideas. How about fig pudding that's really Semtex or tinsel that can be used as a garrote, or a stuffed animal that can be used as containers for nerve gas; just pull off the head and toss it. And…"

"Okay, okay, enough, please, not now. There's plenty of time for all that tomorrow." Santa finished his cocoa and handed the empty cup to his wife, who took it with a warm smile. "One thing I've learned since the dead began to walk is that we have all the time in the world."

"Amen to that, dear," Mrs. Claus said. "And Merry Christmas to you."

Santa smiled, his cheeks puffing up as he let out a hearty, "Ho-Ho-Ho. Thank you, dear. It's nice to have someone say it to *me* for once!"

Herman began to chuckle and Melvin joined in, and soon they were all laughing. The dead may rule the Earth and death and decay were everywhere, but here, at the North Pole, life still flourished…and so did Christmas.

HOLLY JOLLY CHRISTMAS

KELLY M. HUDSON

Dallas racked the shotgun in his hands with a keen sense of satisfaction. The rotting zombie shuffling in front of him flinched with instant recognition of the sound. Those things may be dumb as a blonde and slow as a rock hard turd, but they knew the sound of a shotgun clacking. They understood what was coming. And that made Dallas grin wide as a tractor trailer.

It was dressed like an elf, the kind you'd see when it was Christmas time at the mall. One of Santa's Helper's. This poor bastard had gotten bitten in the neck and died shortly after, coming back to be cursed forever, wearing that stupid outfit. There was a hunk missing from just below its right ear, which had been partially chewed off as well. The skin had since turned a dark green and the stench of its rot fogged the hallway and made Dallas' eyes water. This one had been dead a long time.

He pushed the shotgun into the dead elf's face and it raised its hands by instinct. He laughed. This was turning into a real good time.

The zombie moaned, hissing out its last utterance before it died for good. Dallas pulled the trigger, excited to watch its head explode. Dried brains, brittle bones, bits of green skin, and tufts of black-matted hair, splashed the walls behind it. The zombie collapsed to the floor, arms and legs twitching for all of a minute, before it stopped altogether. Dallas sprinted down the hallway.

He'd entered this sprawling shopping mall yesterday, hiding out in one of the front stores. He was good with electronics, so it had been no big thing to trip the wires and get the gate in front of the jewelry store to rattle open. The noise brought the zombies, of course, but that was okay. Once inside, he closed the gate, looked the store over from top to bottom to make sure no other creatures were inside with him, sacked out behind the register stand, and slept for almost twenty-four hours.

It had been rough out in the rest of the world. The dead were up and walking and there was no end to them. He'd run from the big cities just like anyone with half a brain would do, but after a while, he realized he had no way of eating. He wasn't a very good hunter, despite how hard his father had tried to make him into one, and he didn't have time to grow food. So he hiked the twenty miles to the nearest small city and decided to set up shop some-where there.

That meant more zombies and more danger, but if he was smart and moved fast enough, he could be relatively safe. The secret was to keep from getting cornered by the bastards. If that happened, and unless he had a machine gun, his goose was cooked.

After he woke from his deep slumber, he ate the last can of tuna fish he had and headed out into the mall proper. He used a back door that connected to a hallway that led to the main floor of the mall, and that's where he ran into the zombie elf he'd just killed. He knew the shotgun's report would bring them shuffling, so he ran to the end of the hall to take a look around to see what the inside of the mall actually looked like, then dashed back to the jewelry store, stunned at what he'd found.

Christmas. There were decorations everywhere. He'd forgotten that the dead rose in December and the gradual destruction of society had begun around the middle of the month. It was easy to forget such things when his every moment, breath and thought was spent on survival. Now he was reminded of what he'd forgot-ten, and he wasn't very happy about it.

He hated Christmas. He had, ever since he could remember. His mother died when he was five, the day before Christmas, and that had kind of blown the rest of them from then on out. His father was a real son-of-a-bitch, a redneck who thought the wrestler Diamond Dallas Page was the greatest man on Earth. What a role model. That's how Dallas got his name. And this redneck father of his thought he should raise his kid tough, so he told him straight that Santa Claus was a lie.

Dallas didn't believe it, though. He prayed to Santa, asking him to come and prove his father wrong. But like God, Santa never replied, so Dallas was left with a dilemma, one that turned ugly fairly quickly.

It all started on Christmas the year after his mother died. She'd given him a locket, one that played the song 'Silent Night' when it opened. Inside was a picture of her and him, as a little baby, taken right after he was born. Dallas had taken it out to hear the song and think of his mother when his father came out of nowhere with a grimace and a cocked fist. All Dallas remembered after that was seeing three of his baby teeth clatter to the floor and the locket being ground beneath his father's boot heel. His father smashed it until there was nothing left. Dallas remembered laying there, crying, listening as the last bits of Silent Night warped and bled into the carpet.

"Christmas is over," his father said. And that was that.

When other kids were opening presents and visiting the mall Santa to give him their wish lists, Dallas was out learning to shoot a gun and hunt a deer. To be sure, the shooting skills came in handy later, when the dead rose and the world went to Hell, but it was a pain in the ass when he was a kid. Especially when his father would beat him for missing a shot.

Dallas walked to the front of the store. The zombies that had shown up at the gate last night had either drifted off or went to investigate where the sound of his shot had come from. Good. He opened the gate just enough to slip under and left it there. If he needed to run back later, he could do it without much trouble.

The mall was decked to the halls with Christmas decorations. His stomach churned when he looked up, absorbing the sights. Garland was roped across the open spaces: red, green, silver, all tinkling in the fluorescent lights — so far the power was still on.

The shops had big red and green stars stuck to their windows, with other decals, like giant candy canes and reindeer. One closed and boarded-up store had a long mural of Santa in his sleigh pulled by the reindeer. Off in the middle of the mall was a mock-up of red felt and fake snow with a big sign over the entrance that read 'Santa Land.' Steps led up to a small platform where a large throne sat empty. That's where Santa would be, if things were different.

Behind the seat, a short distance away, was a giant Christmas tree, obviously fake, because it was way too green to still be alive and months of being cared for. Bright lights circled it, some sparkling and others blinking on and off in a chaotic pattern.

The sight of all of this captivated him for a moment. He was so stunned he barely registered the few zombies wandering around, moaning and heading towards him.

How many times had he laid in bed at night, praying to Santa Claus? When he was little, he didn't believe his father. Santa was real. He had to be. Other kids got visits and gifts, why didn't he? The proof was in the pudding, and the pudding was rich with presents for everyone else but him. So he'd developed a theory. Santa didn't come because his father had been a bad parent, and if Dallas prayed hard enough, Santa would come anyway. So he did. Even after the beatings and the cajoling, he prayed and pleaded and got down on his knees. And you know what happened? Nothing. Nothing at all. Except more punishment and derision.

Pretty soon, he started believing in nothing at all, and least of all, Santa Claus.

Dallas shook his head of all the bad memories. The zombies were getting closer. He had to wake up and either deal with them or get to safety. He raised his trusty shotgun and prepared for battle when he was hit with his third unexpected surprise of the young day.

The music. It started right up, like it was on a timer. Christmas songs. The jingles were bright, chirpy, and loud, echoing in the big open spaces. He watched with horror as the zombies advanced towards him, their limbs twitching in time to the music. He felt like he was in an outtake of some Michael Jackson video, one where Christmas never ended, even during a zombie apocalypse.

The first dead hand fell on his arm from his right side. It was a woman in a tattered blue dress, stained brown by dried blood. Half her face was missing, like it had been torn off by a tiger, and her tongue was swollen with teeming maggots, lolling through the empty space where her left cheek had been.

He jerked his arm away and swung the butt of the shotgun around, shattering her skull. He stared in horror as the maggots tumbled from her mouth like a chunk of wriggling rice, spilling onto the floor.

They were followed by a few rotten teeth and a cowlick of flesh. The woman staggered, still functioning despite the blow, and moaned. He raised his shotgun and blew the rest of her head off. It went up in a puff of dust and desiccated skin. What was left of her brains flew straight up and rained down in tiny, thick clots.

Dallas backed away. By his quick count, there were probably ten zombies, all very close to him now. He was sure there were more, but he couldn't say where. He heard them, though, over the Christmas music, their moans filling the building.

He ran back to the jewelry store, slid under the gate, opened the door, went inside, and closed the gate again. It would hold, unless there were a few hundred of them out there. If so, he was screwed anyway.

He hesitated at the entrance, facing out into the mall. The zombies shuffled over, pressing against the gate, smashing their faces into the grating. After the first dozen appeared, all pushing and shoving and scratching, he lost sight of any of the rest. There were so many of them, all from different walks of life.

He saw Asians and whites and what he suspected were some Mexicans. There were a couple of black ones, too, and an Indian. It was amazing to him. In real life, all those folks wouldn't have been able to come together on a consensus about anything. But in death, their hunger for warm, human flesh made everything else meaningless. That's why they'd won. It seemed stupid and implausible that such slow-moving creatures could defeat so many people, armed to the teeth with guns and tanks. They had, though. Because of their persistence, because of their single-mindedness; they only craved human flesh. They didn't sleep, didn't rest, didn't care if it was hot or cold, raining or dry. They kept coming. And, given the circumstances, whenever they killed, another one joined their ranks. Dallas stumbled to the counter and sat down on his ass, hard. He covered his ears. Even here, in this store, the music was being piped in. He couldn't stand it. The damn Christmas songs. He hated them and now here he was, trapped in a place that was going to be Christmas Land forever. He curled into a ball, shoving his fists up against his head. He couldn't shut out the music and he couldn't ignore the moans. But after a time, exhaustion hit him again and he fell asleep.

When he woke, he had a plan. It was insane, he realized, but who cared? If he died, he died. At least carrying through with his plan would give his life some meaning. He was going to make Christmas pay. He was going to go out there and kill every damn zombie, and when he was done, he was going to burn the place to the ground.

Let's see them have a holly jolly Christmas now, he smiled.

He checked his backpack. He had a box of shells left. That should be enough. He didn't really have to kill them all, just slow them down a bit. He'd seen a camping store in the northwest corner and it would be his first stop. In there would be some propane. A few of those canisters, placed in the right spots, and he could burn the place down, no sweat.

The front gate was still clogged with zombies, so it looked like he would have to go out the side, back into the hallway. So be it. He stuffed his pockets full of shells, made sure the shotgun was fully loaded, and took off.

The hall was empty. Nothing was there but the headless body of the zombie he'd killed before. He crept along until he reached the mouth and peered around the corner. It wasn't so bad out there. Around two dozen pusbags shuffled around the front of the jewelry store. Others had drifted off and were walking around, gazing into closed shops. They were spread out just fine. He had plenty of time and space to get to the camping store, jimmy the lock for its gate, and get inside before he would be bothered.

Above him, *Jingle Bells* was playing. Jingle Bells. Christ.

Dallas took a deep breath, let it out slowly, convinced himself he could do this, and bolted.

He scurried through for zombies, pushing one out of his way and tripping another. They fell into a heap, stunned and confused. He ran, dashing towards the center of the mall.

Just past Santa Land and to the left was the camping store. Nothing really stood in his way. The pusbags up ahead were all really spread out, so this was going to be easy, like the snap of a finger.

He cut through the entrance of Santa Land. It was quicker to go through here, with less obstacles. He was almost to Santa's chair when he saw them, coming down one of the side corridors. Forty, fifty of them, all dead, all walking, and all dressed like Santa Claus.

He stopped and stared.

How could this be? Where had they been? Where did they come from? Then he saw the sign, halfway down that very same hallway. A zombie crashed into it, spinning it around. The chrome borders glittered in the overhead light. The sign read: 'Santa Meeting.' There must have been some kind of employee meeting of all the men who were employed as Santa impersonators right here in this mall. What were the odds of this meeting happening right when the living dead apocalypse broke out? A million to one, he figured, and the odds went up even more when he, the hater of all things Christmas, was thrown into the equation.

Instead of scaring him, the arrival of the zombie Santas only made him more determined. When he set this place on fire and he watched those bastards burn, it was just going to make things that much sweeter.

He pointed his shotgun at Santa's chair.

"Hey, assholes!" he yelled. He pulled the trigger. Sure, he wasted a shell, but it was worth it. The top of the chair splintered and threw a thousand of shards of plastic and red felt across the back of Santa Land.

The Santa zombies moaned as one.

"Yeah! You don't like that, do you?" he shouted. "Well, maybe one of you, just one of you, could have brought me a present. Just one!"

He pulled the trigger again. The rest of the chair blew backwards and tumbled down the small stand it was sitting on. He had to get it together. He was losing it. Something had risen inside him, some sort of hateful bile that threatened to choke him if he didn't let it out. He'd had this pent-up rage for so long he'd forgotten about it and now, here he was, in the middle of the end of time, and he had a chance to get it off his chest.

Dallas shrugged his shoulders. Might as well go for it.

He ran over to the tree and stood beside it, watching and waiting as the Santa zombies advanced. The tree was close to thirty feet tall and thick with fake, plastic branches, tinsel, those blinking and stuttering lights, garland, and on the bottom rows, pictures of kids taken with the mall Santa. The stand was driven into the floor but it was made of plastic, too. He tapped it with the barrel of his shotgun. The *tink-tink* sound confirmed his thoughts: it was hollow. This would be easier than he thought.

He couldn't forget about the other zombies behind him, though. They were coming, closer and a bit faster than the Santa ones. He would need to deal with them first.

Dallas jogged over to the blown Santa seat and took aim. He was going to stick with his original plan here. He didn't need to kill them, just slow them down. He pulled the trigger. The knees of two zombies, one in a marching band outfit caked with dried intestines and the other dressed like a waiter in a seafood restaurant, went down in a heap.

The buckshot had shredded the right knee on one and the left calf on the other. They wouldn't be walking again. During their collapse, the seafood waiter fell into a woman in a black dress with a mess of fake pearl necklaces laced around her neck. The waiter got its arm wound up in the necklaces of the woman and they were tangled so hard that they were both reduced to crawling and moaning.

That was one good shot.

A boy zombie wearing a pair of overalls and a checkered shirt, strangely bright and clean as the day they were made, was next. Dallas decided to go ahead and end it, so he shot the boy zombie full in the face. Its head was erased in an instant, leaving behind a smoking neck stump and a small body that fell to the side, jittering.

He loaded the shotgun again, musing on what had brought him here. He frowned, thinking it over. Seeing these decorations, and the elves and Santa zombies, brought it all into sharp focus for him. He hadn't really come back to the city for food, he had come back here to die. The truth was, he was tired. Tired of running, tired of being afraid, tired of being alone. There was no future, not any more.

He had been a part of three separate groups since the apocalypse happened and each one had fallen apart because of in-fighting or stupidity. Things always fell apart, because people were pieces of shit, just like his father always said. That was the biggest problem.

Since he was a child, he lived thinking his father was wrong about everything. When he got older, he saw that some of what his father said had been true, and now that the world was in the throws of its end, he saw his father had been absolutely right.

Dallas didn't want to live in a world that proved his father true.

So he came back, fooling himself into believing it was for the food, but deep down, he knew the real reason. He'd come here to die. He hadn't, however, expected to go out like this.

A big grin creased his face as he took the legs from four more zombies with two separate shotgun blasts and then another five with two more. That took care of the closest ones and now he could get to his real business.

He turned to his right and sure enough, the Santa zombies were in perfect position. He ran back over to the tree, placed the muzzle of the shotgun against the stand, and fired. He aimed so the shot would hit on the side facing the Santa zombies. Plastic flew in every direction and the tree shuddered. Dallas stepped back, still smiling.

Thin cables that had run from the top of the tree to anchors in the walls twanged and broke, whipping through the air as the tree fell with a shriek of torn plastic and metal. It collapsed on the advancing Santa zombies. He watched as they got either pinned beneath the tree or caught-up in the branches, lights, or garlands. They were trapped; easy pickings.

He checked his pockets and made sure he had plenty of shells left, then reloaded the shotgun. He was going to take his time now and kill them one by one. And with each one, he was going to grin and curse Santa and Christmas and his father and every other damned thing that had made his life miserable.

The first three went quick, the next two not so much. They were so knotted in the limbs and lights that it was hard to find their heads. He did the best he could, and even if he didn't kill them for good, he gave them plenty to deal with. When he was done, he left behind simple smears of old, clotted blood, fragments of skulls, and greasy brains, before moving on.

He checked over his shoulder to the left, marking the progress of the crawling zombies he'd already maimed and those coming up behind them. He had time. They were maybe a little closer than he wanted, but he could get a few more Santas, take care of some of the walkers, and get back to those trapped beneath the tree.

Above him, *Hark the Herald Angels* came over the speakers. He gritted his teeth, wishing he could get to the speakers as easily as he had the tree. He bent down to kill another Santa when he heard a low hiss come from behind. Dallas spun and his heart lurched in his chest.

Four dozen zombie children marched towards him, all in various states of decay. Some were fresher than others, but they all reeked of death and carnage. Most had faces and fingers smeared with dried blood and congealed bits of flesh. They were all dressed as Santa's elves, in tiny green costumes with jingling bells on their little red booties. He hadn't heard them over the roar of the shotgun and now they were so close he could almost taste the rot in the air.

Behind him, several Santas rose out from under the fallen tree, staggering to their feet and moaning as they shuffled towards him. He was pinned between two groups with no way out. Dallas set his jaw. If this was to be it, then so be it. He would take as many out as he could.

He pulled the trigger. The shotgun blast thumped two zombie elf kids in their chests, shattering their sternums and sending them flying backwards. They crashed into a few others and took them down like bowling pins. He stepped towards them and fired again. His shot caught a kid right in the throat, its head popping like a zit and tumbling off to the side. It hit with a wet smack and rolled over by the closed gate of a bookstore. He reloaded.

A white-gloved Santa hand fell on his shoulder and yanked him back. He swung the butt of the shotgun so it smacked the Santa zombie right where the bridge of the nose met the skull. Bones cracked and the zombie staggered away, giving Dallas some room to operate.

It wasn't enough. The other zombies, the ones he'd left alone, had arrived. A woman with crooked teeth, wearing a University of Miami hat, grabbed his arm right as another zombie wearing a cock-eyed wig grabbed his leg.

Dallas tripped and tumbled to the floor, the shotgun flying from his hands and clattering four feet away. Too far away.

They crawled on him, pressing their weight down on his body, pinning him. Zombie kid elves had his legs and Santa zombies had his arms. All he saw were flashing, rotten teeth and leering, gray faces.

He closed his eyes, all at once reverting to the child he used to be, all alone, his father approaching him with a leather belt, ready to beat him. Tears squeezed out like juice from a crushed orange. All he could think of was his mother, wishing she were here, wishing she'd never died, wondering what his life would have been like if she had lived. In his panic, in his grief, he let go of so much, there in the final moments of his life.

The weight, the swell in his chest that had been there since that terrible day when he got the news of his mother's death, that he'd carried for so long he forgot it was even there, finally burst.

"Santa!" he cried out, a child once more, for the final time.

The song *Silent Night* began over the speakers, somehow louder than the commotion around him. It filled the mall with its chiming hymn. Dallas heard it and smiled. At least there was this, in his terminal moment. He would have peace at last.

A burst of brilliant white light filled the area. He opened his eyes, only to be momentarily blinded. The sound of bells, loud and ringing, rattled his teeth. The zombies let him go and stood, staggering back. He rolled onto his stomach, unsure of how exactly he'd been saved or why, but not wasting any time. He scrambled in the direction his shotgun had fallen, his fingers clawing the tiled floor, searching for it. All the while, the light grew brighter and the bells grew louder. He squeezed his eyes closed against the brightness and it was all he could do not to cover his ears.

He needed his gun.

Over the sound of the bells was another noise, that of braying and snorting, like wild animals had been let loose. Immediately following this was a long scraping grind. The moan of the zombies was lost in the noise and Dallas stopped thinking about them and everything else. He concentrated on getting his gun. He would deal with all the rest after that.

The screeching came to a halt just a few feet from him on his right. He didn't pay attention to it. He kept crawling, kept reaching, kept searching with his fingers.

His fingernails scraped leather boots and he jerked his hand back. It was a Santa zombie, he just knew it.

The light faded as quickly as it came and he opened his eyes. Black shoes stood before him, connected to short, fat legs swaddled in red stockings. He kept looking up, his eyes pausing at a belly like a bowl full of jelly and traveling up, up, until he saw a big white beard and met the glittering black eyes above it, surrounded by ruby red cheeks pulled back into a smile.

"Ho! Ho! Ho!" the man said.

It was Santa Claus. His mind tried to wrap itself around the situation and he could only come up with three possible explanations. One, he'd gone insane. Two, he'd died and this was somehow the afterlife. Or three, this really was Santa Claus. Option number three was the real truth; he knew it to the core of his being. The real Santa was standing before him. He could feel the magic bristling in the air. Santa was real and had come here, to this mall in the middle of nowhere.

"How? Why?"

"Why?" bellowed Santa. "Why, I came to give you two gifts to make up for the times I couldn't come before, when you were a child."

Tears filled Dallas' eyes again. He was weeping like a baby. Santa reached down and took him by the hand, hauling him to his feet. Animals snorted on his right and he glanced over at them. Reindeer, all tethered together and attached to a sleigh. Of course, what else would they be? The world spun as Santa laughed again, gathering Dallas in his arms as he collapsed. Santa carried him to the sled and laid him in the back.

"I couldn't come because of your father's hatred," Santa said over his shoulder. He sat in the front of the sleigh and cracked a whip. The reindeer ran as the zombies, all recognizing Santa, stepped aside. The deer ran in a circle until their hooves stopped clattering on the floor and stroked the air. The sleigh rose, flying up through the hole in the ceiling they'd made on their entrance.

"It blocked my magic. Hatred always blocks magic," Santa said, shaking his head. "But I always promised I'd come do something special for you, when the time was right."

"But I hated you," Dallas croaked.

Santa laughed. "Ho, ho, ho! No, you didn't! You tried to, but you couldn't! You cried out for me, at last, and now I've come!"

The sleigh flew through the air, out of the mall, and climbed higher and higher. Dallas peered over the edge and saw the earth fall away, the mall and other buildings becoming small dots in the distance.

"Where are we going?" Dallas asked.

"Somewhere far away."

They flew for a long time. Dallas fell asleep and woke periodically until the sleigh slowed down and descended. They landed in a snow-covered field next to a small cottage. Smoke curled from the chimney as he gazed at it. The place looked so warm and inviting.

"Your new home," Santa said. "Far, far from the zombies."

"Is this the North Pole?" Dallas asked.

Santa laughed. "Ho, ho, ho! No! But it might as well be. I've stocked your pantry with magic so that the food will never run out. And you won't be alone. I've given you three dogs to serve as faithful companions."

"What about a woman?" Dallas asked.

Santa shook his head. "I'm not a dating service."

Dallas nodded. "Thank you, Santa. I'm sorry for not believing."

"And I'm sorry for not coming sooner."

Santa waved his hand over Dallas and he was suddenly very sleepy. He felt Santa place something in the palm of his hand and close his fist around it.

"Here is your other gift," Santa whispered.

And that was all Dallas knew for a long time as darkness descended on him.

He woke to a big golden retriever licking his face. He was lying on the most comfortable couch he'd ever slept on, in a small room filled by the warming glow of a blazing fire. The two other dogs, one a cocker spaniel and the other a pug, ran over, tails wagging, licking his hands and howling with joy.

Dallas sat up, as happy as a person could be. It was true. There really was a Santa Claus, and he really had answered his prayers. It took a while, but the answers came right on time.

He remembered his fist and that something was closed within it. He opened his hand and there, as if from a lost memory, lay the pendant his mother had given him long ago. Fingers trembling, he opened it. *Silent Night* chimed from somewhere inside.

Tears filled his eyes as he stared at the picture of him and his mother, taken the day he was born.

"Merry Christmas to me," Dallas said as tears rolled down his face.

SECRET SANTA

JONATHAN TEMPLAR

Santa came early and that, Jacob figured, was why he'd gotten stuck.

The chimney was narrow, after all. Jacob had stuck his head in and peered up often enough to know that for a fact. And Santa was big and fat, a fact as well.

There were still two weeks till Christmas, so the only possible conclusion was that he'd decided to make an early delivery, the magic wasn't working fully yet, and he'd become trapped halfway down.

Jacob didn't like the chimney, never had. It felt like a hole in the house. You could see a little square of the sky when you peered up the sooty passage, and it always unnerved him how he could be indoors with all the windows and doors firmly closed but know there was still a way for someone to get in.

This worried him more these days, what with the strangeness going on. The windows were permanently shuttered, there were bolts on the doors, and the family only left the house when there was someone to protect them, but the tiny little hole had never been closed off.

When Jacob pointed this out to his father, his dad laughed, and ruffled Jacob's hair and told him that the only visitor likely to squeeze down the chimney would arrive courtesy of reindeer and expect a glass of milk and a cookie for his trouble.

Jacob was comforted by this, after all, if his father said they were safe, they were safe. 'End of sentence,' as his classmate Evan would always say. But he resented it as well, resented that his father had laughed at him when Jacob felt he had a legitimate concern. He realized the next time he had such a concern he might just keep it to himself instead.

When he heard the first groan from the chimney, he remembered what his father told him.

He'd been in the room on his own, what they once called the family room, but was now mainly reserved for Jacob and his many, many toys. He'd spread out from his bedroom like a mold, and one room could no longer contain him or his multiple playthings.

The family room was his now, his playroom, scattered with his debris. He was playing there one afternoon, content on his own, basking in the glory of the newly-erected Christmas tree and its pine smell, happily absorbed in the dynamics of a toy tyrannosaurus' visit to a plastic carwash, when the groaning started.

The groan echoed down from the chimney and Jacob reacted with understandable terror. For a moment, the prospect that what was in his bowels would soon be filling his pants was a marginal fifty-fifty.

The groan was like no sound on Earth, a mournful lament from something long since separated from mortality, a brainless, primal sound a long, long way from articulation. Jacob was too young to comprehend all this. Terror gave way to curiosity, and to a fledgling, cautious excitement.

After all, what had his father said? Milk and cookies? Only one visitor would arrive via the chimney and expect milk and cookies to be waiting for him.

"Santa?" he said quietly, and edged toward the chimney.

The groan echoed again, hollow and oddly distant. Jacob took a step back. He'd been led to expect a more jolly sound from Santa. Some ho-ho-ho's at the very least.

"Santa, are you okay?"

Again the groan.

Jacob decided the situation needed further investigating. He crept to the wall and poked his shaggy-haired head under the metal grate.

It was dark looking up, darker than usual. He quickly realized he couldn't see the sky, that the small square of outside was gone. But even in the sooty gloom he could tell that the sky wasn't really gone, but had only been obscured.

There was *someone* up there.

His eyes struggled to make out any detail. He could see the outline, could just distinguish the shape of a person jammed tight into the chimney chute. If he tried really hard, he thought he could make out a face peering down at him, two eyes glinting in the darkness.

"Santa, are you stuck?"

He was answered with the same monotonous groan. No jolly laughter. Jacob was perturbed, but then something occurred to him. He recalled a day last summer, before things had become strange.

His father had taken him to the lake, and they had spent an afternoon watching the yachts racing and weaving across the clear water. A golden day, with the sun blazing and childhood memories forming. Memories that would stick in his mind even as he grew and became distracted by a hundred other details.

What made the day even more memorable were the ice cream sandwiches, one for each of them.

It was hot so they began to melt quicker than Jacob could eat his, and the ice cream started to run down his hand in a sticky stream, so he'd rushed, and gnashed quickly at the sandwich.

In his rush he'd bitten down too hard and caught his tongue, his baby teeth strong enough even then to penetrate his skin. Warm blood had poured into his mouth and there was sharp pain, not at all dampened by the cold of the ice cream. Jacob had hollered and cried and his tongue had swollen up to fill his mouth, or so it had seemed.

When the tears were finished, and the loss of the sandwich which had melted away on the grass appropriately mourned, they had journeyed home and Jacob had greeted his mom with a tongue still swollen.

The sound that had come out had been...wrong. He'd said the words the same as he'd always said them but they came out garbled and backward, as if spoken with a mouthful of marbles. They had laughed, the entire family, and it became one of their legends.

The day he tried to eat his own tongue.

"Santa, have you bitten your tongue?" Jacob whispered to the visitor, who groaned back, slightly louder than before. Perhaps there was some movement in the dark chute, a scurrying sound and a suggestion of something thrashing. Something reaching out to Jacob who took this as confirmation. "It's okay, Santa. I bit my tongue last year by the lake. I know it hurts, but it gets better soon. Have you got any ice cream you can rub on it in your toy sack?"

"Uuuuhhhhh."

"Okay, I don't know if that's a yes or a no. I'll go and ask Mom if she has any. She usually has whatever I need if I get hurt." He turned and made for the door, heading to the kitchen where he'd last seen his mother.

Then he paused and remembered again. How the last time he'd asked about the chimney his father had laughed and rubbed Jacob's hair the way he hated. That hair rub meant Jacob was being silly, or he'd gotten something wrong, or he was being *cute*. If there was one thing Jacob definitely didn't want to be, it was *cute*.

Soon, when he told his mom that Santa was stuck in the chimney and had bitten his tongue and couldn't talk, well, she'd take over. Or worse, she'd call Dad and he'd come home and take charge. Then when Santa got free of the chimney, it would be his dad who would get all the thanks. All the presents. And if there was anyone who knew presents, it was Santa.

It occurred to Jacob at the same time that having Santa in the chimney might afford a few fringe benefits outside the family as well.

All year Jacob had struggled to hide his envy of Evan, who had gotten a Space Ranger Five for his birthday; their relationship had never really recovered. Jacob had wanted the ship, too, wanted it bad, and since Evan had gotten his, he'd lorded it over the playground.

He'd made them know every day in every way that he had something they wanted and he wouldn't let them forget it. Now Jacob had Santa—the actual, genuine Santa—stuck up his chimney. That trumped a Space Ranger Five! That trumped anything.

"Santa, Mom doesn't have any medicine," Jacob lied. He crossed his fingers as he said it and hoped that despite everything—he'd been warned in the past—Santa really didn't know when you were being naughty. "You'll have to stay up there for now. But I'll come back and check on you later, okay?"

"Uuuuhhhhhh"

Jacob took the groan as a yes and left the family room a happy boy.

It had been a while now since things had turned weird, but for Jacob and the rest of the children in school, it hadn't affected their lives in a big way. The adults were acting differently, that much was obvious. They looked worried all the time, and there were soldiers everywhere. The soldiers never looked happy, and they often scared Jacob—the intensity they showed.

None of the children were allowed outside on their own, and spent all their time between school and home restricted to indoor activities. But it was winter, so they would have been indoors anyway.

Even at school, the playground was out of bounds. They spent their breaks in the cafeteria, which had been customized to make a suitable play area, but was cramped and noisy all the same, the sound of hundreds of screaming voices amplified by the sealed windows and doors.

All Jacob had ever been told were that some people had gotten very sick, and the sickness could spread very quickly and very easily, so it was best for the children if they stayed inside and didn't ask many questions.

One day, their teacher Miss Northern, became really upset during their lessons and started to cry, and while she was crying she told them that everything her parents had told them was true. Something she called *Judgment Day* had come, and Hell and Earth had become the same place. Or something similar, anyway.

One of the other teachers had come in and led Miss Northern away, and she hadn't been seen since. The children mostly laughed when she was led out, the uncomfortable laughter of children who didn't understand the way adults sometimes were, though some of them had cried, too.

Evan said that Hell couldn't be on Earth because Hell was made of fire, and was really, really hot and it made sense. One of the other boys explained what *Judgment Day* was. He believed it had something to do with wrestling, and that seemed to reassure everyone. Things were strange, sure, but everything carried on regardless.

Jacob approached Evan as soon as he boarded the school bus the following morning. The school bus was different these days; there were metal plates on the windows and you couldn't see out, and soldiers sat at the front with *real guns*—Evan told everyone that was really, really cool but Jacob still thought it was a bit scary. The guns looked very, very big when seen up close. But the bus still picked them up and dropped them home just the same as before.

"Santa is stuck in my chimney," he whispered through clenched teeth.

"What?" Evan replied, the usual sneer in his tone.

"Santa Claus. He's stuck in my chimney. He must have come early, maybe because of all the weirdness. And he's bitten his tongue so he can't talk properly. But he's up there."

"Santa?"

"Uh-huh."

"Don't be a tool, Jacob. There's no such thing as Santa. Lloyd told me about it years ago. It's just something adults make up so you behave."

"Then why is he up my chimney?"

"If he isn't real he can't be up your chimney. End of sentence."

"Why don't you come and see for yourself?"

"Have you been asleep the last two months? I can't come to your house, my mom's been talking about stopping us from going to school, too. There's no way she'd let me visit anyone, let alone you."

"Oh."

Evan had never visited Jacob even before the 'shit hit the fan' as his father had once memorably put it—memorably for Jacob anyway, who until then believed that adults were unaware of the existence of swear words, which were instead the exclusive province of he and his friends.

He and Evan weren't friends as such, and Jacob knew his mother didn't think so much of Evan's mom. Evan's mom was young and pretty and wore colorful clothes when she used to pick him up from school. She bought Evan whatever he asked for, so he always had the coolest toys.

This seemed like a good thing to Jacob. But when Jacob's fifth birthday party invitations had been sent out, there hadn't been one for Evan. This drove a wedge between them, and it was one that Jacob had been trying to remove ever since. Although he would have struggled to explain why, he thought Evan was cool.

"Well, he's up there all the same," Jacob said in conclusion.

Evan had little more to add and whispered, "Loser," as he turned away.

There was no one else at school to ask, so Jacob figured he was on his own. Santa had to be freed and only he could do it. He gave it some deep thought during the day, his mind drifting from the lessons and the steamy enclosure of the cafeteria to the more practical considerations of freeing a jolly fat man from inside his chimney.

His first thought was how perhaps he could poke him with something from above, to squeeze his bulk down. But it would have to be a pretty long stick, and Jacob knew he was unlikely to be able to produce the right amount of pressure himself. Besides, the chances of his parents allowing him access to the roof were roughly zero. They didn't even let him out onto the porch on his own these days.

The only alternative he could think of was a grim one for Santa.

"I don't think there's any way I can help you down, Santa!" he called up the chimney later that day. "But the way I see it, if you're stuck up there it's because you're fat, and you get fat 'cuz you eat too much of the wrong stuff, that's what Mom says anyway. But all the while you're stuck up there you can't eat a thing, can you, Santa? So I figure you'll get skinny pretty quick, and the skinnier you get, the easier it's gonna be for you to slide down."

The mournful groan appeared to agree with him.

"Then that's it, Santa. I know you're gonna be awful hungry but I'll make sure there's plenty of stuff waiting for you when you get down. I've got some here, I'm gonna leave it by the chimney so you know I'm tellin' the truth, and I figure it might make you want to squeeze as hard as you can so you can have it."

He put the glass of milk and cookies pilfered from the kitchen onto the tiles before the fireplace. He was pleased with himself. This had been some serious problem solving, he felt sure his father would be very proud once Jacob was able to tell him exactly what he'd done.

"Well done, Jacob, you've rescued Santa," he said to himself, feeling pride fill him. Perhaps his dad would shake his hand like he was another adult rather than ruffle his hair.

That would be great.

As the days before Christmas ticked away, Jacob became almost absent-minded about his project. School broke up for the holidays early this year, and his father had come home one day just after lunch. He sat with Jacob's mother in the kitchen talking quietly for a *loooong* time. Jacob tried to listen in, but his father sent him away. Mom was crying, her eyes red, though she tried to pretend everything was okay. His parents wouldn't let Jacob watch TV anymore either. They didn't explain why. It just seemed that things outside were getting weirder...and worse.

Jacob checked up the chimney each day, but it was too gloomy to see if Santa was getting loose or not. He called up some encouragement when he could, but the moans were answering less frequently now.

Jacob replaced the milk with a fresh glass every day, and had to replace the cookies on more than one occasion when his own temptation became too great. Christmas was coming, and Jacob remained confident that Santa would free himself in time. The alternative was unthinkable.

Mom tended to leave him alone while he was in the family room, and his father never came in, so they never heard Santa's groaning when he did it. But she did appear once on Christmas Eve, just before his father got home and the doors were bolted for the last time. When she saw the milk and cookies, a smile lit up her face. She didn't smile much anymore, and it made Jacob warm inside to see it.

"Oh Jacob, let's hope that Santa manages to do the rounds this year. We could sure use him."

"I'm sure he will, Mom. In fact, I'm certain of it." He glanced at the chimney, hoping he wasn't being too obvious, hoping that Santa wouldn't choose this moment to call out. His tongue was still swollen and he wasn't talking much, but Jacob was sure his mom would soon see to that once the fat man was free.

His mother's nose wrinkled. "It smells awful here, Jacob. I hope you didn't spill something and not tell me. If so, you need to clean it up. We can't open the windows again for a while, you know."

"Sure thing, Mom," Jacob said, and then she was gone. He scuttled to the chimney.

"That was my mom. Once you get down here, she'll take care of you, Santa. You'll feel like your old self again in no time!" he called up.

It was gloomy as ever, but for the first time Jacob could see that Santa really was working his way down. He could see the detail of a hand, pale and coated in grimy soot but a hand all the same. It was only inches away from the opening. He beamed in delight. "You're doing great, Santa, I think you'll be out by Christmas day for sure!"

Santa hissed hungrily, only inches away from Jacob, who could sense just how ravenous he was.

A cloud of sooty dust belched from the chimney and Jacob had to back away to prevent it powdering his face.

At that moment, Jacob's father arrived home. He was shouting to them as he opened the door, and Jacob cringed when he heard the door slam shut with an impact that rocked the entire house.

The bolts were thrown back. Jacob darted from the room and into the hallway.

His father was leaning with his back to the door, as if he could keep it closed all by himself. He was ruffled, and his tie was awkwardly angled on his collar. One shoulder of his jacket was torn and the white lining had spilled out.

His light-gray trousers were stained with what could have been oil, or grime, as if he'd walked on his hands and knees through a car park.

His face—the stoic dependable face that Jacob trusted and feared in equal measure—was distorted into a mask of panic, terror, hopelessness. His eyes darted from his wife to his son, refusing to rest on either.

"It's over, it's all over. It's all fallen apart!" he panted.

Jacob's mother moved toward him, then stopped. She put her hand out to him but then snatched it back to cover her mouth. She whimpered. "What...what ..." she stuttered softly.

"They're everywhere, there's too many of them. The Army retreated, just ... retreated. Ran away. All the barricades are down."

"What do we do?" his mother wailed.

Still he didn't move toward her, just pressed his back against the door as if turning away would let the outside in. "We make our own barricade. Anything we can find. Keep them out until the Army can regain control."

His mother ran her hands through her hair frantically and moaned to herself. Jacob wanted to go to her, to put his hands around her and console her, but he didn't understand, couldn't fathom what was happening. He felt tears start to run down his face but he wasn't sure why.

"Dad?" he called gently.

"It's okay, Jacob. It's all going to be fine," but his father had never been less convincing, had never told a more transparent lie. "We're safe inside the house. Nothing can get in here."

His parents began hours of frantic activity: moving furniture, shifting everything that wasn't fixed down to block doors and windows, making sure there wasn't an inch of access anywhere in the house.

From outside, there were occasional sounds that carried even into their sanctuary. Screams. And gunfire? The first few times his parents paused their activity to listen. His mother had started crying again, but his father placed his hands on each side of her face and whispered to her until she stopped.

They were both red-faced and sweating by the time they finished.

The house that had once been ordered and calm, a place where Jacob would face serious time on his punishment step if he left things anywhere other than their prescribed places, was now a chaos of barricaded windows and furniture tilted any which way to provide purchase.

Jacob sat and watched all of this from the doorway of the family room, the only room in the house without a window, without access to the world outside.

Or at least, any that his parents had considered.

Scared though he was by all the activity, Jacob felt oddly calm and comforted. He had his secret after all, and he knew that soon enough, he would be able to share it with his parents.

Through the open door to the family room, Jacob could hear the frantic scuttling sound from the chimney, the sound of someone pushing ever closer to freedom.

It would be Christmas in the morning, and Jacob hadn't been naughty, and in fact, had definitely been nice. Everything would be okay, everything was going to be fine after all.

It didn't matter what was going on outside, not really. No matter how weird it was getting, Jacob knew Santa would soon be here, and then everything would be fine.

He couldn't wait to see what was waiting for him underneath the tree in the morning.

THE CHRISTMAS HELP

THOMAS SCOPEL

Malba, the lead toy workshop room elf, saw the glazed-over look in his assigned help's eyes and knew the time was drawing closer. With the toy still clutched in his hand, he stopped assembling and concentrated on the moving corpse across from him laboring on its chore.

Continuing to scrutinize, Malba's mind gathered to the days of old, long before the horrors, when the time was happy and gleeful, exciting and full of joy. He didn't smile, not even faintly. Those days were over; had been for a while now and he knew it.

Typically bombarded and invaded with melancholic former happy thoughts, the closer the season approached, he actively tried to keep them at bay. He assumed the others had them, too, at least the ones who were unlucky enough to have experienced them firsthand. He half-heartedly appreciated them, but more so wished he'd never experienced them at all. At least then his mind wouldn't try and wander, but would stay focused. Now was not the time for reminiscing. It could get him killed.

A memory pushed in—he and the rest of the elves were gathered around the fat, rosy-faced jolly old man, laughing and singing, congratulating and waving as he climbed aboard the sleigh and took flight. He forced it away with a vision of teeth tearing into the fleshy portion of an upper arm, and directed his observance back to the matter at hand.

Time grew shorter every year. No longer was it a joyful trip around the world filled with giving and sugary treats. The annual event was now more of a scavenger hunt, a cat and mouse game filled with one single thought. Feeding…before it was too late.

Long ago, when St. Nick knew the world like the back of his hand, he didn't need direction. The magic of Christmas guided him.

But with the onset of the terribleness this was no longer the case and 'the list' became 'the map,' St. Nick's only concern. The joy had been ripped away and was now completely gone. The yearly chore was now just a desperate grasping attempt at saving Christmas. Of course, the gifts were left and the stockings were stuffed, but he certainly didn't linger or take the time to eat cookies. He couldn't.

It was one of the primary contributions to his massive weight loss. The cookies had lost their taste anyway…

Like a season over season growing tolerance, this year's occurrences were the quickest yet. Malba was the first elf this year to see the beginnings of conversion. As fear took hold; he hoped they all could hold on until the sleigh returned. If they couldn't, Christmas would fade into oblivion; be forgotten. A thought he dreaded the most.

Looking narrowly at his help again, he paid special attention to the eyes. The white murky haze had grown slightly into and fully around the darkened iris, like tremendous clouds in the sky building before a rainstorm. If the pupil were allowed to become covered; control would be lost and bloodshed was almost certain, probably a combination of both the help's, as well as theirs. He had seen it before.

He puckered his lips and held them in place, awaiting the right moment to whistle the predetermined warning melody every living elf was required to master, just like they had with toy making. The whistle, specific and distinct, was a grave cautionary warning indicating to be fully on guard, for somewhere within the shop it was noticed that the time was drawing dangerously near. He felt the inner panic flourish. It would have been worse had he heard another one whistle instead. At least now he could gather some form of composure.

The first year after the signal was implemented, Malba had needed to use it. He whistled loud and true, but many couldn't hear it over the boisterously-maintained seasonal music and thus, became a victim. Eliminating the Christmas melodies altogether solved the problem, but also took away what little joy was left.

Fighting his quivering and tight chest, Malba took a deep breath and whistled. The harmony broke the otherwise drab quietness of the room and sent an immediate horrible chill down the spines of the other supervisors. Malba's eyes darted around at the other workstations, taking a visual of who had heard it. He saw pointed ears perking, wiggling and propping up. He knew they had heard. He took a small step backwards away from the table, an unconscious effort to get farther away from the atrocity. He peered back into its eyes. The cloudiness was beginning to bleed into the pupil.

Listening intently for a returned whistle from each station, scattered throughout the room, he silently prayed that each elf was taking a visual note of their own help's appearance.

Different whistled compositions started flowing back, each specific and indigenous, another required learning conveying understanding and location.

Malba's perked and pointed ears distinguished and perpetually listened for those he couldn't see, on the opposite side of the room behind the massive and brightly decorated Yule tree located at the center. When their whistles were heard, he was satisfied that complacency was nowhere to be found. His ears relaxed a bit and drooped, but his fear didn't subside.

Not wanting to attract his help's attention, he laid the toy down onto the bench and cautiously reached back behind him to the small of his back. Probing under his smock, he broke through the waistband of his green tights and gripped tight the small handle of the issued two shot derringer pistol nestled into the stitched-in felt holster. The limited protection measure felt warm and comforting. He didn't draw it out, but simply clung to it; aware and prepared.

His eyes darted about again. Many of the others had done the same. He saw their serious and worried looking faces. Obviously they weren't going to be caught off guard this year.

No one bothered to count the years since this place, once filled with bliss and cheer and giving, had grown dark and become joyless. But it had been many. And although many did believe it to be the cause, no one knew whether the sickness, horrid and ruthless, spreading fast through many of the elf families, began on that fateful night. The night when the Northern Lights lost their luster, flowed oddly vertical and eerily flashed green. Some of the elders called it an omen…an abomination brought on by the world's quest for materialism and the loss of the true meaning of Christmas. This foretoken rested lightly in the clan's psyche, but swelled heavily as the unforeseen coming events appeared.

The first few deaths were accepted and treated with normalcy. Promptly, just as they had for centuries, the elves took to traditionally wrapping the dead body in brightly-colored foil paper; usually red or green, depending upon which color suit the deceased had worn, and customarily prepared them for the placing. The placing was an age-old custom of putting the wrapped body under the Yule tree for twenty-five minutes, a number signified by the date of Christmas. This placing was much like the modern day calling hours at typical funeral homes and allowed the fold to pay last respects before burial.

This tradition proved to have deadly, long-standing consequences. They just didn't know what was about to happen. When they finally did, the sadness of death was replaced with trepidation and the nightmare began. It didn't take long for the North Pole to become chaotic and the serene bliss was irrecoverably broken forever.

Unprecedented for such a pristine environment, the dead unexpectedly started to rise, often during the immediate wrapping process. Shockingly, they took to gnawing into and eating the flesh of their attendants, subsequently creating more grisly deaths.

Wholeheartedly unfamiliar with violence, the peaceful elves had no idea how to deal with these atrocities and resorted to running away, the dead stalking them.

It was during the darkest first few days that Tendor, a lead toy designer attending his stricken father's prepping, realized exactly how to cope with and handle the monstrosities when, while being chased by his arisen father he stumbled upon the solution by accident.

In an attempt to get away, Tendor had run outdoors into trickling snowflakes and crouched behind a large pine tree. His pursuer followed and Tendor climbed up the tree to escape. With wild, dark-clouded eyes, flailing arms and snapping jaws, his chaser stood at the base of the tree, looking up at him and making attempts to mount the lower branches.

Now high in the tree, Tendor chillingly watched as his demented hunter grasped the concept and began slowly scaling the lower branches. Then Tendor saw a large icicle glimmering in the moonlight. He inched himself out onto the branch. It bowed and creaked with his weight, sending chills rippling down his spine. Reaching out, he broke it off from the end of the branch.

Just as the branch snapped, he threw the icicle like a spear. He shot plummeted through the branches and landed with a thud on the ground, knocking the wind out of him; he lost consciousness.

When he awoke a few minutes later, the corpse was lying prone a short distance from him, sprawled on its back, oddly resembling a macabre snow angel in the white covering. He scrambled to his feet and prepared to run, but then looked closer at the repugnant figure. The point of the icicle had found its mark, embedding deeply through the elf's eye and into its head. Suddenly Tendor was overcome with both sadness for losing his father as well as the relief that he wasn't being chased any longer; he wept violently. When the tears stopped flowing, anger had replaced the sadness, something he'd never felt before.

Armed with this newfound knowledge, the wrapping procedure was disregarded and halted. Attending loved ones stood fast nearby, clasping sharpened peppermint sticks and awaiting the deceased to rise.

Upon rising, the pre-designated one, typically the family's eldest, was responsible for putting the undead elf back down. This personal accountability sent a slight sense of security throughout the compound, trusting each family would take care of their own and assuring that there would be no flesh-seeking stragglers to stumble on the unaware.

With an abnormal method of control in place, and assuming the worst had passed, a struggle to regain routine was underway. However, a substantial population loss had occurred and the remaining began having difficulties maintaining the ever-increasing Christmas lists.

This outbreak happened in early January, and by mid-month, Santa and the remaining department head elves had met to discuss this apparent problem.

Being obvious that any attempt at an elf population explosion assisting the following season would prove futile, the suggestion was made to not kill the rising elfin dead, but to try and utilize them, to train them to do a single productive chore.

Initially, the dreadful idea was viewed as ludicrous and bordered insanity. After all, most, if not all had seen what the reincarnated monsters were quite capable of and the prospect of working alongside them offered no appeal whatsoever.

Only after a substantial debate, including a compelling scientific argument hypothesizing that remnants of previous lives lingering within the dead brains could be tapped into, concessions were made and the theory was accepted and placed into a trial.

Of course, much more convincing was needed before a training team willing to place their lives in jeopardy was found. After substantial volunteer psychological testing, four members, all able, willing and having become emotionally numb to the recent events, were selected. In the end, it was the weight of saving Christmas verses not saving it that prevailed.

They began with just one—a teen familiar with all named Chinzi, who had recently passed due to being bitten, selected for his smaller size and therefore thought to be more manageable. Under the watchful eye of the scientific crew, the team began the attempt.

As two members held firm Chinzi's roped-laced arms, one on each side, another spouted the joys of Christmas giving, sort of like a Sunday preacher giving a sermon, in an effort to break through the deceased psyche. The final member, armed and standing nearby, was ready to aid if needed, and the training officially began.

Chinzi remained ferocious and brutal, constantly snapping and clacking exposed teeth, nothing like he'd acted in life. After the third day, no tangible progress was made and hope became fleeting.

That evening the team was preparing to pen an especially combative Chinzi when one of the ropes broke loose. The sadistic corpse easily attacked the horrified and screaming elf opposite him, savagely chomping into and tearing away large portions of the poor elf's flesh. Short of mounting an attack and chancing injury themselves, there was nothing the other three elves could do. Revolted and repulsed, they watched from a distance and planned their next move.

After consuming a good part of the fallen elf, including the brain, Chinzi sat upright, red-faced with flesh dangling from his teeth. He looked up at his prior captors and was eerily calm. They saw that Chinzi's eyes no longer harbored the frightful coal black color.

The three elves circled and drew nearer, each carrying a pointed, peppermint stick weapon and bent on destruction. The aberration watched their slow approach and then looked down. It lifted and held out the loose arm. The team jumped back, threatened by the odd, seemingly beckoning forgiveness gesture.

The three looked at one another, perplexed.

The scientific community took note and urged the team to inch closer. The flesh-eater held position and didn't budge.

With one elf facing the sitting corpse, armed and ready to attack at the first sight of violence, another took hold of the undead elf's wrists and attached the rope, pulling it taut. The third remaining elf, the largest of the three, made a fresh slipknot in the rope and went around to the rear.

Fear forced heartbeats to pound loudly as the loop holder crept gingerly up behind Chinzi. He lunged quickly, looping the rope around the outstretched arm before dodging to the side and pulling hard, forcing the knot to tighten. Chinzi rocked to the side at the tug, but didn't fight against it and remained passive. With firmly held wide spread arms, Chinzi stood and let the captors guide him into a heavy duty wire mesh pen.

After being safely locked away, the team released the ropes, leaving them attached to Chinzi's wrists. Chinzi groaned, as if trying to actually speak, and lumbered up to the inside of the door. He stuck both tied arms out through a small rectangular opening at the front of the pen and moaned again. Two members of the team, under the direction of the overseeing scientific crew, removed the ropes and the creature stumbled off into the darkness of the pen's shadows. Also, as directed, they tossed the hollowed-out remains of the dead elf into the pen.

The following morning, with renewed vigor, the three made their way to the pen and found the remaining portion of the body was picked clean, leaving little more than a pile of bones. Chinzi had eaten heartily and returned to the shadows.

As the team stood in disgust of the sight, a clear-eyed Chinzi came out of the shadows to the door and placed his arms through the opening. Promptly, the ropes were attached and Chinzi was led out.

That day, a constant vigil was kept on Chinzi's eyes and training began to show small signs of success. When the eye haze started to show, Chinzi was quickly taken back to the pen and observed. The eyes grew blacker and Chinzi's disposition graduated to all out ferocity.

This revelation, the realization that if the dead were kept fully fed…serenity, controllability and acceptance were the standard norm, caused a ripple to rapidly run through the compound. They now knew how to control these monsters and the prospect of saving Christmas was elevated.

But soon another conflict arose…the scarcity of enough fresh flesh to keep them satisfied.

Various attempts were made to find a suitable source, including their undead counterparts after they were killed again. However, the atrocities wouldn't eat dead flesh. Through trial and error the team came to learn that the undead would in fact eat their own…only if the flesh was from either the freshly dead, before they arose, or immediately after they arose and were put back down. The timeframe was critical and fully eliminated any storage idea, and another rather gruesome and chilling solution was employed.

With many still alive and being nursed, having been injured during the initial outbreak and sporting various bite wounds, the likelihood of recovery was grim. Therefore, as each succumbed and passed, they were incorporated into a feeding program and the problem was temporarily solved.

At first, feeding timeframes were kept on a tight schedule. But it soon became apparent that this time table was unreliable and a task force of highly trained elves was developed. Their only occupation was to work alongside and constantly keep watch for the cloudy-eyed warning signs, a very prideful and supreme position.

A number of elves with delusions of grandeur, having already seen that control was established, volunteered for the highly lucrative and status-filled positions. All who volunteered were accepted. But not all survived the training.

Although fully aware of the dire consequences of inattention, occasionally an elf trainee would become complacent and miss the warning signs. The mistake was realized only after it was too late and a portion of their flesh had been bitten into or off. Of course others would come to the aid in bringing the hungry biter back under control, but that offered little consolation to the injured elf.

Now considered infected, and medical attention having been proven to be futile, the misfortunate one was immediately surrounded by weaponized guards and firmly led off to a side room, where they were butchered fresh and used for feedings.

The entire scenario may have resembled a typical execution, complete with a babbling and blubbering condemned prisoner being led down the last mile, but it was as precise as military clockwork; very effective and a powerful deterrent to constantly remain attentive. This forlorn and morbid approach was not well received by any means, but it did assure that the virus remained under constant careful quarantine and the act was mostly respected for doing so.

A young Malba, one of the very first trainees to enter the program, saw this happen firsthand. His view was gruesomely bittersweet and became an attribute he contributed to his ability to maintain chronic awareness—something held firm to this day that allowed him to elevate in his position.

While in this training program, it was suggested that some sort of warning signal needed to be implemented, and he took it upon himself to author and perfect the art of the whistle signal, another aspect that boosted his future status.

Although the help appeared to be well-trained, the feeding timeframe effectiveness was weak, and chains and ropes were used as precautionary measures. From time to time, during the throes of hunger, chains were broken, ropes were snapped and a rampage would happen. Sometimes the help was put down before any injurious damage was done and sometimes they weren't.

It was immediately following one of the very first occasions that the Derringers were issued as a means of quick personal action.

Regardless, the undead certainly proved capable of learning mundane tasks such as chopping firewood, lugging packages, or dipping clear lights—one at a time—into a color vat and thus making the bulb either red, green or blue.

Soon a bevy of additional Christmas help was in place, productivity soared and some sense of normalcy—if you could call it that—gradually took over, at least for those who weren't responsible for working closely with the potential zombie elves.

When not in use, the horde was locked away in a newly built, secured corral deep inside a cave, chilled, but not cold, and were typically allowed to remain unfed and vicious until needed.

Each morning, an attached, heavily-barred and strong metal cage—much like that used for loading cattle—was employed. By lifting the corral-sided gate, a pack of zombies would rush into the cage. The gate was dropped, cutting off the remaining ones and the cluster was fed and observed. When the haze had fully disappeared from their eyes and calm had set in, each was led, one by one, into another section of the cage where they were chained and taken to their assignments and trainers.

Once at the assigned location, the supervising elf would tap into prior teachings previously embedded in the undead elves psyche, and teach the day's menial tasks.

By using cubed, bite-sized morsels to entice, much like training any pet, the help was taught the daily chore and would usually abide. Rather efficient and highly effective, provided vigilance was maintained and feedings were offered when necessary.

Maintaining his grip on the gun, Malba reached with the other hand under the covered flap into his side pocket and pulled out the last chunk of rationed red meat. It was small, diced, and just starting to have a bouquet of rot, like the help—something they could never seem to find a solution for.

Pine, Poinsettia, peppermint and even cocoa scents were tried. Nothing worked and all were forced to tolerate and accept the fact that the wonderful baking gingerbread and roasted goose fragrances of old were gone forever, having been replaced by the constant stanching sweet aroma of death, and many disgusted vomitings occurring due to the rancid odor.

Malba tossed the flesh morsel onto the wooden table directly in front of his help, an elf formerly known as Whipper, who he vividly recalled speaking with a number of times. Whipper quickly caught sight of the tidbit and eagerly snatched it up. He chewed once and with a single gulp, swallowed, leaving a faint red foamy remembrance on his pale gray lips.

Malba looked deeply into Whipper's eyes, saw that the haze was starting to diminish and felt only slightly relieved. Swiftly he glanced at the other stations and saw the supervisors. Some exchanged concern glances with him, but most exchanged looks between their help and the overhead skylight. All were listening intently for the familiar jingling of bells. Malba didn't have to ask why.

I hope he gets here soon, too, he thought.

Whipper slowly lifted his head and stared at him, a product of training. As fear grasped hard, he reached back into the pocket and fumbled around, hopeful to find a piece of missed flesh. He didn't.

Trying to keep positive, he recalled the glimpse he'd of this year's list.

If all goes well, we won't have this trouble next year, he thought. *There should be an ample supply.*

Whipper's eyes only had a small bit of the dreaded haziness and he was back to placing the red toy wagons into the boxes. Malba knew it wouldn't last long.

Hurry up, Santa… Please hurry…

Santa tucked the last one into the red bag, put a finger to the side of his nose, felt the teardrop's moistness and wiped it away before disappearing up the chimney.

On the roof, he tossed the heavy bag into the rear of the sled with a loud thud and took his place on the center of the front seat. He leaned forward, grabbed the leather reins and gave them a quick snap. Dasher, Dancer, Prancer, Vixen, Comet, Cupid and Donner took off with the sled in tow. No longer did he yell out, calling each by name. It had grown too painful.

The cold winter's night wind cut past him, causing his beard to flutter to the side. He thought about Blitzen, the memory flowing into deep sadness and forcing tears. Caught by the wind, the droplets streaked down the side of his face and he wiped them away before they froze.

He recollected the early discussion of using venison as the help's food, before they realized what would work. He hadn't agreed. But in the end, the needs of the many outweighed the needs of the few and he gave in. It hadn't solved anything and in his mind's eye he still saw how Blitzen had looked at him when the blade pierced his heart. Santa hadn't stayed for the butchering.

"The damn things wouldn't touch it!" he subconsciously blurted out angrily, his loud voice echoing radiantly through the night. He didn't care if anyone below could hear.

Only after taking solace in a memory of how, in a fit of rage, he laughingly snatched up an axe and furiously chopped through a cluster of elf zombies did he become tranquil, remaining silent for the rest of the trip.

Fresh snowflakes fluttered down from the large skylight when it opened and a collective sigh flowed through the workshop room. Santa guided the sleigh in and onto the landing port and pulled back on the reins until the reindeer stopped.

Immediately, many elves, their faces as devoid of joy as Malba's was, quickly approached the sled and formed a single line. Malba watched, secretly wishing the first to receive would come directly to him.

Santa turned and reached over the front seat, pulled on the string and popped opened the bag. He slid the machete he carried from the side of his black belt, smearing the white fur ruffle at the bottom of his coat red in the process, and started slashing in through the bag's opening.

The massive bag's side took on a shiny appearance as liquid leeched through the material. In one swift swoop, he tucked the bloody and gruesome-looking blade back into his belt, pulled out the bloody meat masses by the handful, and passed them to the line of undead elves.

After receiving the meat, the elves promptly took off running, in all directions, to the supervisors waiting impatiently at the workshop tables.

Within minutes, the help was fed and led off to be penned. Upon returning, the living elves collected and carted off the sleigh bag full of freshly killed—but unspoiled bodies—to a frozen cave where they would be hanged on hooks for use throughout the next year.

With the bag gone and the night dying down, Santa stepped off the sleigh and made his way to Malba.

The no longer jolly fellow heaved a heavy sigh and said, "We made it."

Malba scanned Santa's red-blotched white beard and splattered face, more concerned with how loose the skin—previously full and plump—had become.

Malba solemnly nodded.

"I don't know what it is Malba," Santa said, eyes moist with impending-yet-held-back tears. "The world is changing and each year I wonder more and more whether we're only prolonging the inevitable. You should see some of the places. Materialism has certainly taken hold and I'm not all surprised at how the naughty list seems to keep growing considerably longer each year. By next year…"

Malba was silent, only shrugging his shoulders.

"…I'm going to need a bigger bag."

"Try not to think about it, Santa," Malba replied, trying to reassure and patting him approvingly on the shoulder. "Look at it this way. We're keeping Christmas alive and well…at least for the nice list, however short it becomes."

Santa sighed gloomily, a tear trickling down his face, flowing through a splotch of blood splatter and streaking red. He turned and slowly walked off.

Woefully, Malba walked to the brightly flashing tree, turned around and looked across the room. Various elf supervisors had congregated before him.

One handed him a steaming mug of hot cocoa. Malba offered the elf a faint, but obviously unhappy smile in return. It wasn't reciprocated.

He raised the steaming mug and nodded. The rest followed suit.

"And to all a good night…"

ABOUT THE WRITERS

Vincenzo Bilof is an educator from Detroit, Michigan. Publication credits include six horror stories published in SNM Magazine in 2011, with appearances in three anthologies, including: Book of the Dead 6 (Living Dead Press), Zombie Buffet and Bigfoot Tales (Open Casket Press). Poetry credits include Nuvein Magainze, The Detroiter, SNM Magazine, and Miller's Pond. He's currently finishing a post-apocalyptic novel titled "Under a Red Sun."

Mark Christopher is employed as an industrial hygienist by day and a horror writer by night. He is the author of "Faye Believes," "Riser," "The Wanderer," "The Glass Coffin," and "How Stopping a Zombie Invasion Will Get You Grounded." His newest short story, "The Demon in the Water," is published by Severed Dead Press. He is also the author of the thrilling zombie novel, "Hollow Point." He's a graduate of Louisiana State University and currently resides in Baton Rouge, Louisiana with his wife, Jessica.

Anthony Giangregorio is the author of 35 novels, almost all of them about zombies and has edited over 20 anthologies.

His work has appeared in Dead Science by Coscomentertainment, Dead Worlds: Undead Stories Volumes 1-7, and Wolves of War by Library of the Living Dead Press. He also has stories in End of Days: An Apocalyptic Anthology Vol. 1-5, the Book of the Dead series Vol. 1-6 by LDP, Zombie Zoology by Severed Press, and two anthologies with Pill Hill Press. He is also the creator of the popular action/zombie series titled Deadwater and his action/ horror novel Dead Rage is being optioned for a movie. Check out his website at www.undeadpress.com

Ash Hartwell lives in England with his beautiful wife and children. He's been writing horror stories for a year and his work appears in a number of anthologies from Wicked East Press and Static Movement.

Kelly M. Hudson hails from Kentucky and his favorite Christmas movies are Black Christmas (the original, of course) and Gremlins. You can't go wrong with either. He has numerous short stories in print and two novels called The Turning and Men of Perdition. You can find out all about his work at www.kellymhudson.com. He wants to wish you and yours the merriest Christmas possible!

Ken L. Jones has written everything from Donald Duck comic books to many published grisly horror stories. He's been doing this for over forty years and maybe he will do it longer than that if he can accomplish his lifelong ambitions of becoming one of the living dead.

Kevin Lewis is a member of New England Horror Writers (NEHW). His fiction has appeared in publications such as Blood Moon Rising Magazine, MicroHorror, and Sonar4 Science Fiction and Horror Ezine. Kevin's story, "Get Me Out Of Here!" will be published in the anthology, Groanology 2: Monsters, Madness, and Mayhem. He lives in Massachusetts.

Daniel Loubier is an avid fan of all things horror. His first novel, a zombie horror titled, "Dead Summit," was released in the Fall, 2011. He is currently working on, "Exorcising the Demon: The Biography of Eileen Dietz," which is scheduled for a Spring 2012 release. To find out more about Daniel, visit his website at: www.danloubier.com

Christopher Nadeau is the author of "Dreamers at Infinity's Core" through COM Publishing as well as over a dozen published short stories in such august publications as The Horror Zine, Sci-Fi Short Story Magazine, Ghostlight Magazine. He was interviewed as part of Suspense Radio's up and coming authors program and collaborated on two "machinima" films with UK animator Celestial Elf called "The Gift," and "The Deerhunter's Tale," both of which can be viewed on YouTube. His novel "Echoes of Infinity's Core" is slated for a 2011 release. He Resides in Southeastern Michigan.

James Jeffrey Paul is a native of Orlando, Florida and an alumnus of Duke University and the University of North Carolina at Chapel Hill. His play about Jack the Ripper and his last victim, "Miller's Court," is available as an audio download from Amazon and iTunes. His true crime book, "Nothing Is Strange With You: The Life and Rimes of Gordon Stewart Northcott," has sold over 5,000 copies since its publication in 2008. He's just finished a novel about the search for the Loch Ness Monster. He can be reached at jfpl@aol.com.

Suzanne Robb's debut novel "Z-Boat" will be released by Twisted Library Press under their Library of the Living Dead Imprint. Her stories are in several current and upcoming anthologies. In her free time she reads, watches movies, plays with her dog, and enjoys chocolate and Legos. For more check out Ramblings of an Anxiety Ridden Mind at http://suzannerobb.blogspot.com/

Thomas Scopel has been published in many horror and fright-based electronic and print publications. His tales include Twitch (Suspense Publishing), The Pumpkin Patch (NorGus Press' Look What I Found" anthology), Lickety Split, While You Sleep, All the Creatures Were Stirring...Even the Mouse, The Eight Legs of Night, The Argument, A Cup of Sugar, The Horrors of Easter, Don't Forget the Fingers: A Guide to the Perfect Zombie Family Picnic, Welcome, and more. His alter ego is an evil clown by the name of Wee Willie Wicked http://weewilliewicked.blogspot.com and he fictitiously and gruesomely killed off his fellow co-workers in a series entitled The Daily Death for his blog http://stayingscared.blogspot.com.
He can be reached through his website at www.thomasscopel.com

Rebecca Snow lives with her cats and her husband in Virginia on a patch of property dotted with rusted barbed wire fences. Her short fiction has been published in various small press anthologies. She can be found online on Twitter @cemeteryflower and on Facebook (look for the bloody hand).

Jonathan Templar has worked for local government, been a full time parent and written copious vampire and zombie fiction. He won't reveal which profession was the goriest. He can be found at www.jonathantemplar.com

ZOMBIE BUFFET: A ZOMBIE ANTHOLOGY

Edited by Anthony Giangregorio

If you're hungry for zombie stories, look no further than this anthology.
There's enough rotting meat to satisfy even the most discerning connoisseur,
and our all-you-can-eat buffet is sure to please.
Rotting intestines, severed heads and exploding spleens are just some of the
courses waiting for you within this book of undead mastication.
So grab a knife and fork, slap on a napkin, 'cause you're gonna get dirty, and
prepare yourself for the Zombie Buffet.
A zombie feast of epic proportions.

RATS

By Anthony Giangregorio

Killer black rats the size of dogs are roaming the streets and no one knows
about their existence.
Wild dogs, the authorities warn. Stay indoors and all will be fine.
Domenic Salvatore soon finds himself in the middle of a cover-up of epic
proportions; where no one will believe the truth.
And why would they? After all, he's just a kid.
For what no one understands is that the rats have taken on a taste for human
meat, but it's a particular kind of meat…young flesh…the flesh of children.
As the kids are hunted one by one, killed and dragged off into the night to be
devoured, Domenic realizes that it's only a matter of time before he's next.
Something evil stalks the town of Wakefield, Mass…and it's hungry.

CLAN OF THE BIGFOOT

ANTHONY GIANGREGORIO

ZOMBIES, MONSTERS, CREATURES OF THE NIGHT
OPEN CASKET PRESS
OPEN CASKET PRESS.COM
THE NEW NAME IN HORROR

9 781611 990331